About the author

Anne Booth was born in Blackburn and has lived in Lancashire ever since. Her love of history was always encouraged by her father who was also the inspiration behind the research she has done into her family tree. After retiring from teaching, she decided to continue to trace her ancestors and began to discover stories within the lives she traced. The writing of these stories seemed to follow on quite naturally and it has given her a new focus in life. 'I have loved both the research and the writing,' she says. 'I become personally involved with each character; their loves, lives and losses, living each day with them as I write their story.' The Joiner's Secret is the second of these stories.

The Joiner's Secret

By Anne Booth

 New Generation Publishing

To my father, Brian Booth, who died in July 2012. His enthusiasm for knowledge about his ancestors gave me the inspiration to research our family tree.

Acknowledgements

I would like to thank my daughters Andrea and Lyndsey, and my sisters Christine and Kathryn, whose help in the editing of this work has been invaluable. Their encouragement, criticisms and suggestions as always have been of great help.

Without the work of the many people who transcribe and record the valuable records which appear on the multitude of genealogy websites, tracing a family tree would be much more difficult. So, on behalf of all amateur genealogists everywhere, I would like to offer my thanks to these people.

Preface

Finding out who our ancestors were, what they did and where they lived can be the key which unlocks the secrets of our past. It can be a roller-coaster ride of excitement, sadness, pride and disbelief, but the rewards it can bring are hugely gratifying. The mysteries which are solved along the way often leave a lasting impression and life is never quite the same again.

The Joiner's Secret is the sequel to my first novel – A Tragedy Too Far, but is able to stand alone in its own right as a novel which tells the story of Joseph Clarke Freeman who was my great, great grandmother's second husband. Joseph's story was inspired again by family tree research and the discoveries made along the way. The number and variety of records which are available today is amazing, making the task of researching these lives a never ending journey of surprises, but giving a real picture of the way our ancestors lived. The Joiner's Secret must be considered a work of fiction although the main characters are real people, their dates of birth, death and marriage all sourced by the relevant documents. It is then that their story is woven around this framework, giving substance to the story and personality to the individuals within the story. I have enjoyed every minute of writing this story and I hope that its readers will share in my enjoyment as they read it.

Prologue

Newchurch July 1903

As the rain poured, the Rector could be seen leading the line of bedraggled mourners through the churchyard towards the burial place.

"I am the resurrection and the life says the Lord..."

The words became muffled by the sounds of sobbing and the incessant howling of the wind. After what seemed like only seconds, the coffin was lowered into the ground and the voice of the rector could be heard quite clearly.

"Forasmuch as it had pleased Almighty God of his great mercy to take unto himself the soul of our dear sister here departed, we therefore commit her body to the ground; earth to earth, ashes to ashes, dust to dust...."

He could hear the heavy thud as clods of earth were dropped onto the coffin, and from his hiding place the faces of Hannah's family became clearer. Which one was *his* son, he wondered; for he was almost sure it was a son that Hannah had given birth to. Joseph was no longer a young man and the encumbrance of the secrets he had borne had begun to weigh heavily on him. His conscience told him that he should go and make his peace with the family, but he was a weak man; the pathetic shadow of the man Hannah had known; and he faltered. After all these years would they want to know him? How could he acknowledge that he didn't even know his offspring's name? Joseph was unsure whether he would be able to explain the reasons for the way he had behaved all those years ago. He needed to know the answers to so many questions, but was unsure whether or not he deserved them. After all, he was the one who had dishonoured the family, and it was they who really needed the answers. The wretchedness and guilt he felt at the sight of Hannah's coffin overcame him and Joseph slumped onto a nearby gravestone. The questions would have to remain unanswered and he would have to live with the guilt he felt, until his own life came to an end and he was free from the burden of the secrets he had carried.

The burial was completed and Hannah was at last laid to rest. The family joined the rector in the final words: "*Lord have mercy upon us*", and Joseph turned his back once again on Hannah.

"Lord have mercy on me," he whispered to himself; "and may God forgive me for what I have done."

Chapter 1

Scout Hall Halifax 1854

Joseph thought back fondly to the day when he had married his eighteen year old bride in 1854 and the birth of their first child Mary Ellen later that year. They had been happy until their first born made her way into the world. It soon became apparent that Mary was not going to be a bright child. Her development was slow and she was unable to walk until she was two years old. Her speech was unclear and her understanding was limited. Joseph knew even then, that it was not going to be easy to take care of his daughter. By the time Mary was two, their second child, a son was born. Charles Frederick was a normal happy little boy who gave them great joy and his birth was followed by the birth of Thomas in 1858, Hannah Maria in 1860 and Henry in 1861. Esther had suffered two miscarriages during the gaps between the births of her other children and Joseph had hoped that Henry was to be their last child. Esther was only twenty six and the ravages of childbirth had taken their toll giving her the appearance of a much older woman. The pressure of her pregnancies had taken away her youthful appearance and she was not strong.

In spite of the fact that he had no proper papers to prove it, Joseph considered himself to be a skilled joiner and cabinet maker, and most of his furniture was well made. He should really have been apprenticed and served his time with an experienced joiner, but his training had been short. He had spent a couple of years working as a joiner in one of the factories, learning the trade as he went along. Still, he seemed to have an aptitude for the job and loved working with his hands.

Joseph had made a few pieces of furniture for the wealthy of Halifax as well as other serviceable sturdy furniture which his own class could use. He came from a farming family and knew only too well that most people made a table and chairs last a lifetime, so good, well-made pieces were essential for his reputation and so his livelihood. He had no doubts that he wanted to make furniture and not work in one of the woollen mills repairing machines. However, unless he was prepared to work in the town, it was unlikely that his dreams would be fulfilled. He needed a shop or premises to work from and he did not have the money to support these plans.

Joseph's father had farmed about forty acres of land in Scout Hall near Halifax for many years, working and living in the same place and bringing up their children in this secure environment. In spite of the industry nearby, the air never felt clouded by the smoke and pollution which was to be found in the towns. The countryside was green and lush, the fields producing a verdant supply of grass to feed the cows and sheep; and the valley sides had a blanket of trees. There was always food on the table and although never wealthy, James Freeman was not a poor man. It was in this content family atmosphere, that Joseph grew up with his four brothers and four sisters. As a young man, he did not need to look for employment, but worked on his father's farm spending much of his time learning how to fashion things from wood. His mother had given birth almost every two years since she had married James, and it was probably the healthy lifestyle and sufficient food supplies that enabled her to rear nine healthy children.

There were only nine families living in Scout at that time and most of the adults and children of working age were employed either in the manufacture of worsted, a type of woollen cloth; or in the coal mines nearby. No other joiner or cabinet maker lived in the district, so most of Joseph's customers were local people, none of whom were wealthy.

Although Joseph enjoyed this work, eventually he realised that he would need to travel around to find employment: living in the countryside was suited to a farmer, but there was not enough work for a joiner. He had grand ideas about making furniture for the wealthy, but in reality, these commissions were few and far between. Most of the available work was in the factories and Joseph did not seem able to hold a permanent job for long. At the beginning of his marriage, he tried hard to work to feed his family, and was happy; but he was often out of work and money was short.

Esther spent all her time looking after their growing family and life was good for a while. However, their lives were to change dramatically when at the beginning of 1865, their youngest child Henry died from pneumonia. He had never been a strong baby and his death was followed by the deaths of Hannah Maria in 1866 and then Thomas Arthur in 1867.

Henry's death was a tragic event and Esther was distraught. When the burial was over and she had laid her son to rest, she took to her bed. She became almost an invalid herself and was unable to look after the rest of her children. Her life held little purpose, giving her no motivation to continue with even the smallest of everyday tasks. Joseph could see that if she did not get better soon, his small family would suffer. Frustration took hold until he could bear it no longer.

"Esther," he bawled at her. "If you do not desist from taking to your bed, our children will be the ones who suffer. Do you really want that to happen after we have lost our dearest son so soon in his young life?"

Esther was shaken by the tone in Joseph's voice and could not bear to look at him. She put the blame for Henry's death firmly on his shoulders, although she had not spoken her accusations aloud to her husband. The bed covers were firmly pulled up around her neck as the last thing she wanted was for Joseph to see any part of her body. She felt only disgust at the shrivelled breasts that once fed her beautiful dead son. How could her husband ever look upon her with love in his eyes ever again? As she looked straight ahead towards the foot of the bed, her whispered reply came almost inaudibly.

"I cannot help it Joseph. My body is unable to depart from the bed in which it lies. I will try my utmost to be up and behaving as a mother should, as soon as my strength returns." In reality, Esther wanted to punish her husband and had already made up her mind to try and get up the following day. Her remaining children were her only thoughts now. Hannah Maria was already suffering from a disability in her joints and she found it difficult to get around without the support of crutches. Esther knew it was time to bring herself out of the doldrums and look after her children.

Joseph left his wife in her bed, in despair of the situation she had got herself into. He had not been able to bring in a regular wage and so food had become less plentiful. His children were in danger of becoming mal-nourished and he knew that this poor lifestyle had probably contributed to Henry's tragic death. It was obvious that things needed to change to enable Joseph's family to survive.

No matter what the weather brought during the following weeks, nothing could liven up Esther's spirits, but eventually she rallied round and returned to her monotonous routines of cooking, cleaning and trying to feed her children. Henry was never far from her mind and she often went up to the Church in Haley Hill where he was buried. She would talk to him and tell him of her worries and the idea that she could converse with him gave her comfort. She made sure that no one was around to hear her when she spoke to him; this was her own private time with her beloved son.

"Your sister is not well," she whispered to him one day several weeks later. "She suffers from a great deal of pain in her hips and is becoming bound to the house. I worry so about her. Please God I don't lose her too."

Her quiet conversations with Henry continued for several months until she gradually found that she did not need to visit his grave so often in order to remember him. By the time the first anniversary of his death arrived, she was just beginning to think that her children were going to survive beyond the age of ten. Joseph's mother had left the farm for a while to visit her son in London and her husband was left to manage the farm with the help of a couple of labourers and his daughter. Joseph also helped out when he could and as his own commissions were scarce at the time, he did this readily.

"Some of the cows are unwell, Esther," he told her one warm evening in early June. He had been helping with the milking and his father had expressed some concerns. Joseph was aware of his father's reluctance to discuss things further and suspected that things were difficult. He placed a large jug of creamy milk on the table and poured Hannah a mug of the foaming white liquid. This was something which he knew was good for all of his children and would keep them well nourished, so brought as much as his father would allow.

"Has your father said what the problem is?"

enquired Esther. "Perhaps they are suffering from parasites or some such illness." Esther knew little about animal husbandry and was desperately trying to calm her husband.

"He has given no details except to say that he thinks some are unwell. The affected ones are lethargic and not gaining weight as they should."

"We should try not to worry, as your father is a very experienced farmer and knows what he is doing. If there is a reason to worry, he will let us know in his own good time." Esther tried to turn the conversation towards something else knowing that Joseph was concerned for his father.

Within the space of the next couple of months, James' worries about his cows were to be confirmed. He had suspected that the problem was serious. Another farm less than five miles away had cattle with consumption and his cows had all the symptoms. He had tried to confine the affected beasts to the barn, but it was not long before the majority of his herd were showing the signs. He knew that he should have brought in the veterinary long before now, but money was short and he had tried to reason that his cattle should have been safe from this dreadful disease. How would he ever explain his actions to his family? He need not have worried as Joseph understood his father's actions and within a day, the affected cows were shot and disposed of, the whole community helping to burn the carcasses.

After the ordeal of disposing of almost half of his herd, James had to try even harder to eke out his living, made all the more difficult by the sudden death of his wife whilst in London. It had taken a week for the news to reach him and by that time her body had been buried in Chelsea. It seemed that the bad news would never end. Joseph and Esther tried hard to keep their lives as normal as possible, but Joseph too had been badly affected by the loss of his father's cattle to consumption and even more so by the loss of his mother.

The summer of 1866 gave way to autumn and Esther became ever more vigilant in the fight to keep her children healthy. September appeared with a late burst of fine, warm weather, just right for the gathering of a harvest, but Hannah Maria began to show the signs of a severe cold. In spite of all her mother's efforts to treat it, the cold became worse and she developed a severe cough. Hannah's hip complaint seemed to worsen and by the end of the month it was clear that her cold was in fact a symptom of consumption. It would seem that Joseph's purpose of enriching his children's diet with milk had caused her illness. The milk had more than likely been from one of the infected cows!

The doctor was sent for in spite of the cost, but his prognosis for Hannah was not good. It seemed that her hip disease had been aggravated by the symptoms of consumption and he prescribed plenty of fresh air. Hannah was much weaker and her continuing fatigue made it difficult for her to walk at all. She sat, day in day out, in the doorway of the cottage, with a shawl wrapped around her poor thin shoulders whatever the weather; in the fervent hope that the air would cure her. Esther spent her nights at her daughter's bedside trying to appease her fever and soother her with calming words. Her hands were relentlessly clasped in prayer, but all to no avail. As October disappeared and the chill winds of November made their appearance, seven year old Hannah lost her fight for life. She was buried beside her brother in the little churchyard on Haley Hill on the third day of November.

Esther's belief in God was sorely tried in the days surrounding her daughter's death and she vowed she would never set foot in the church again. Why had God taken two of her children? Was it something she had done? Again she blamed Joseph. It was he who had given their daughter the infected milk and she could not see that he had only been trying his best to provide for the children.

Christmas came and the Freeman family had nothing to celebrate. Esther would not celebrate the birth of a God who had taken her children. They ate as normal and tended to the animals, for they would suffer too if left without food. James spent the first Christmas without his wife, instead spending the day with his son and a wife who were barely communicating. It was inconceivable that their suffering could continue and the family gradually took on the semblance of normality. Life had to go on……

Early in January in 1867, one of Joseph's neighbours came to speak to him. He worked at the nearby woollen mill and had heard some disturbing news.

"It is said that scarlatina is passing through the neighbourhood Joseph. I thought that with the afflictions your family have had to suffer, that you should be the first to know."

Joseph blanched with fear. This was not a disease that was easy to survive. He knew only too well that if Esther got to hear of this, she would crumble with anguish, for she knew that with scarlatina came the shadow of death.

Thomas was within a few days of his ninth birthday when he showed the first signs of a rash. He had already developed a cough, but so had many of the other children and adults in the small hamlet of Scout – after all, it was winter and this type of complaint was to be expected. For Thomas however, the cough was just the first of several symptoms he endured and as soon as the rash became apparent, Esther knew that Thomas had scarlatina. The neighbours were quickly alerted and the Freeman's cottage was isolated from the rest of the community to reduce the spread of the disease. Esther was unusually calm, waiting for the grim disease to take its course. Perhaps she too wanted to die; she certainly took no precautions herself although it was unusual for an adult to contract the disease. After three days, Thomas' condition worsened. He complained of pains in his arms and legs and the rash had spread to the rest of his body as the poison within his small frame took hold. Finally, his body was unable to rid itself of fluid and he became dropsical. Within a day he was the third victim of death in this ill-fated family.

The burial took place three days later on the twenty second of January and Thomas was buried beside his brother and sister. The day was bitterly cold, but Joseph and Esther felt only the pain in their hearts. Poverty and illness had taken away their children and Joseph and his family were devastated by these losses. To lose a parent is bad enough, but to bury three of your children before their time was a bitter blow, with far reaching consequences.

**

The devastating feelings which plagued both Joseph and Esther after the loss of their three children were not easily overcome. Scout would always hold the memories of these unfortunate children and so reluctantly, in 1868 Joseph and Esther decided to take Mary and move away from Halifax to start a new life in Cheshire. When Joseph decided to leave Scout Hall for Hyde, James realised he could offer his grandson Charles Frederick a home and at the same time find a new labourer for his farm.

"It stands to sense lad," he told Joseph, "you can't afford to feed a family and I can give him a job and a home. Ask the lad and see if he is willing! But mind, he will have to work hard and I will not call him by that namby pamby name you have given him; he will be known as Fred whilst he lives with me."

Grudgingly, Joseph and Esther left their son Charles with his grandfather and set off to find a new home and a better standard of living in Cheshire. Esther was unhappy to leave her only surviving son behind, but she knew that he would be well looked after. She also knew that Joseph was unable to cope with the knowledge that his idleness and lack of effort in finding work, was partly to blame for the decimation of their family. They had very little money left and what they had would just about pay a month's rent on a house and feed them for a couple of weeks. It was imperative that Joseph should find work as soon as they reached their new destination. Esther had been reproachful of Joseph's behaviour since Henry's death and realised that the remorse he felt was genuine. He was not to know that he was feeding infected milk to his daughter or that Thomas would eventually die from scarlatina, but she also knew that if her children had not had to go hungry so often, their bodies would have been stronger and more able to recover from illness.

Regardless of this, she could not shake off the thought that perhaps they would be no better off in a different place and that Joseph would be unable to change his ways. Only time would tell. For now she must be strong and direct her thoughts towards the future and the possibility of a better life for them all.

Chapter 2

Hyde, Cheshire 1868

Esther's spirits rose and the move to Cheshire filled her with hope: hope that her husband would find a steady job, and hope that the rest of her family would remain healthy. Her only sadness had been that her son had to be left behind. As they settled into their new home in Beelay Street, she concentrated on making her new house into a real home for them. Mary was able to help with the chores and between the two of them; they scrubbed the small terraced house from top to bottom, placing their newly washed curtains at the now sparkling windows.

Hyde was an industrial place with many mills and heavy industry. Smoke filled the air from the factory chimneys and dust and dirt left its mark on the windows and walls. Mary developed a hacking cough within days of their arrival and it was a constant reminder of the cleaner countryside air they had left behind. Mary's health was always going to be a worry for them, and Esther told herself that she would get her some cough linctus as soon as she could.

The only house available to them in the area was the one next to the policemen's houses and lock ups. Although this might have deterred some families with a more dubious background, it did not worry Joseph and Esther. They were generally law abiding people and knew that they had nothing to hide. However, within the next few years, Joseph was to wish that perhaps he had been able to find a property a bit further away from the eyes of the law.

With a positive view for the future, Joseph set off to find work as soon as they had settled into their new home. From talking to the neighbours, he knew that there were as many as four other joiners living on the same street. Most of the other neighbours were employed in a variety of occupations including a tailor, a coal miner and several who were employed in the local mills. William Batty, a young joiner who was living only next door to Joseph, had just started his own furniture business in the town. He had recently employed three other joiners and Joseph found to his delight that he was in need of another. Life seemed rosy as he turned his feet homewards the day after being offered a position at the premises of William Batty, who described his goods as being 'furniture of distinction'.

Although the day was cloudy, Joseph's face was filled with sunshine as he opened the door of his new home that afternoon.

"I'm home!" He shouted, the door creaking on its rusty hinges.

Mary approached her father and noticed the smile on his face. He gave her a hug and asked her where her mother was.

"She is in t' y- yard, sort out washing tub, big crack in it!" she stuttered hesitantly. It was unusual these days to see her father with a smile on his face and she hoped that he had some good news for them.

"You happy. Why?"

"Wait and see. I will explain all when I see your mother," he teased.

Esther heard the voices and came into the parlour. She looked at her husband with a sense of trepidation, not knowing if the loud chatter meant good news or bad. Her day so far had not been good and she hoped that Joseph had at last found a steady job which would give them security and put regular food in their bellies. All they had in the pantry at that moment was a selection of wilting vegetables and a small sack of potatoes. She would have to go out and buy some meat to make a stew, but was reluctant to waste money if Joseph was still out of work.

Joseph looked at his wife with a serious expression. He wanted to surprise her and so did not tell her his news straight away.

"The wash tub is broken and I am unable to do the washing!" Esther blurted out. "And by the look on your face you do not have good news for me again. Was there no work to be had? What will we do?" Esther's face crumpled and Joseph could contain himself no longer.

"It is good news," he grinned. "I have found employment with one of our neighbours who is the owner of a furniture shop in the town. He also employs three of our other neighbours who are joiners. It looks as if we might have struck lucky in renting a house in this street."

Esther's tears soon turned to tears of joy as she hugged Joseph. Within minutes, she was in a much better humour and out of the house, running down the street to the butcher's for a piece of meat to make a stew for tea. Their meal was a celebration and as they ate, they talked about all the things they would like to do when they had the money.

"Do you think you will be able to buy furniture for us at a discount? Or even get the chance to make us some in the workshop? Esther asked.

"Let's not assume anything for now, but I am sure that Mr Batty is a reasonable man and there is a chance that he will give us a discount on anything we buy. When I find out where he gets his wood supplies from, I can see if they would be willing to sell me some at cost price. Then I can make our furniture in my spare time." Joseph was full of hope for his new job and was sure that soon he would be earning a good wage. They might even be able to move into a bigger house with a garden.

Mary sensed the excitement in the family and clapped her hands with glee. It had become apparent that she would be unable to find a·job herself, as not many employers wanted to take on a person who many described as 'an idiot'. She was generally happy, but rarely went out of the house without her parents. Mary had been well known in Scout and had been accepted as the 'idiot' child of Joseph and Esther. However, in Hyde she had been stared at and called unkind names. Mary had an enlarged tongue, typical of children like her and as a result her speech was unclear and she often stammered. She rarely spoke when in the company of others, being more relaxed at home with her parents. Along with others of her kind, she could often be the subject of people's curiosity and as a result, she was often the subject of scorn. Many children with disabilities like this had been sent to an institution from an early age.

Mary's beautiful round face and blue eyes often reflected her mood. On the day her father found work, her eyes shone with happiness and even though she could not always express her feelings in words, she understood most of what was said to her. On hearing the news about her father's new job, she hugged him hard. She loved her father without reserve and she knew that she was loved in return.

"Steady on Mary, you will choke the life out of me!" spluttered Joseph as she squeezed his neck with some force. He gazed at his daughter with a smile on his face. Many people had already told them that in their opinion, Mary should be in an institution, but he could not bring himself to do it. She was definitely a handful, always getting into mischief, especially when she had been a small child. At fourteen, she was showing some of the physical signs of becoming a woman although mentally, she was still a little girl. Mary was shorter than most other girls of her age, but was of sturdy build and unaware of her own strength. Joseph worried that one day she may unintentionally hurt Esther with her rough and tumble. For now they must deal with the problems which arose, but at the same time take delight in the affection which their only daughter afforded them.

The sun shone when Joseph awoke on his first full day at Batty's Furniture Emporium. As he opened the curtains the rays of the early morning sun were beginning to creep into each corner of the room. Esther was up and already making her husband some tea and a thick slice of bread with dripping. He was rather nervous, but at the same time he felt a sense of optimism about this new start in life. Joseph walked the twenty minute journey into town, his boots ringing on the cobbles as he went and it was with a bright smile and happy demeanour that he opened the shop door. The bell sounded as the door opened and Joseph could see Mr Batty at the far end of the sales room.

"Good morning Mr Batty sir," he said brightly. "If you can show me to the workroom and explain my task for the day, I will begin work immediately."

William Batty regarded this new employee with uncertainty. He had been in desperate need of another joiner when Joseph came looking for work, but had since had time to think. Joseph had no indenture papers to prove his worth and so William was taking a chance taking him on. He would certainly need to establish himself! He seemed a likeable chap, if somewhat cocksure, but confidence wasn't necessarily a bad thing. Only time would tell, along with his skills at making furniture.

Joseph's co-employees stared at him as he entered the workroom. They had caught sight of him with Esther during the few days since his arrival on Beelay Street and knew that he was about to work with them, but knew nothing more about him. As Joseph worked, he made friendly banter with his fellow employees and they with him. By the time the day had ended, Joseph felt that he had attack the man in the pub made some new friends and felt more relaxed in their company. The walk home that day was in the company of these new friends who all lived within a few doors of each other and they agreed to meet again at the pub down the street in less than an hour.

Esther was pleased to see him and helped Joseph out of his boots and sat him down to relax while she prepared the tea. He was full of the news about his job and of course the men he worked with.

"There's John Keen who only lives across the street with his wife, and John MacMillan who only lives a few doors away," he started. "John MacMillan is from Scotland and so everyone calls him 'Jock'. That makes life easier when you have two men named John working together. Johnson Bland lives near John Keen and he has a young family. The lads are all grand and they seem to get on with me too."

Esther put his tea down in front of him and both she and Mary listened intently whilst he continued to talk about his day. Esther was relieved that his day had gone well and that he seemed in better spirits.

"I have arranged to meet the lads at the pub for a drink in a bit," he added. "I didn't think you would mind and it seemed a good way to get to know them better. I will just finish my tea and have a wash; then I will be off."

Esther was a bit disappointed that Joseph wanted to go out and spend some of their savings on beer, as he had not yet had a week's wages and the money pot was almost empty.

"We have very little money left until you get paid," she reminded him. "So don't get carried away and spend every penny we have. We still need to feed ourselves until you get paid."

"For goodness sake woman, can't a man have a drink with his mates after work without being nagged!"

Esther was hurt by Joseph's curt reply. After all, she was only concerned for their wellbeing. She did not reply to his outburst, but turned away and took the dirty dishes to the scullery to be washed. As Joseph left, the door closed with a bang behind him and Esther felt a sinking feeling in the pit of her stomach. She hated confrontations with her husband and thought that this new start would make things better. His temper was short and he often became irritable when he was 'in his cups', and she fervently hoped that he would be sensible tonight.

Both Esther and Mary settled down for the evening with their embroidery. Esther was teaching Mary how to make a sampler and they were soon engrossed in their efforts. They were both tired and so by nine o'clock, they made their way to bed, Esther hoping that Joseph would not be too long. Just as sleep seemed possible, she was roused suddenly by loud voices coming from the street outside and amongst all the noise, she recognised Joseph's voice. He was laughing and bidding goodbye to the other men who had been at the pub with him and eventually she heard him noisily opening the front door.

The thudding of heavy footsteps and furniture being pushed around also woke Mary. She got out of bed and went to the top of the stairs where she saw Joseph reeling about, trying to find his way up the stairs, but his feet seemingly unable to go where he intended them to.

"Esther! Esther!" he shouted angrily. "Who's moved the bloody stairs? Why aren't you down here waiting for me?"

Mary started to cry. She always felt uneasy when her father was like this. Sometimes bad things happened when he had been drinking beer and she went to her mother, and was cowering by her side when Joseph finally made it to the bedroom.

Joseph looked across the room towards his wife and vaguely saw the figure of his daughter by her side. It was the sight of Mary, huddled into the security of her mother's nightdress that seemed to bring him to his senses, so he turned and went out of the room. Mary crept into bed beside her mother and was soothed by Esther's calming voice.

"Everything will be fine now Mary. Don't worry. Your father will spend the night on the couch downstairs and in the morning he will be sorry for scaring you." Within minutes, the reverberating sounds of heavy snoring could be heard from the parlour and Esther knew that Joseph had gone to sleep.

Sure enough, when daylight dawned and Esther made her way down the stairs, it was to find Joseph still sleeping. His mouth was open and the snorts and snuffles she could hear almost made her smile, but her anger at him for coming home drunk had not subsided. She woke him gently and gave him a cup of tea, expecting a gruff response to his awakening. Joseph screwed up his eyes against the sunlight and held on to his head. The eyes which looked back at her showed repentance and as he looked up at Esther he realised that his behaviour the previous night had been unacceptable.

"Esther, will you forgive me?" he begged. "I got carried away and spent all the money I took with me. I felt I had to buy drinks for the lads to help our friendship and so I had too much myself."

Esther did not reply immediately, but turned her back on him. She felt let down by his actions and was annoyed that he had scared Mary. She turned back just in time to see him getting up from the couch. He staggered, and she sent him to wash his head under the tap outside. The cold water revived him, so after a quick breakfast of porridge, he was soon ready for work.

"You scared Mary last night," scolded Esther. "She doesn't understand what is going on when you come in drunk. Please stay at home tonight and make your peace with her. Until you are paid now, we will have to live on what we have in the pantry which is very little, because I am not going to beg any shopkeeper for left over's here!"

Esther had made her feelings quite clear and Joseph was not in any mood to argue with her. The atmosphere in the house was chilly and Joseph felt belittled by the way Esther had spoken to him. As he walked to work, he told himself that he would not allow his wife to dictate to him when or if he should go to the pub! He was the man of the house and he would do as he pleased.

The atmosphere in the shop was lively. Both John and Jock were talking about the way Joseph had got drunk the evening before and wondering what his wife would have had to say. They had got the impression that he was 'under the thumb'. Joseph's face affirmed their suspicions.

"Well man, did you get in bother last neet from your wife?" asked Jock, who was grinning like a Cheshire cat.

"None of your business," replied Joseph gruffly. "She'll do what I tell 'er and no mistake." Somehow though, Joseph felt a stab of guilt talking about Esther that way. She didn't usually interfere but he had his reputation to think about. He was quiet for the rest of the morning and the men didn't try to engage him in conversation – he would talk when he wanted to. Joseph was determined that if the men wanted to go to the pub again, he *would* go with them.

Mary woke that morning expecting her father to be bad tempered as he usually was when he had been out drinking the night before. She was surprised therefore to find that he had already gone to work by the time she got up. Esther was busy washing the dishes she had used to make the porridge. Mary thought that her mother looked sad, but as soon as Esther saw Mary's face she smiled.

"I thought we could go to the market today and see what they have to offer," said Esther. "It will be a chance for you to see some of the streets where we are living and get to know your way around."

Mary wasn't sure that she wanted to get to know her way around this new place where they were living. That meant she would be expected to run errands for her mother and she was afraid. People didn't know her here and they might call her names. However, she would do whatever she could to make her mother happy, and she looked like she needed cheering up.

"What you sad about?" she asked Esther. "Is it father? You upset?"

Esther looked at her daughter. She may not be all that clever, she thought, but she understands when someone is happy or sad. "I am not sad, just a little bit worried that your father may not be able to keep his new job for long," she replied, hoping that Mary would understand.

"Why? Not like working in shop?" Mary continued slowly. "Happy last night."

"I am sure that he likes working in the shop, but sometimes he can do things that the master doesn't like and so he has to leave his job," said Esther trying desperately hard to explain herself.

Mary shrugged her shoulders and muttered an 'Oh'. She didn't understand her mother or father sometimes. What they said didn't make sense. She turned again to look at her mother and saw the worried expression on her face. Mary hugged her mother and smiled at her, trying desperately to find a way to make her happy. To her delight, Esther smiled back and gave her a kiss on the forehead.

"Come on," she said, let's get ourselves ready to walk to the market. You will need a warm hat and shawl today as there is a chill wind."

Esther could not remain sad for long whilst her daughter was smiling. Her eyes lit up the room and the sun shone out from them, taking away the cold from the air. They set off for the shops, Esther carrying a basket to put any shopping in that they might get. She had taken the last pennies from their tin in the scullery and hoped that Joseph wouldn't want any money for the pub that evening. The tin was empty now and would stay that way until Joseph was paid at the end of the week.

The walk to the market took about ten minutes and although the weather was cold, they did not feel it. Esther encouraged Mary to walk briskly and this kept them warm. The street was busy with people going about their daily business. From the other side of the street, Esther heard a small group of young men jostling and jesting loudly. It took a few minutes for her to realise that they were poking fun at Mary. She hoped that Mary had not seen them and tried to ignore their gestures. It soon became obvious that they were not going to stop and very soon the hand gestures became taunts.

"Take 'er back to the looney bin missus, she'd be better off there!" shouted the ring leader of the group.

"Why is she dribblin'? That's what babies do," added another of the group.

Esther hurriedly guided Mary along the street, trying to outpace them, but the gang only walked quicker.

"Why they shouting?" asked Mary. "Not like us?"

Esther again tried to make light of the taunts, explaining to Mary that they were only young men trying to have fun and teasing. Mary however, understood only too well that the teasing was aimed at her and although she could not express her fears, they were only too apparent to her mother. By now, the group had crossed the street and were walking only a few feet behind them. Esther began to feel the threat and suddenly felt a stinging sensation on the back of her head. When she put her hand up to feel the spot which hurt, she felt the wet stickiness of blood and knew that she had been hit by something. As she turned around, she caught sight of another of the group taking aim to throw yet another stone – for that is what had hit her. She ducked her head and shielded Mary from the onslaught, but the gang began to run - shouting taunts of 'looney', 'thicko' and 'stumpy legs'.

Esther gathered all her strength and pulled Mary to the side of the tiny pavement gathering her daughter in her arms and wrapping her shawl around her to shield this vulnerable girl from the scathing, hurtful taunts of these ignorant men. Too late, the women were surrounded by the gang who were by this time taking part in the frenzy of taunts and physical bullying. Mary was terrified and clung to her mother, hoping that these men would stop and go away. Her body shook with fear and she was unable to move. The men were obviously drunk and Esther could smell the offensive odour of stale beery breath and unwashed bodies. A crowd of people, mostly women, had begun to gather a short distance away, not knowing whether or not they should intervene.

"What on earth is going on here?" demanded a booming voice from the side of the crowd now gathered. "Leave the poor woman alone!"

As the voice was heard by the gang, they suddenly realised that it belonged to Mr Walford the policeman who lived and worked next door to Esther and Joseph. The taunting stopped as Mr Walford approached and the men began to walk away, each in separate directions as if nothing had happened. The policeman blew on his whistle and brought the men in the crowd to their senses. Within a few minutes each of the men involved in the assault on Esther and Mary had been apprehended.

"I am so sorry that you have had to suffer this indignity Mrs Freeman. It is not a good way to be welcomed to Hyde. I can assure you that they will be charged with affray and put into the lock-ups overnight. If you have any further trouble with despicable men like these, you must let me know and I will deal with them personally." The policeman offered to walk them back home as he could see that Mary especially was in a dreadful state, shaking from head to toe. The poor girl had obviously wet herself in fright and she stood in a puddle on the pavement. Paul Walford was aware of this, but said nothing. He did not want to upset the family any further and he knew that Esther would sort it out when they got back home. He was a married man himself and was disgusted that the offenders should taunt women in this way, especially someone as defenceless as Mary.

Esther and Mary walked straight back home, leaving the shopping until another day. Mary was in no fit state to continue the trip to the shops that morning. Mary's plight was made all the worse by her urine-soaked clothing. She was acutely embarrassed, even with her mother, because of the state of her dress.

"It does not matter to me Mary. I can wash your clothes and you can have a wash and change into something clean in no time," she pronounced. "No one else needs to know!"

Once back in the house, Esther helped Mary to undress and took her wet clothes out to the tub in the yard and suddenly realised that she would be unable to wash them immediately as her tub was broken. That was one of the things she had hoped to do today – arrange for the cooper to come and mend it. Joseph would have to do that now.

Mary sat quietly beside the range in the kitchen, huddled on the chair, her face still showing acute signs of distress. Tears flowed down her pale cheeks and she was not the happy, smiling child she had been earlier in the day. Nothing would comfort her, except the hugs her mother could give her. It had been a traumatic experience, and one which she would not forget in a hurry.

Joseph had not made further plans to visit the pub that night, which was just as well given the scene which met him when he got home. Mary was still sat in the chair where she had been sitting all day since they arrived back from their eventful shopping trip, her face pale and blotchy. Her fingers plucked at her dress and she stared into the glow of the fire in front of her. As he entered the room, Esther immediately put her forefinger to her lips in a quiet sign for him not to talk. Joseph followed her into the scullery where Esther proceeded to tell him about the events earlier in the day. He listened intently at first until Esther went on to explain that Mary had been so distressed that she had in fact wet herself.

"Who did this?" he roared. "I will kill the man!"

Esther, flustered by the sudden noise of his shouting, tried to calm him. "Shhh... You must not upset her any further. I have told her that I wouldn't inform you that she wet herself. She feels humiliated by it all and does not want anyone, even you, to know."

Joseph gazed through the doorway at his daughter. "She may not be as clever as some," he spoke gently, "but she is my daughter and I will kill anyone who hurts her!"

Esther proceeded to explain the further details of the whole incident, including the fact that Mr Walford from the police house next door had walked them home and put the ringleaders in the lock- ups.

"I think I will go and see these men and let them know just what I will do to them if they come near my daughter again," he grimaced, walking quickly to the door.

Esther tried to stop him, but he would not listen. The front door slammed and Esther heard his fist hammering on the policeman's house next door. Shortly afterwards, she was aware of loud voices and a heated exchange of words coming from outside. It was obvious that Mr Walford would not let Joseph into the lock-ups and that Joseph was not happy about it. About ten minutes later, Joseph appeared at the door, closely followed by Mr Walford.

"I have tried to explain to Mr Freeman that he cannot take the law into his own hands and that the offenders of the assault on you and your daughter are being dealt with." Looking once again at Joseph he continued, "It will not help matters if you too are charged with affray or impeding the course of justice, will it?"

"Justice!" bellowed Joseph. "I hope for your sake

that justice is done. My wife and I have had to suffer the loss of three of our children before we came here. I thought we were coming to somewhere safe and to a place where we could settle happily. Now I find that some low living men are trying to make our lives a misery already!" He slumped to the floor in torment, unable to keep his distress to himself. Paul Walford and Esther helped him to the sofa and Esther tried to explain the circumstances which had brought them to Hyde.

Paul Walford left the Freeman house in stunned silence. He could truly understand Joseph's reaction to the thugs which had assaulted his wife and daughter, but was also aware that as a policeman he must protect his prisoners. He would need to keep a close eye on Joseph to ensure that his vehemence towards these men did not get the better of him. The last thing he needed was to be locked up as well. The group of men responsible for the attack had been drunk. This was no excuse for their behaviour, but it had made them forget any constraints which might have stopped them from behaving this way normally. They had been locked up and charged with assault on both women and were due to be sent to the local assizes for a hearing the next day. Paul hoped fervently that he would not see them again after that. All the men except one were travelling workers trying to find employment. The ringleader however, was a man already known to the police as a trouble- maker. He had been involved with this kind of crime before and Paul was relying on the magistrate to sentence him to a long term of imprisonment this time.

Joseph sat with his daughter in silence. He cradled her in his arms as if she had still been an infant and wondered what life would hold for her. Perhaps she would really be better off in an institution? At least there she would be safer from the taunts of other people. However, he knew that Esther would not contemplate such an idea and so put it from the forefront of his mind, but in the years to come the thought would rear again many times.

After a poor night's sleep, Joseph rose the next morning knowing that he would have to go to work as normal. Mr Walford had said that his wife would pop in to see if Esther wanted any shopping, and get it for her. It was obvious that Esther could not take Mary out again so soon, but somehow they had to get food. Hannah Walford was a young woman who had been married to her husband for several years but had no children. She had given birth to a still born baby boy a year after her marriage and had not been able to get pregnant since. It had always been a source of sadness to her that she had not had children, but had learned to come to terms with it. When her husband had told her about their new neighbours, she made it her mission to help. Hannah had no close friends and this would be her opportunity to form a new ally in Esther Freeman.

Esther heard the knock at her door at about nine in the morning. Joseph had gone off to the shop, promising to return straight after he had finished work. His thoughts returned constantly to his intention of finding out who had been responsible for the assault, and making them pay for what they had done. His mind was plagued with these thoughts throughout the day and he could not concentrate on anything else. Esther must not know of his plan that was certain; he would do this his own way and woe betide the thugs when he found them!

Esther opened the door tentatively, unsure about who might be calling at this time. She was nervous and peeped through the crack in the door until she saw Hannah Walford standing there.

"Hello Mrs Freeman! It is only Mrs Walford, the

policeman's wife. I just called to see if I could get any shopping for you."

Esther opened the door, relieved that it was a friendly face; feeling comforted by the fact that someone else cared.

"Come in, Mrs Walford. I am pleased to see you and thankful to hear a friendly voice."

The two women soon chatted freely, and Esther realised that she had a firm friend in Hannah. Mary was in the scullery washing the dishes and singing to herself. Hannah popped her head around the doorway and smiled at her. Mary was unsure of this new person and wary of her intentions, but her mother had taught her to be polite and so she smiled back.

"This is Mrs Walford, the policeman's wife, Mary. She had come to see if we need any shopping today so that you do not need to go out."

Mary ran to her mother and gave her a hug in response to this piece of good news. She did not need to speak to let Esther know that she was happy about this arrangement; her facial expression showed her relief. As Hannah gazed at the scene before her, she felt saddened by the way this innocent girl had been treated and vowed to help all she could.

In the days that followed, Esther and Mary began to walk with Hannah to the market when they needed anything from the shops and the company of the policeman's wife, who was well known, gave them security.

Chapter 3

Joseph tossed and turned. He was drenched in perspiration, little rivulets of his sweat running down his back soaking the bedclothes. Esther tried to wake him, but he was sound asleep. The faces of his young children were before him, pale and waxy. Dark circles surrounded their eyes and they too were damp with the ravages of fever. Thomas's face bore the hideous rash that was brought on by his illness and Hannah was crying for her mother. He was unable to help them and the more he tried, the louder they cried – "Help us father, we are hungry." It was then he noticed just how thin they were and that they were barely able to stand. In desperation, he rose to pick them up and could not reach them. "I am here," he cried. "I will help you!"

Esther, concerned by her husband's ramblings shook him hard. "Joseph! Wake up! Wake up!"

Joseph opened his eyes, showing in them the terror that had been his nightmare. He was unable to speak for a moment and when he did, it was amid a rush of tears which came in an unrestrained cascade.

"I saw them – our children. They were crying out for help and I could not reach them. Oh Esther, what have I done?"

Esther cradled her husband knowing that he carried the burden of guilt which she had assigned to him. It was still difficult for her not to apportion blame, but she knew that he would never have hurt his children intentionally.

"Joseph, it is not your fault that our children died. We have to get on now and look after Mary as best we can. Charles is safe with your father and we must try to rebuild our future here."

Joseph listened to his wife's words and tried to take comfort from them. But the dream was to return often

41

in the coming years and he held within himself, bitterness towards the men who had scorned his daughter, vowing to make them pay somehow.

It was an exhausted Joseph who returned to work the next day. He looked grubby and had not had time to shave. Listening to the conversations around him, he gradually gleaned bits of information about the other people in the locality.

"You look tired today Joseph," remarked Jock with a grin. "Been on the drink again have you?"

"No!" grunted Joseph. "I have my worries at home and did not sleep well, that is all. But I might want to go to the pub tonight if you want to accompany me."

The men agreed to have a quick drink with Joseph after work. He looked like he needed it! Joseph remained in a cantankerous mood for the rest of the day, snapping at anyone who spoke out of turn, his thoughts remaining with Mary and his plan of revenge.

The pub was busy that Friday evening, bustling with men desperate to spend their hard earned wages and get some relief from the stresses of the working week. Loud jeering and laughter came from the snug, where someone was telling a funny story. As Joseph sat in a quiet corner with Jock and his friends, he listened intently to the conversations around him.

"You're quiet tonight Joe," said Johnson. "I got the impression at work that you needed to talk, but you haven't spoken a word."

"I am sorry lads, but my wife and daughter were assaulted the day before yesterday and I am trying to come to terms with it. My daughter is rather slow and behaves differently to other girls of her age and they were set upon by some idiots who could not resist the urge to pour taunts upon them." Joseph kept his head down in an embarrassed silence. After what seemed like an eternity, Jock broke the anguished calm.

"Joseph. You should have told us earlier. No wonder you have been feeling out of sorts! What sort of mindless thugs would do such a thing?" The men were all stunned by what Joseph had told them and tried to reassure him that justice would be done. But it was just a string of words to Joseph. What he needed was to see the criminals punished. As they sat quietly talking, it became obvious to Joseph that a couple of men at the bar were listening to the conversation. He watched them intently and for a brief moment caught the eye of one of them. The man had a rough looking complexion and a face which bore the scars of a seedy life. Joseph instinctively knew that he would recognise him again and was sure that their paths would cross before long.

The following months were spent in the normal routines of work and home for Joseph. Both Esther and Mary were beginning to leave the house along with Hannah Walford to do the shopping, and after a fashion life appeared to be getting back to normal. An undercurrent of anxiety was still running along with the everyday tasks, but was kept in check by Esther's positive manner. The men who had been in the prison lock-ups had been before the magistrate and all had been sentenced to a year in prison and Esther began to feel that Joseph's threats of revenge had been forgotten.

Esther and Hannah became firm friends in the months that followed and were often seen together, whether it be at the shops or taking the fresh air along with Mary. Esther felt secure in her company and there had been no more incidents of abuse. Joseph however, continued to have the nightmares about his children on a regular basis and became a more sullen, unsociable man. He spoke little to the men he worked with and did not visit the pub very often. In time, he lost the camaraderie he had gained when he first began to work at William Batty's shop and became more solitary.

Esther was concerned about him and now actively began to encourage him to go to the pub occasionally with the men after work.

The autumn of 1872 was a mild one, September bringing unusually warm days and thunderstorms. Joseph had decided that he would go out with Jock to the pub one Friday after work. He was sick to death of feeling bad, and deep down knew that he had to somehow forget the traumas of the past year or two. When he awoke early that Friday, it was to the sound of thunder clashing overhead and the sight of forked lightening which seemed to light up the room even in the dull glow of the early morning. As he glanced out of the window, he saw to his surprise the figure of a man whose thin jacket was pulled up around his ears to protect him from the rain which proceeded to pour down in torrents. The man was looking up at Joseph until he realised that Joseph was also looking out at the scene below him. Their glances met briefly and the gloomy figure of the man outside suddenly ran into the shadows of the buildings opposite. A prickle of uneasiness made Joseph look even closer and for a moment, he thought that he recognised him. What on earth was this shabby looking man doing gazing up at his window so early in the morning? Joseph could not shake off the idea that he had seen him before and felt ill at ease leaving his wife and daughter that morning. However, he had made up his mind to be more sociable at work and so tried not to worry.

Esther and Mary had their cleaning to do and set about it with gusto. The floors were swept and rugs taken into the yard to be beaten within an inch of their lives. Furniture was dusted and everything was left as neat as a pin. It was during this frantic cleaning, that Mary discovered she was being watched. The rug she was beating was draped over the back yard wall and as she beat the rug, she sang her own little song. Totally engrossed in her work, she did not immediately notice the untidy little man staring at her from the other side of the wall.

"Looney girl," came a voice from the other side of the wall. "Looney girl."

Mary suddenly looked up at the face of the scruffy looking man. His hair was unkempt and he was dirty. As she glanced at him, he grinned at her. His teeth were yellow and he had several missing which gave him the appearance of a tramp. Mary was terrified, not just at the emergence of this man, but at the words he had spoken. These were the same words which had been spoken by the men who had attacked her all those months ago. Petrified, she ran indoors to her mother, leaving the carpet beater stranded on the ground.

"Man! Man!" she shrieked at her mother.

Esther looked at the terror in her daughter's eyes and knew that something had happened. She too ran out into the yard only to find the carpet beater abandoned on the ground. As Esther nervously peeped over the yard wall, expecting to find something horrific, she saw nothing. There was no sign of the man Mary had so loudly protested about. Mary would not come out of the house and so Esther went back inside to try to decipher the mutterings which came from her daughter's mouth. In obvious distress, Mary could not explain to her mother what had scared her apart from the fact that she had seen a man. The two of them stayed indoors for the rest of the day; Esther trying to keep Mary calm and relaxed. She would need to tell Joseph when he got home!

The day had continued to be rainy and it was a group of rain soaked men who entered the pub after work that day. As Joseph drank his beer and engaged in conversation with Jock, he heard a sniggering sound from behind him. Joseph was sat by the bar and as he turned around he heard snatches of a whispered conversation: "…looney girl" and "…father of that idiot girl".

The two men involved in this conversation were poorly dressed and Joseph was sure that one of them was the man that he had seen sitting in the corner of the bar not long ago. He had the same worn face and unkempt appearance. The other man however, was the one who had uttered the insults and he was grinning from ear to ear.

Joseph leaped off the stool and in seconds had his hands around the throat of the man who had spoken. "How dare you speak of my daughter like that? Was it you that attacked her all those months ago? I will kill you!"

Jock immediately sprang to his feet and held on to Joseph's arms pulling them behind him in order to restrain him. The two men tussled together, Jock trying to keep Joseph away from the scruffy man, and Joseph intent on doing this man harm. Eventually the innkeeper, a burly man, managed to help Jock pull Joseph away. The scruffy man and his companion immediately rose from their seats leaving tables overturned; and escaped from the pub in a hurry.

"Get the constable!" shouted the innkeeper, and several men ran outside to fetch Mr Walford and chase the man who had been the cause of all the trouble. Joseph was manhandled to a seat and kept there until Mr Walford arrived. It soon became obvious from further discussions amongst the other customers, that the man who had taunted Joseph was indeed one of the original thugs who had attacked his wife and daughter. He had served his time in prison and come back to the area where he had previously lived. He had no job and was it seemed, homeless; trying to find lodgings but to no avail. Paul Walford had no option but to put Joseph in the lock-up overnight to calm down.

It was dark and well after tea time when Esther heard the knock at the door. By now she was getting worried about Joseph, feeling sure that something had happened to him. He should have been back from the pub. She fervently hoped that there would not be a repetition of the last time he had arrived home very late, drunk and unable to get up the stairs to bed. The loud rapping at the door made her jump and she tentatively opened the door, unsure of who would be calling at this late hour. When she saw the face of Paul Walford, she panicked. Surely her fears were correct! Joseph must have been hurt; or even worse be dead! Mr Walford saw the look of panic on Esther's face and led her to a chair where she could sit calmly and be told the news that in fact her husband had been involved in a brawl at the pub.

When Esther had been informed of the unexpected news that Joseph was now next door in the lock-ups, she wept.

"What am I going to do?" she cried. "We too have had a scare today." She went on to explain the incident of the man in the yard and was sure that the two events were linked.

"Try not to fret Esther. Joseph will only be in the lock-ups for the night as I have just given him a warning. He is fortunate that I know him quite well and am able to see his side of the story. However, he must behave in the future or he may well find himself in prison for assault."

Fortunately, Mary was by this time in bed and not a witness to the scene below in the parlour. Next door, Joseph had time to mull over the events of the day and calm down. He realised that without a doubt the man in the pub was the same man he had seen earlier in the day. He must have been watching the house! Not knowing that Esther too had had her troubles that afternoon, he felt that his family were somehow in danger. He also realised that if he had attacked the man in the pub as his instincts had almost let him; he would by now be held for affray or even malicious wounding and then possibly a term in prison. In frustration, he pounded his fists into the floor until his knuckles were bloody. "I will get him though, somehow," he muttered to himself.

As she lay in bed that night, Esther mulled over the events of the day. Could the stranger who frightened Mary have had some link to the brawl in the pub? Although PC Walford had explained the reason for Joseph's detention in the lock-ups, she was not sure of the details. Joseph had some explaining to do the following day! Then she panicked. Would he be released in time for work? Saturday was a busy day at the shop and she was confident that he would lose his job if Mr Batty was made aware of Joseph's involvement in the scuffle at the pub. Her sleep that night was troubled with images of the family without an income again – no food and hardly any savings to pay the rent. When Esther woke early the next morning, she was bathed in sweat and exhausted. After washing her face in cold water from the ewer, she hurriedly went down to the scullery where she began to make breakfast. If Joseph was released early enough, he would need breakfast.

The minutes passed slowly, but eventually at about eight o'clock, Joseph opened the door of the house, head held low, looking dishevelled and weary. Esther dashed to meet him and he put his arms around her.

"Esther, I am sorry for the distress I have caused you. Mr Walford has let me out early without any charges and so if I hurry, I should be able to get to work. Just pray that Mr Batty isn't informed of what has happened!" He held on to her tightly and for a moment, they were reminded of the passion they had felt for each other in the early part of their marriage. Esther looked up into the worried face of her husband and their lips met in an urgent kiss. What Joseph wanted to do most of all, was to make love to his wife. She had understood so far and he must not let her down, but his obsession for revenge was all consuming.

Esther broke the silence. "Joseph, you must wash and make yourself look presentable. I will make you something to eat and then you need to get off to the shop. Tonight we will talk about yesterday, for there are things which you do not know yet!"

Joseph glanced at Esther's worried face, not understanding her fears, but knowing that she too was concerned about something he had no knowledge of.

"What is the matter Esther? What else took place yesterday that I am not aware of?"

Esther, needing to talk to her husband, but aware of the urgency to get him off to work, made light of the news she had to tell him and persuaded him to go. Their conversation would need to wait.

Mr Batty paced the floor. Where was Freeman? Joseph's behaviour of late had encouraged his employer to keep a watchful eye on him. Something was amiss and Mr Batty did not want his employees to bring their personal troubles into his shop. The other men had no idea about his whereabouts or why he might be late, but William Batty suspected that Joseph had been drunk the previous night and slept in. When Joseph did finally enter the shop, an hour late, he was full of apologies to Mr Batty.

"I am sorry sir for my lateness and understand that

you will have to fine me, but my daughter has been ill these last few days and we have been up in the night tending to her needs." The lie tripped easily off his tongue and Joseph surprised himself at the ease at which he was able to convince Mr Batty of Mary's illness. As he spoke, Jock and the other men stared in astonishment at Joseph, all knowing the true reason for his lateness and not really expecting him to arrive at the shop at all that morning.

Mr Batty grudgingly allowed Joseph to continue with his work, but gave him a stern warning. "If there are any more incidents like this," he bawled, "you will be out! Change your surly attitude and work hard then there will be no problem. As it stands, I will fine you half a day's pay!"

Joseph thought this was rather a big fine to have to pay as he was only an hour or so late, but dared not argue with him. His job was important and he must suffer the consequences of his actions. As they worked that day, Joseph quietly told Jock about his stay in the lock-ups and of his determination to find the man who had taunted him and somehow get revenge. Jock thought he was idiotic to pursue the matter any further and told him so, but soon realised that Joseph was single-minded in this matter and that there would be no change of heart.

"Watch your back Joe," he told him; "there are people in this area that would just as easily turn on you, if you made enemies of them."

The day passed slowly for Esther, and although she got on with her chores, her mind was constantly churning. Eventually, Joseph arrived home tired and hungry. They sat together with Mary at the small table in the scullery and ate a stew which Esther had prepared earlier in the day. They also tucked into home-made bread, and apple pie.

"This is a feast fit for a king," smiled Joseph, "let alone a humble joiner."

They tried to keep their anxious reflections away from Mary until after she had gone to bed. Esther was the one to bring up the thoughts which were uppermost in their minds.

"We had a scare yesterday," she said, after Mary had gone upstairs. "A man spoke to Mary over the back yard wall and she was terrified. I do not know what he said as Mary has been too frightened to be able to tell me, but whatever it was; it made her scream in terror."

His mind returning to the figure he had seen early in the morning, Joseph was almost certain that it could have been the same man. Perhaps the man in the pub that evening was the same man too! Joseph and Esther talked long into the night about what had happened and Esther was even more concerned by her husband's mood. He said little, but she knew him only too well and understood his need to protect his family, but could see problems looming ahead.

"Don't do anything rash," she told him. "We can cope with mindless imbeciles who taunt us with names, but I cannot manage if you are sent to prison."

Joseph took his wife to bed and for the first time in many months, she felt loved. In the days that followed, it seemed that Joseph really cared about her. His caresses brought a renewed vigour to their lovemaking and Esther began to relax. Joseph's calm exterior however, belied the turmoil in his head and he kept a constant vigil for the man who had taunted them.

Chapter 4

The letter from Scout was a welcome distraction from the problems which had recently beset them. Esther was unable to read, but she was fortunate that Joseph had been instructed in reading and writing as a boy and enjoyed reading whenever he had the chance, especially the novels of Mr Dickens which had been given to him by his father. James had written to tell him how Fred was getting on at the farm and with general family news. It would appear that the farm had begun to recover after the dreadful episode of consumption among the cattle. However, there had been an outbreak of measles and several of the children in the locality had suffered; some not surviving the illness. Fred was healthy enough and working hard, but in his grandfather's words was 'not best suited to work with animals'. It would appear that Fred disliked the dirty jobs which came with animal husbandry. However, he did what his grandfather told him, if somewhat reluctantly. Fred added his own words to the letter, poorly written and barely legible, but the few short sentences gave Joseph and Esther comfort in the knowledge that they had done the right thing in leaving him behind.

For Mary, watching the smiles on her mother and father's faces when reading the letter, made her feel happy. If they were happy, then so was she. Mary was determined to try and forget the face of the man who had scared her and so when her mother suggested that they walk to the park later that day, she reluctantly agreed. After all, her mother would look after her and ensure that she was not hurt. Perhaps Hannah Walford would come with them as well. She was well known as the policeman's wife and when they were with her, she felt safe.

Winter was fast approaching and the three figures were wrapped warmly with their heavy shawls fastened tightly around them. Bonnets were fastened with ties to make sure that they did not blow away in the gusty wind, but it was apparent that in spite of the chill wind, they were enjoying the saunter around the park. Mary's face was pink and her cheeks glowed with the cold. She laughed at the ducks on the pond that were trying to stay upright on the frozen surface, but slipping onto their tails as they hurried along. It made Esther feel good at last to see her daughter smiling again. Hannah had accepted their invitation to walk to the park saying that the exercise would do them all good. The park was quiet with the exception of a few mothers with young children also taking the air. It had generally become accepted that fresh air was a good cure for many ailments and so a walk around the park was becoming more fashionable for people of all classes.

The walk was uneventful and soon the women decided to head for home and a nice warm drink. Mary held on to her mother's hand tightly for extra warmth and as they approached the park gates Esther turned to look behind her as a noise in the rhododendron bushes nearby made her wary. The dark shape of a man quickly vanished from sight, only the rustle of the bushes giving any indication of his presence. Had she been imagining things? By the time they stepped through the gates and onto the narrow path that edged the road, she was convinced that it was simply her nerves which had made her panicky. Looking down at her daughter's face and not wanting to worry her, she tried to ignore her fears and they continued to walk briskly home.

From behind the camouflage provided by the dense undergrowth, a man smiled to himself. He knew he had been seen, but was not concerned about it. She was not his target, but the man she called her husband. His face was still bruised by the punches thrown at him and the swelling of a broken nose making his rugged face even uglier. It would soon be time for a return match. No one got away with clouting Barney Smith without getting a bloodied face themselves. Perhaps a little more taunting of that stupid daughter of his would bring him into the open.

As Christmas passed and the cold weather gave way to spring; the Freeman household seemed to thrive. Joseph had been forgiven by Mr Batty and had worked hard enough to be able to make a new cabinet for Esther for Christmas. She had been delighted with it and they had been able to afford a few luxuries for their Christmas meal. Life was beginning to look up! Mary was confident enough now to go to the nearest shops alone, after all, she was eighteen and any normal young lady of this age would have relished the idea of spending time away from her parents. Esther no longer had to rely on Hannah as an escort although she still enjoyed spending time with her as the two women had become good friends. Batty's Emporium as it was now called, was thriving also and had taken on another joiner. His name was George Smith and had lived in Hyde for many years, but not lived close by. He had always lived with his mother and she had recently died leaving George with nowhere to live. This had prompted him to find lodgings near the Emporium when he began his employment there. George appeared to be a pleasant, quiet man who worked hard and said little, but his eyes appeared empty of any emotion and it was difficult to guess what he was thinking. He was a stocky man with a ruddy complexion, like a man who had been used to working outdoors. Joseph and Jock introduced themselves to him on the day he started work and during that first day, told him about the local area – the pubs in particular and tried to make him feel welcome. George only really spoke to answer a question, and by the end of the week they still really knew very little about him except that he was not married.

When Friday arrived, Jock invited George to visit the local pub with them as had become their custom lately. He refused saying that he already had plans for that evening, but that he might go with them the following week. As Joseph and Jock sat drinking their tankard of beer that night, the conversation soon got round to George.

"What do you think of the new bloke then?" enquired Jock. "He seems amiable enough but doesn't give much away, does he?"

"There's something I can't quite work out about that man," replied Joseph. "I think perhaps I need to get to know him better to come to a decision, but he looks shifty to me. There's something about his eyes that makes me feel uneasy."

The two men brushed off their doubts about George and decided that he was probably the sort of man it took a while to get to know. Later that evening, when Joseph was finding sleep difficult, his thoughts once more returned to George. There was a familiar look about him, but he was certain that he had never met him before. He would ask him tomorrow at work and then that would settle his mind.

"George! Something troubles me about you," began Joseph as they settled down to work the next morning. "Your face seems familiar, but I am sure that we have never met. Do you have a brother living in these parts who might be known to me?"

Joseph made light of his enquiry, not wanting to offend George, but George misunderstood his intention.

"What business is it of yours whether or not I have a brother? I have come here to work and all you want to do is quiz me about my brother. I have never met you before and would have said so if I had!" George's curt response surprised Joseph and the other men in the shop. They immediately took this outburst to mean that George would rather keep to himself. As a result, they continued their friendly banter among themselves allowing George to get on with his work uninterrupted, and Joseph let him be.

The walk home from work that evening took Joseph longer than usual as he sauntered along enjoying the late spring sunshine. It would be dark before long and he wanted to make the most of the peace and quiet. His thoughts dwelled upon his daughter. It would not be much longer and she would be nineteen, but she still maintained the behaviour of a child. To look at her, she seemed much like any other young woman except for the rather masculine way she had of walking. Her face was quite pretty, but she was a stocky girl now whose clumsiness had become more obvious in the past few years. Joseph worried about her. What would she do if he or Esther passed away? Even worse, if both of them died! The events of the last year or so had made him realise that she needed the support of her parents even more now, than when she was a young child. He knew that Mary would never be able to hold down a job independently and would probably rely on her parents for financial support for the rest of her life. The burden of this responsibility rested firmly on his shoulders and would stay there unless Esther managed to find employment. But how could she when that would mean Mary would be left on her own during the day which was not a good idea. Trying not to show his concerns, he finally opened the door of his small terraced home to find a warm welcome from his family. The next day was Sunday and he was determined to make it a family day. They would go out, even if it meant a stroll around the park. He knew that Esther and Mary had already ventured there, but it was a place which he had never had the time to explore.

Sunday was a beautiful fine day. The sky showed no sign of rain and the blue patches between the clouds told him that it was going to be sunny. He was suddenly reminded of the countryside around Halifax; the bluebells would be coming out now and he could almost smell the green grass. A pang of homesickness washed over him and he had an urgent desire to go home. Hyde was not home, and he would always think of the countryside around Scout as his real home.

Esther quickly brought Joseph from his reveries as she grabbed hold of his arm squeezing it tightly. Mary walked ahead of them as by now she knew the way and it made her feel independent to walk in front, almost as if she were actually on her own.

"You were deep in thought then Joseph," she said to her husband. "What was on your mind?"

"I was just reminded of home," he answered. "The air was so fresh and the grass so green. I miss the countryside terribly. Do you think we might return there some day?"

Esther considered his thoughts. "I think it's unlikely. We are just beginning to settle here now and it would be another upheaval to move back. After all, where would you work? You have got a good job here and you would be going back to a farm where there isn't enough work; which would mean a job in the town. We would end up living in one of the nearby towns, not the countryside and I don't think we would be much better off, do you?"

"Perhaps," he answered quietly, but his thoughts still remained with the idea of returning to Scout.

Mary was enjoying the walk. She pretended that she was on her own, and on her way to meet a young man. He would be tall and well dressed, not like the man who had scared her; and he would be very kind. Every young man she passed along the route to the park was identified as a possible beau and she smiled at every one. Before long, her smiles brought a smile in return and she took this to mean that the young men were interested in her. Just as they passed the park gates, she smiled at a man who was indeed tall, well dressed and very handsome. He was alone and also walking into the park. He returned Mary's smile and nodded his head. Mary made a bee-line for him and within no time at all, he had spoken to her and was trying to engage her in conversation. Mary was rather shy and although she was flattered by his attentions, she was brought firmly out of her dream when she realised that he wanted to talk. This was something she was not very good at and the idea of joining in a conversation with him scared her to death. Although this only took minutes, and the man actually meant no harm, Mary began to panic. Her parents were only yards behind her, but the young man had no idea that she was indeed with them.

Esther could sense Mary's alarm from yards away. She could see the young man trying to talk to her and was unsure about his intentions. Mary had begun to flap her arms in an agitated fashion and suddenly shouted at the innocent man before her. The man was immediately alerted to Mary's panic and not understanding her difficulties, took hold of her arms to try and calm her. Joseph was instantly by Mary's side, pushing the man away and shouting obscenities at him. The man was bemused by all that was going on; after all, he was only talking to the young woman and it was she who took fright. In desperation he began to walk away, shouting to Joseph as he went.

"I was only talking to her. Where is the harm in that?"

Esther calmly took charge of the situation and led Mary by her hand to a park bench. "What did he do? Why were you upset?" Between sobs, they were able to ascertain that the man had in fact not done anything. They realised that perhaps it had been Mary who had led him on and that the man had been innocent of any crime. The realisation that their daughter was now a young woman and perhaps had begun to have feelings of interest in the opposite sex, suddenly became obvious to Joseph and Esther. This was another worry for them and was to prove problematic in the future.

Chapter 5

George tucked into the pie which his landlady had made for him. The gravy trickled down his chin and he wiped it with the back of his shirt sleeve. He was content. The job he had managed to find was paying him a reasonable wage and he was able to keep a keen eye on the Freeman bloke his brother had mentioned. Barney was plagued with the thought of doing mischief to this man and his family in return for having to spend a year in prison. No man wanted to be incarcerated in a small, dank and smelly cell for long; and Barney had endured a whole year of it: all for teasing his daughter! She was an idiot anyway, so what did it matter? Those sorts of people should be in the workhouse and not be a burden to normal people like him.

It had been George's task to follow the girl and her mother to make them feel uneasy. He was sure that he had done the job well as he knew they had all sensed his presence, and the girl was scared witless when he had teased her over the backyard wall. It wouldn't be long now and they would have the job done. Barney had been stupid enough to get himself caught in the pub by Freeman when he heard him talking. Still, he had paid for that with a bloodied face. Freeman had been late into work the next morning, uttering some excuse about his daughter being ill. If only William Batty knew! Well, thought George, I can remedy that before I leave. Barney had arranged with his brother to go north after they had sorted out Freeman, perhaps finding jobs in one of the mills in Lancashire – anywhere but here.

The night was cold and George turned up the collar of his threadbare jacket as he strolled down the street to meet Barney at the corner of the market. It was not wise to be seen together in public anywhere close to where Freeman lived or the pub where he drank. This could so easily blow his cover and George did not want Joseph to realise that he was Barney's brother. The fact that Joseph was a bit suspicious already didn't help. He had already enquired as to whether or not George had a brother. They were very much alike in appearance and it was this which had sparked Joseph's uncertainties. George had been forced to be rude and give the impression that he was an introvert, discouraging any banter between them. What he really wanted to do was to become one of Joseph's friends and use his friendship to find out about the family. Instead, he had chatted to one of the other workers in Batty's emporium who seemed to know everything about most of the employees there.

"Psst! Over here!"

George was distracted from his thoughts by the quiet, urgent whisper of his brother who was lurking in the shadow of a shop doorway. Barney had his cap pulled down over his eyes to try and shield his face and disguise the twisted nose.

"Well, what do you know?" hissed Barney to his brother. "Is the Freeman girl frightened to death yet?"

George began to divulge any gossip he had gleaned from the last few days at work, but was unable to reveal anything which would really help Barney except the information that the girl was more confident again, but also now seemingly interested in talking to young men. The fact that Mary had approached a man in the park had not gone unnoticed by George as he had followed the whole family on their jaunt that day. This was the news that Barney had been waiting for and an idea began to form in his mind...

The outing to the park had been for the most part and enjoyable one for Joseph and his family. Mary soon got over her fright as after all, the young man hadn't done anything to her and she had enjoyed his attentions. Esther was still worried about Mary's new found interest in young men and vowed never to let her out of her sight. This was becoming more difficult as Mary was starting to enjoy a sense of independence when allowed out of doors on her own. She had only ever been to the shop when her mother had sent her for simple things such as bread or flour where she had no need to make a choice. After the incident in the park however, Esther was reluctant to allow Mary to even go shopping unaccompanied. This only led to confrontations between them and Mary's temper was often unleashed. Esther bore the brunt of her emotional outbursts, often being left with bruises to her arms where she had tried to restrain her daughter.

As the Christmas of 1873 approached, Esther was busy with preparations for the festive season. She had been saving with the goose club so that they would have a fat juicy bird to be the focus of their Christmas meal. Small gifts had been wrapped ready for the family and there was a small present for Hannah. Esther did not know what she would do without her friend especially as Mary seemed to trust her implicitly. The gift was a table runner which had been lovingly embroidered by Mary and hemmed with tiny stitches so fine that it was difficult for the human eye to see them. The brown paper which Esther had saved all year had been put to good use and a length of red ribbon had been purchased to secure the paper.

Esther went into the parlour to remind Mary to wrap the gift so that they could take it round to the Walford house later in the afternoon. She expected to see her working on her latest piece of embroidery, but Mary was not to be found. Esther's heart began to beat faster as she realised that the front door was ajar. Dashing upstairs to see whether or not she was in the bed chamber, Esther began to panic. Mary had never done this before and so Esther gathered her cloak hastily, noticing that Mary's cloak had also disappeared, and went out onto the street. Alarm was evident as her voice trembled and Esther began to shout her name. Passers-by became alerted to Esther's anxiety and came to her assistance. Hannah Walford, hearing the commotion, came out of her house and saw Esther in tears.

"What has happened? Why the panic?"

Esther told her that Mary had disappeared from the house and that she had gone without speaking a word to her mother. Hannah as usual took charge of the situation and brought her husband to speak to Esther.

"Mrs Freeman, try not to worry. I will look for her myself and bring her home safely within a short time. Perhaps she has gone to the shops."

He led Esther and his wife back inside where they were instructed to wait in case Mary returned, and the house was left unoccupied. PC Walford knew that Esther and his wife Hannah had taken Mary to the park several times before and so he was confident that this could be the place she was heading for. What he didn't tell the ladies was that there had been reports of a peeping Tom in the park just lately. He hoped that Mary would not try to engage anyone in conversation as this would alert them to the fact that she was a vulnerable young woman.

Mary was cross with her mother. Why was she never allowed out of the house alone? She was grown up and could not understand the reasons for her confinement. 'Well,' she thought, 'I will go out when mother is not watching and she will not find me until I am ready to come home!' As soon as Esther's back was turned and she was engrossed in her Christmas preparations, Mary took her chance; and opening the door as quietly as she could, she swiftly snatched her cloak from behind the door and left. She could see no one about except a beggar leaning on the wall across the street. She had seen him several times before, but he had never spoken to her…or so she thought. She knew her way to the park and had always enjoyed her outings there, so her steps took her hastily along that path.

Across the street, leaning on the corner of an unoccupied house, was Barney. He was also dressed for the cold weather, but this also served to add to his disguise. Pulling his jacket collar further up around his neck and tugging at his cap to ensure it was hiding his face, he watched Mary leave the house. This was his chance! Allowing her to walk alone for several yards, he then followed her at a discreet distance. She seemed agitated and ill at ease. He got the distinct impression that she was hurrying to get out of sight of her home as quickly as possible. In her haste, she stumbled and almost tripped over the cobbles, so Barney took his chance and waylaid her swiftly.

"Hello Miss", he sneered. "Can I be of assistance?"

He firmly held on to her elbow and guided her towards the park entrance, for that is where she had been heading. Before she knew it, he had pulled her into a rhododendron bush at the side of the path and was tearing at her clothes. Mary screamed for all she was worth and it was the piercing sound of these cries which saved her from a more vicious attack. The sounds of her cries alerted a man who was walking into the park at that very moment, and he looked around to try to determine the direction of the shrieks. Barney knew that he could not continue with his intended assault and pushed Mary to the floor.

"Tell anyone and I'll kill you!" he threatened, although it was obvious to anyone that an attack on her had been carried out. As Barney retreated from the bushes, the man who had heard Mary's screams was penetrating the thick foliage of the rhododendron bush. He just managed to grab hold of Barney by the collar and a scuffle ensued, but Barney was a brutal man and got the better of the stranger. As Barney ran off, leaving the stranger with a bruised and scratched face, Mr Walford was approaching the park gates.

"Stop that man! Stop him!" Yelled the stranger.

His cries went unheeded, as the park was very quiet that cold winter's day; but were heard by Paul Walford as he ran towards the gates. He watched as Barney dashed out of the gates, looking around shiftily to see if he had been noticed. Paul blew on his whistle hoping to alert any other constables who might be in the vicinity and immediately Barney recognised the familiar figure of the policeman. He turned and ran as fast as he could in the opposite direction, with PC Walford in pursuit of the criminal. Barney's face was familiar to the policeman but he was too fast for him to apprehend. Returning to the park after a brief chase, PC Walford entered the park to find the stranger sat on a bench next to Mary; he would capture the felon later.

Within minutes, he had ascertained that the man he had seen was the one who had attacked both Mary and the stranger. By this time, the park had begun to fill with people and a crowd had gathered around. Mary was distraught and did not know what to say. The sight of all these strangers pointing and whispering behind their hands made Mary feel embarrassed. She was paralysed with the anxiety she felt and held on to her cloak, pulling it tightly around her shoulders to protect her modesty, for her dress had been torn and her undergarments were plainly seen. Paul took out his notebook and began to take some details from the stranger, including his name and address. He knew that

Esther and Joseph would want to thank him in person, for he had saved their daughter from a dreadful fate.

Esther was pacing the floor in agitation. It had been at least an hour and there had been no word of her daughter's whereabouts. Joseph had not been informed yet of her disappearance and she knew that he would be in a murderous frame of mind when he was told the news. She would wait another hour before she sent someone to Batty's to find him in the fervent hope that Mary would be home by then. Where was she? Why had she gone out when she knew that her mother and father would be worried by her disappearance? All thoughts of the Christmas preparations had been put aside and Esther felt sick. Her mind would only allow thoughts of murder or rape to register, her instincts telling her that another child was to die before her allotted time. Minutes ticked by and she knew that she should let Joseph know of his daughter's predicament, but could not bring herself to do it just yet.

The front door was flung open and the force almost took the door off its hinges. PC Walford stood there with Mary at his side, slumped against his shoulder, fear and apprehension unmistakable on her face. Esther dashed to her side, pulling the quivering form of her daughter towards her.

"Mary! Where have you been? Are you hurt?"

The questions poured from her mouth in a torrent of jumbled utterances like a waterfall in full flow. Mary was unable to answer any of the queries put to her and was overcome by all the attention. Esther instructed Paul Walford to lay her on the couch before she fainted and Hannah brought her a glass of water. The doctor was immediately sent for as was Joseph, for now it was no longer possible to keep things a secret from him. Mary was unable to discuss her ordeal with the doctor, and although her physical wounds were easy to heal, her mental state was a cause for concern. Mary was prescribed some laudanum to calm her anxieties and she was put to bed to sleep for a while.

Joseph was unaware of the occurrences which had taken place that day and so was shocked to find a neighbour appearing at the shop asking to see him. William Batty took no persuading to give Joseph the rest of the day off. All thoughts of revenge reappeared in Joseph's mind and this time he *was* going to find the man who had harmed his daughter and teach him a lesson. If he allowed this idiot to go unpunished, he could do worse another time and Joseph wasn't going to risk that. He would need to make sure that Mr Walford knew nothing of his plans; he didn't want to end up in prison – where would that leave his family? It was now becoming an annoyance that the policeman lived next door to him. Events would be more problematic, but he would see to the murderous brute that had hurt his daughter!

As Joseph arrived home, he was just in time to see the doctor leaving the house. Inside, all was now calm and Mary was resting more peacefully in her bed. Esther was worried about her husband's reaction to the news he was about to receive and braced herself for the worst. Nevertheless, she made sure that he was told all the details of Mary's brutal attack and of the way in which she was rescued by a stranger. Esther went into the scullery to make tea for Mr Walford as none of them had taken any refreshment in some time. Joseph took the opportunity to talk to him.

"Who do you think did it? I know that you saw him. Was it someone you recognised?

Paul Walford hesitated for a moment. If he told Joseph that he knew the name of the criminal, then he would surely chase after him and end up in prison himself. Joseph sensed the reluctance to be open with him and tried to reassure Paul that he would not do anything which would jeopardise his family's future.

"I am almost sure that I know the man, but it is not police policy to allow the names of assailants to be made public before they have been charged with any crime. I am sorry Joseph, but I can't be of any help to you, except to tell you that he will be caught soon. I know where he lives and will be arresting him this very day."

This was excellent news for Joseph and he began to plan his tactics immediately. He would follow the policeman and find out where the attacker lived, and take his chance whenever he could.

Joseph paced the floor backward and forwards from the window, keeping a close eye on the comings and goings to and from the lock-ups. Paul Walford had not yet left the police house to go and find the man who had assaulted his daughter. What was keeping him? Patience was not one of Joseph's virtues and he was beginning to get irritated. Esther was alarmed by his mood although she understood his anger at the policeman. Surely he should have done something by now to bring the criminal to justice? She fervently hoped that Joseph would not do anything irrational.

"Esther, I think it is time that we really thought about moving away from Hyde. Our daughter is not safe here and it is only a matter of time before something else happens. I do not think that I can restrain myself if she were to be the subject of more abuse. Surely I will find work again if we move nearer to Halifax." Joseph was by now in a state of increased distress and was sweating freely. He was unable to sit down and was almost stamping his feet in rage.

"Try to calm yourself Joseph," soothed Esther. "Perhaps you are right about leaving Hyde. Mary has not been able to settle here and you are in danger of committing some kind of assault on this man. I know that you are enraged by what had happened, but revenge is eating you up and is not the way to solve the problem."

Joseph ignored his wife's pleas and continued to look out for any signs of movement from next door. His patience was rewarded when he finally watched as PC Walford left the police house and crossed the street. Within seconds, Joseph had his jacket on and had also left the house. Esther had no time to stop him or even to try to persuade him to stay indoors. Her mouth felt dry, and no coherent sound was heard, as she tried to call after him and her instincts told her that he had gone after the policeman to find the attacker.

**

Barney Smith had run for his life when he left the park and knew that he must hide up somewhere out of the way of PC Walford. When he knew that he was no longer being chased, he slowed his pace and walked quickly to his brother George's house. He would need to get in without his landlady being alerted to his distressed state. When he arrived at last on the tiny back street of shabby terraced houses where George had taken lodgings, Barney paused for a few minutes to try and make himself look presentable. Pulling at his shirt tails, he managed to use the corner to clean his face of the blood which had come from the cuts on his hands. After tidying his clothes a bit, he knocked at the door, fervently hoping that Mrs Jennings the landlady would not be at home. He waited for a few minutes and knocked again, the door being opened by none other than the dour faced woman, he did not want to see.

"Can I speak to George please?" he asked in a sickly sweet manner which belied the menace beneath. "I do

69

hope he is in."

Mrs Jennings regarded Barney with suspicion, but opened the door a little further and allowed him to enter.

"Upstairs in 'is room," she croaked. "I don't allow visitors after nine at night, so make sure you are gone by then!"

Barney went up the stairs as sedately as his demeanour would allow and entered the cramped room. George had not been in long from work and knew that Joseph's daughter had been attacked. It was the talk of Batty's Emporium. Knowing what he did about his brother, George had already suspected that it was he who had committed the crime and was expecting a visit from him.

"What in the blazes have you done now?" he leered at Barney. "The police are after you and I am not going to hide you so get cleaned up and leave!"

George was impatient with his brother by now and had no intention of becoming incriminated himself. He had already helped him enough. Barney glared back at him, growling his reply .

"She deserved it, constantly flaunting herself at the men she met. She should be in the workhouse and that Freeman fellow knows it! I have got my revenge on him now and so I suppose I will have to be content with that. Let me hide here for the night and then I will go north. If I go back to my lodgings, that policeman will find me. I am sure he recognised me so I am not safe there."

Mrs Jennings could hear the heated exchanges from down stairs and shouted her annoyance up to the two men. George was not going to allow his brother to stay a moment longer than he needed to and so after cleaning his cuts and washing his grubby hands and face in the cold water from the ewer on the wash stand,

Barney took his leave; threatening his brother as he left.

"You were supposed to help me get even," he whispered between clenched teeth. "I will not forget this!"

Mrs Jennings was glad to close the door behind the burly man who had just left her home. He looked and acted like a thug and she did not want that type of person in her home. She had not experienced any trouble with Mr Smith her lodger and had not thought that he was the type to cause any nuisance, but she would keep her eye on him in future.

To be able to leave the area and escape from the eyes of the police in Hyde, Barney had to collect his belongings from his own lodgings. All of his money was hidden there and he could not manage without it. Knowing that the police would soon be on his tail, he hurried through the streets in the darkness, keeping to alleyways and the shadows to assist his way. On reaching the street where he was lodging, he waited for a few seconds to make sure that no one was watching the house before he walked confidently up to the door.

**

When Joseph left his home that evening, he had no exact plan of action. He had been incensed by the actions of the thug who had hurt his daughter, and needed to get his revenge. The urgency and strength of these feelings had been eating at him for a long time now and he needed to be free of them. Following PC Walford was not difficult as the sun had long gone and in its place was a dimly lit moonlit evening. There was just enough light for Joseph to see the policeman at a safe distance without having to take any risks. PC Walford strode out towards the criminal's last known address hoping to catch him in. He had left it for a few hours before setting out in the likelihood that after hiding out for a while, the man he wanted would return to his lodgings to eat and rest before making a run for it.

An elderly woman with her shawl wrapped tightly around her shoulders answered the door when PC Walford knocked loudly.

"What do you want?" She shouted." No need to rap so loudly, I'm not deaf!"

From a short distance away, Joseph could see that the policeman was unlucky in his quest to find the assailant. His disappointment soon vanished when he realised that now he knew where the man lived and if PC Walford left the house without waiting for him, he would take his chance. Paul Walford waited for an hour in the parlour of the lodging house before he finally left. He decided that he would return early the next morning before anyone had got up, in the hope that he would catch him then.

Outside, Joseph watched and waited. The policeman left and the way was clear for Joseph to take his revenge if the thug did appear. He had all the time in the world and was prepared to wait. His patience was soon rewarded when he noticed a burly looking man approaching from the other side of the street. Joseph saw his chance and immediately disappeared into an alleyway at the side of the house. The man was obviously looking around him, to check if he was being watched. This had got to be the man he wanted and sure enough, he paused at the same door which PC Walford had only minutes previously left. Joseph acted quickly and without any thought to his own safety, surprised the villain by the suddenness of his attack. He grabbed the man from behind and took hold of his neck, immediately taking the wind out of him. Barney tried his best to turn and face his attacker but was surprised by the strength and ferocity of the attack on him. When Barney was close to collapse, Joseph let go of him, for he had no intention of killing him. The struggle which ensued ended when Barney was thrown to the ground. He landed awkwardly and knocked his head on the sharp corner of the alleyway wall.

Joseph bent to the ground to see what had happened and was horrified to see that the man, slumped against the wall, was unconscious and hardly breathing. His cap partially hid his bloodied face, and Joseph tugged the cap free from the matted hair to reveal the features which had so far eluded him. It *was* the man from the pub! This was the man with the hefty look and rough features he had seen ages ago when he was drinking beer with Jock and Johnson! Satisfaction poured through his veins like the effects of a strong drink, making him heady with the gratification that he had got the right man. But now was not the time to linger! He must get away quickly before anyone saw him.

In a blind panic, Joseph hid around the corner of the alleyway, trying to get his breath back, for he was not used to physical violence of this nature. He hoped that the man was not dead; that would mean possible hanging for him if he was caught. Realising the severity of his actions, Joseph knew that he would need to appear as normal as possible when he got home that night. He just hoped that no one had seen him!

Esther went to bed early, not waiting for Joseph. The events of the day had made her exhausted and as she trod her way up the stairs, she tried not to think about what he might be doing, but it was impossible. She washed her face by the light of her candle and undressed quickly. The night air was chilly and the room was freezing. Frost clung to the inside of the windows and Esther shivered; either with the fear of what might have taken place, or the icy temperatures;

but her teeth chattered as she lifted the blankets and slipped into bed. Thoughts of their dead children entered her mind as she worried about the future. What if Joseph had actually killed someone? He would be hanged and what would become of them? Apart from the shame of having her husband labelled a murderer, how would she cope with Mary Ellen? Knowing that it would be difficult to get and maintain a job, her worst fear of having to incarcerate Mary in the workhouse seemed a real possibility. Esther lay awake for some time, her mind ever more wakened to every sound she heard. Was that him? No, perhaps it was a drunk on his way home. How she wished that Joseph would return.

After the trauma of the day, Joseph expected Esther to be waiting; waiting for an explanation which would explain his absence. As he opened the door into the small house which he had shared with Esther and Mary for several years now, it seemed more dingy than ever and the silent darkness met him unexpectedly. Esther had not waited up for him as he had expected and he was disappointed. Looking around at the dimly lit room, he slumped into a hard wooden chair whose only comfort was a cushion which his daughter had embroidered. He had to remind himself that it was for her that he had put his whole future in danger that night. Joseph knew that he must have blood on his hands and torn clothes, but was unable to see clearly what he knew to be true. The urgency to divest himself of the evidence of his nights labours, made him get up and go upstairs. His footsteps seemed to echo: murderer, murderer; as he trod the stairs to his bed chamber. Please God he thought, he is not dead, only injured; for he had not meant to kill him!

Esther was wide awake in spite of the exhaustion which pervaded her whole body. Her mind was too active to allow sleep to take her and so when Joseph entered the room, she turned her head towards the door and her pale blue eyes, full of sorrow, met those of her husband. Tears began to flow: tears for her daughter, tears for her dead children, tears for herself and most of all, tears for Joseph and what he may have done that evening. She was so frightened of asking about his evening's activities because of the answer she might get. Eventually it was the expression in her eyes that did the asking.

As Joseph undressed, slowly ridding himself of the evidence of his night's toil, Esther watched him. The muscles on his chest and arms rippled in the glow of the small candles which served as a light, and she was reminded of the passion they had shared in this very room. Was all of this to be a thing of the past now? Now that he had, she thought, committed an assault on a man deemed to be their daughter's attacker; or God willing, perhaps he had been unsuccessful and their future would still be secure.

Joseph put his arms around Esther as he got into bed and before she had the chance to speak, he began to explain. He told her everything, including the fact that he did not know whether the man was alive or dead. Esther's tears turned to sobs and Joseph could not console her.

"What are we to do Joseph? She gulped. "If he is dead you too will die, and at the very best if you are caught, it will be the transportation ships for you!"

Her sobs, uncontrollable, meant that Joseph could get no more sense from her and as she clung tightly to him, he tried to think what to do. Eventually she calmed and he tried to console her.

"I do not think that anyone saw me, let alone the brute that hurt our Mary, so if I try to behave as normally as I can, and pretend that I was in the house all night, then perhaps I will get away with it!"

Esther was too upset to think straight, but Joseph knew that he must get this right. Although neither of them slept that night, Joseph was up early making his usual preparations for work. He had hidden his clothes under the floorboards in Mary's room and washed all traces of the blood from his body. Thankfully, his face had not been bruised in the affray and so there were no outward signs of any conflict. Esther made her husband a cup of tea to calm his nerves and he set off to work as normal. She knew that she must find strength from somewhere if she was to confront PC Walford when he arrived, as he surely would. She must protect her family and the only way to do that was to play her part in her husband's duplicity, which meant of course giving him an alibi for the previous evening.

Chapter 6

Barney lay in a bloodied heap on the tiny pavement until almost daybreak. No one had seen him, and if they did, they ignored him. Consciousness returned to him in a blur of confused images. As he tried to stand, he stumbled and fell once more against the wall which had done so much damage to his head. Putting his hand to his forehead where the pain was, he felt a sticky wet substance which he realised was blood and pulled his hand to his unfocussing eyes to see. A wave of sickness overcame him and as he tried to enter his lodgings, a man on his way to the mill stopped to help him.

"God man! What on earth has happened to you?"

No reply was forthcoming and he realised that Barney was in a bad way. Hearing the commotion outside her front door, Barney's landlady cautiously peeped through the curtains and on seeing her lodger being helped up by a stranger, she automatically assumed that he was in a drunken stupor. She opened the door, expecting to find Barney lolling in a pool of vomit, but saw instead a growing pool of blood.

"Send for the doctor! Send for the police!" she screamed at the top of her voice, alerting the neighbours to Barney's plight; and immediately tried to help the stranger in with the semi-conscious man. Barney felt awful. His head was swimming and he was totally unaware of what had happened to him as he was helped onto the couch in the parlour. Betty Wood had been taking in lodgers for the last ten years ever since her husband had passed away and until now, she had never been faced with an episode like this. She thanked the stranger and encouraged him to be on his way, assuring him that Barney would be well taken care of. The doctor arrived just before the police, only to find that Barney seemed to have regained full consciousness and was just about able to talk.

"Well, Mr Smith," said the doctor. "It would seem that you have been very lucky and although you have had a severe blow to the head, no bones seem to be broken. You have serious concussion and must take it easy for at least the next week to ensure no damage has been done to the brain. The cuts on your head have been stitched and should heal, although you will be left with scars."

The doctor was paid and sent on his way, Betty Wood vowing to increase Barney's rent and make him pay double the doctor's fee when he was able. Barney lay on the couch and tried to reflect on what had happened. Gradually memories were coming back to him and although he still couldn't remember how he had been injured, he did remember that he had assaulted Mary Freeman the day before. How on earth was he to escape now? Before he had time to put any further plans into action, the peace was shattered by a loud rapping at the door.

Betty Wood went to open the door, and as she did, Barney could see through the gap between the door frame and the door itself, the tall figure of PC Walford. Not knowing that Betty had sent someone for the police and terrified that the policeman would have come to take him away, Barney tried to get up from the couch. His head was spinning and he was unable to keep to his feet. The sound of a loud thud made Betty turn around and PC Walford followed her into the parlour, to find Barney slumped in a heap on the floor.

"Well, what have we here? Mrs Wood tells me that you have been assaulted and that she found you lying outside the house at about five this morning. Can you tell me anything about the incident?"

PC Walford was patiently waiting to deal with the obvious assault on Mr Smith before tackling the crime which had brought him to this very house the evening before. On obtaining no information as to the perpetrator of the attack on Barney, PC Walford then began to question him about the assault on Mary Freeman. Barney was guarded in his answers, pretending to have lost his memory.

"It seems to me, that we had better take you into custody, and look after you in the hospital under police guard until your memory is regained," declared the policeman with a wry smile. "It is possible that your attacker knows something about the previous act of violence on Mary Freeman."

Privately, PC Walford wouldn't have been surprised if Joseph Freeman had been behind this attack and knew that he must question him about it. For now though, he would see that Barney Smith was put under lock and key! He was a recurring offender who would be better off the streets and away from vulnerable young women.

Esther and Mary had decided to walk to the market and Hannah Walford had asked to join them. Although Esther found it very difficult to keep a positive demeanour, she knew that this was her chance to give the impression to others that nothing was wrong. Hannah had expected Mary to be a little quiet; after all it was only a day since she had been attacked in the park and both Mary and Esther seemed to be putting a brave face on things. On returning to the house, they were greeted by PC Walford, who, he said, had news for Esther and Joseph.

"Joseph has gone to work, I am afraid," said Esther, trying to smile. "He will be back at the normal time if you would rather come back then and speak to us both."

"Where was he last night?" quizzed the policeman, ignoring her information.

"At home of course," she replied, swallowing slowly to try and hide the lies. "We had a terrible time yesterday as you know, and when Joseph had calmed down, we did our best to come to terms with things and tried to keep Mary calm.

PC Walford turned his face towards Mary. "Did your father go out last night Mary? Tell me the truth and you will not be in any trouble."

Glancing at Mary for a moment, Esther was certain that her alibi was going to be proved wrong, but Mary was unable to answer. Her face crumpled and the tears began to flow. Seeing the policeman again had reminded her of the attack on her the day before, and she was not really able to understand why they were asking about her father. Esther ran towards her daughter and turned on PC Walford.

"See what you have done!" she shouted. "Mary is too upset to talk. This whole affair has made her withdrawn and she is unable to cope with any more strain which is put upon her. I have told you where my husband was and if you want to speak to him, you must come back later!"

PC Walford glanced round the room, trying to find any signs which might help him in his enquiries. He knew that he should go back to the house where Barney Smith had been lodging and search for evidence outside the house. It should have been done earlier, but in his haste to get Barney to the hospital, it had been forgotten. Hannah glared at her husband and pushed him towards the door.

"We are sorry Esther," she said quietly. "I am sure you are telling the truth, for why would you lie? Paul will come back later to talk to Joseph, but for now keep calm and try not to worry."

She was annoyed with her husband for almost accusing Joseph of a crime which she was certain he had not committed, but at the same time understood that he was just doing his job.

The day went slowly for Joseph even though the shop was busy with the Christmas rush. He tried to concentrate on his work, whilst expecting the police to come charging into the shop at any time to arrest him. During the course of the day, gossip had spread from customers that a man had been found almost dead outside his home and that police were looking for the perpetrator. As is usual with gossip, the truth is never far away, but it is often shrouded by exaggeration. How much was true was Joseph's worry, but as the time for him to return home eventually came, he was relieved that the day had gone by without a glimpse of the police.

It wasn't until about seven o'clock that the Freeman's peace was interrupted by a visit from PC Walford. The house was searched, albeit not effectively, and Joseph questioned about his activities the night before. Joseph was nervous, but disguised this as the turmoil within him and impatience to discover whether or not the thug who had hurt Mary had been caught.

"Tell me! Has the assailant been caught? Who is he?" he urged PC Walford, trying to ignore the pressure put on him to admit to Barney's assault.

"We have a man in custody, but this man has himself been the victim of a most serious crime. He is badly injured and in hospital and at this moment not able to tell us much."

PC Walford did not want to give too much away to Joseph, hoping that he would eventually say something which would incriminate himself. However, that was not to be and the policeman went away dissatisfied with his night's work.

Thankful that he was still in his own home and not

in the lock-ups, Joseph revealed to Esther the plan on which he had spent the day cogitating. He had decided to write to his father and persuade him to make enquiries about suitable work in the area close to Halifax. Perhaps, just perhaps, something might come of it. If no work was available, then he had decided that they would still leave Hyde, telling their friends that they were needed back home. It was, he felt, better not to have work and still be free, than have a job and then be transported for assault or even worse, for murder.

The next few days were interminable and Joseph's mood matched the weather – cold and grey. Christmas Day passed in a muddle of forced gaiety; for both Esther and Joseph tried hard to keep up the pretence of seasonable merriment for the sake of their daughter, Mary. Each evening after Mary had gone to bed, they sat in an uncomfortable silence, each not voicing their fears and by the time the New Year was upon them, Esther felt as if she would explode with the mental strain that the situation had brought about. The smell of fear hung in the air and clung to them like the damp mist on a foggy evening. It pervaded every nook and cranny of the house, taking charge of their every being, affecting everything that they did. Surely they would receive word soon – a note to tell them that work was to be had closer to home!

PC Walford had not visited them in several days and the torture of waiting for news was unbearable. Esther was frightened and the longer she waited for something to happen, the more scared she became. The fear she felt began to make her ill and she could not eat. As her appetite waned, her strength, both of body and spirit did also. Joseph knew that she was close to breaking point and became afraid of what that might mean. Would she be overcome the next time the policeman came to visit and blurt out all she knew? Or would she take to her bed like she had when their babies had died?

When PC Walford finally arrived on their doorstep a few days later, his arrival sent Esther scuttling to her bed chamber. She could not face him and so Joseph would have to confront him alone. Showing PC Walford into the house, Joseph bade him sit down with a wave of his hand towards the parlour and tried to smile.

"Have you brought us news?" he enquired. "Have you charged the villain with Mary's attack?"

"I have brought you news Joseph, but not all of it good."

PC Walfords face was grave. He scanned Joseph's eyes for any sign of guilt, still unsure about the outcome of his investigations, but Joseph held his gaze, his eyes seemingly innocent of any crime. Joseph however, was in an extremely nervous state. His palms were sweaty and his heart was beating fast. He must keep up the appearance of the injured father for the sake of his family. Hardly able to reply, anxiety forcing a lump into his throat, he voiced his concerns.

"Are you come here to tell me that you have let him go? My wife is ill in bed with the strain of the circumstances we find ourselves in. Mary has been the subject of vile taunts since we came here and I am beginning to think we would be better off back in Yorkshire!"

"No, Joseph; I have come to inform you that the man we have in custody has been charged with Mary's assault and will go before the magistrate at the forthcoming assizes. However, he has remembered something about his own attacker."

The policeman paused to allow Joseph to take in what he had just told him. Joseph's immediate elation at the news that the man had been charged, was immediately dampened by the sudden realisation of his own precarious situation. Had he recognised him or had the police been given some other evidence to implicate Joseph in the attack on the offender? Joseph paced the floor, agitated and hardly able to keep his composure. He absently combed his hair with his fingers and cracked his knuckles.

"Well, what is it? What has he remembered?"

"He only got a glimpse of the man, but remembered that he wore a red checked shirt. He saw the sleeves of the shirt when his assailant wrapped his arm around his throat trying to throttle him. That shirt must be covered in blood and so when I find the blood stained shirt, I will find his attacker! I must ask you Joseph, if I can conduct a search of your house in order to eliminate you from my enquiries."

Joseph thought that the game was up. PC Walford had only to look under the floorboards in Mary's room and he would find exactly what he was looking for, but could not really refuse to allow him to search as that would only indicate his own guilt.

A search of the house was started immediately, even disturbing Esther from her sick-bed. She was almost hysterical when she realised what was happening, but Joseph drew strength from within and calmed her. When PC Walford entered Mary's room, Joseph followed him, expecting the worst. He made a thorough search, moving furniture and emptying the drawers of what little furniture they had. He was just about to leave the room, when he noticed that the floor underneath the rug was uneven and creaked when he stood on it. Without further ado, he removed the rug and saw that the floorboards had recently been disturbed. Getting out his penknife, the policeman prised up the floor and took up the loose board. The tension was unbearable for Joseph who was certain that he would soon be ensconced in the lock-ups next door.

PC Walford was by this time lying on the floor with his arm almost fully in the space underneath the boards and feeling carefully for the evidence he sought. When he withdrew his arm, he was clutching something: not a shirt, but to Joseph's relief, a box; probably put there by the previous tenant for he did not recognise it.

Paul Walford was flummoxed. He was sure that he would find the shirt somewhere in the house. He had seen Joseph wearing a similar one only a few days before the assault; however, the evidence was not there and so he could not charge him with any offence. He left the Freeman house unhappy with the outcome but at that moment he was unable to do anything else.

The relief that both Joseph and Esther felt when the policeman left the house empty-handed was intense. Esther held her head in her hands and cried rivers of tears. When she had finished and there were no more tears to come, she felt drained. Her initial instinct after Joseph had hidden his clothes was to leave them there, but something had made her take them, and burn them on the fire. She had done this whilst he was at work and not told him. The evidence had been there for him to see in the ashes in the grate, but not for long. As the days went by, and the weather grew colder, the fire had been on for longer and by the time Paul Walford had begun his search, there was no sign of the clothes Joseph had worn. Esther clung to her husband for comfort and as she explained what she had done with the shirt, he felt a gratitude to her that would keep him forever in her debt. They were safe, at least for now and Joseph intended to keep it that way.

Chapter 7

Stacksteads 1874

The box which had been found under the floor in the house in Beelay Street contained a surprise. It was several days before Joseph had taken the time to look inside and reveal its contents. When he did, it was to his astonishment that he discovered some money. It had obviously been pushed far beneath the loose boards for he had not noticed it when he had hidden his blood stained clothes. It seemed as though the previous tenants of the house had been saving and left the house without taking the box. Either that or it was the proceeds from some illegal activity which had been long forgotten about! There was not a huge number of notes, but enough for them to feel that their future was about to take a more positive direction. Joseph knew that really he should try to locate the previous tenants and give the money to them, but he was also of the opinion that if they had really needed it, then they would have looked more thoroughly to find it. All Joseph knew was that the money would be useful in helping them to set up their new home and they would be able to afford to make the journey on the train.

Joseph had thought hard about where they should make their new home. He had known about the 'Golden Valley' as the area around Bacup had been nick-named, from the time he had lived in Halifax. In the past thirty years, many mills had been built in the valley and with them came not only the belching smoke of the factory chimneys, but a steady stream of workers, newly attracted to the region by the offer of work in the many mills. The war in America which had caused the 'cotton famine' had been finished these ten years and so Joseph felt that it could still be a good place to find work. In his haste to leave Hyde, he had almost forgotten his reasons for leaving Halifax in the first place, and overlooked the fact that the air around the factories would be polluted with the constant smoky clouds which swirled above the chimneys. A safe place to stay where Mary would feel secure; and jobs which would provide a living, were his only concern.

As the train rattled along, steam passing by in soft white clouds, Esther scrutinised Joseph. He was deep in thought and although she knew he was nervous about the move to Bacup, she could see that he was relieved to be on the way. He sat opposite her in the draughty carriage and was gazing out of the window at the many different sights to be seen; and as they approached the station in Manchester, they could virtually taste the coal dust, and the smell of the smoke became very nearly unbearable. Mary coughed and as they stepped from the carriage, Joseph hurried them along to a different platform to catch the next train to Ramsbottom, Rawtenstall and then Bacup. What a place this was! Steam bursting from the funnels of the engines waiting to depart, carriage doors slamming, hooters blasting their warnings and whistles telling everyone it was time to go. Although Mary was uncomfortable with the acrid smell of the smoke filling her lungs, she was excited by the new and thrilling activities which were happening all around her; but at the same time she became alarmed by the unfamiliar noises and held on to her father's arm for reassurance. People were bustling and jostling to make sure they were not late and porters carrying portmanteaus were knocking and bumping against each other, so Esther and Joseph walked on either side of Mary to ensure her safety.

The train to Ramsbottom was already waiting and Joseph managed to find seats for them which were next to each other, and before long they were on their way again. Once out of Manchester, the factories gradually disappeared and the open countryside came into view. Towns made way for fields and the vivid green scenery reminded Joseph of his home near Halifax, which was perpetually encircled by trees and fields.

It was several hours, and yet another change of train, before the family finally arrived at the station in Bacup. However, the journey had been much shorter than their original trip from Halifax to Hyde thanks to the wonders of the train and the money in the tin! The exhausted trio left the station and managed to obtain the services of a carrier to help them transport their heavy bags to the house in Tunstead Bottoms. They had Joseph's father to thank for that as he had been to arrange their accommodation the previous week and although it was nothing special, the rent was reasonable and to them, at that moment in time, it looked like a palace.

It took Esther several days to get the house in order and Joseph made use of the few days leisure time he had awarded himself. Why look for work just yet, he thought, when I have money in the tin? Esther's practicality soon made him see sense and eventually he was persuaded to go and look for work. She knew that the extra money wouldn't last long if they squandered it and they would more than likely have need of it before long. They seemed to go from one ordeal to the next and she was well aware that life would probably deal them another blow before too long.

There were many mills in Bacup, so the obvious choice for Joseph was to find work in one, but he reasoned with himself that he was a joiner by trade; and a good one at that! What he really wanted was to find employment making furniture as he had in Hyde and set off to investigate the local shops. Perhaps there would be a furniture shop locally, which might be in need of a joiner. It was worth a chance! If he didn't find work today, he would buy a local newspaper and read the advertisements which employers sometimes put in. For now he needed the exercise and fresh air and relished the thought of meeting new people.

Spring was beginning to show signs of its arrival; the trees beginning to bud, giving the air that special fresh smell of newness; and so Joseph set off with a spring in his step. It had been raining so the cobbles were wet, and there was still a distinct chill in the air, but none of this deterred Joseph, and for once he felt as though he was about to step out of the darkness of his past and into the new beginnings of a fresh start. The house he was renting was in Tunstead Bottoms in Stacksteads, only a short distance from the ever growing town of Bacup. In recent years, the two places had almost become one as more industry had been introduced, and with it the houses for the mill workers. It was only about half an hour's walk to the main street in Bacup and as he sauntered along Newchurch Road, he passed several shops on the way. None of them seemed to be selling furniture but he hoped that as he got nearer to the town, he would find what he was looking for. By the time he had walked the length and breadth of the town, Joseph was beginning to feel dejected until he wandered into the new Market Hall; although the hall had, in fact been open for about seven years, it was still referred to in this way. It was a wonderful place, a handsome, stone building with an arched front which contained stalls of many kinds including ironmongery, toy stalls, a butcher and a café. As he wandered around, he marvelled at the variety of different things which could be bought, and looked for a stall which might mend or sell furniture. Just when he thought that he was going to be unlucky, he caught a glimpse of an old man perched on a wooden stool. He was almost hidden in the corner of the market, being surrounded by bits of broken furniture which he appeared to be mending. Spirits raised, he approached the man, taking great care not to knock any of the battered chairs and oddments he saw lying on the floor nearby. The old man did not seem to have a proper stall, but was sitting in the corner with a tool bench at his side where all manner of tools for making and fashioning wood were held. Joseph smiled at the old man.

"Good morning sir," he began. "I can see that you are very busy and have a lot of furniture to repair."

"If you need something fixing, I am afraid you will have to wait a few days. I have more work here than I can manage at the moment," the old man grumbled. "Come back next week and perhaps I can help you!"

Joseph immediately took his chance and sat down on a stool close to the man.

"No sir, I don't need anything fixing. My name is Joseph Freeman and I am a joiner and cabinet maker by trade. My wife and I have just moved into a house in Stacksteads and I am looking for work. I could help you get this lot finished this afternoon if you let me, then you can see how I work. If you like what you see, perhaps you could employ me. I am a good worker and will not let you down. Any work I do today, I will do for no payment to show you that I am an honest man."

The old man appeared startled by Joseph's sudden outburst and glanced at him over the rims of his spectacles, pausing for a minute or two from his efforts. He was exhausted and knew that he had taken on more work than he could manage on his own, but did not really want to pay anyone else to help him. At seventy, he had the best years of his life behind him and could do with taking it easy. His wife, God bless her soul, had tried for months before she died to get him to slow down, but he had continued to work. Now she was gone, and it was all he had.

"A joiner are you?" he said. "Well only time will tell me how good you are. If you can help me get this lot shifted before the end of the day, I might think about taking you on. I can't afford to pay much mind, so don't expect a fortune in return."

Helping himself to the tools on the work bench, Joseph picked up a broken chair and within minutes had it as good as new. It was a pleasant sensation to feel the shape of a hammer and chisel in his hands once more and he set about the work with delight. Soon the conversation flowed freely between the two men and Joseph found out that the old man's name was Jacob Ashworth and that he lived locally in Bacup. The afternoon went by in a flash and before the market had closed for the day, they had repaired all the oddments of furniture before them. Jacob was amazed at the speed at which Joseph had worked and was thankful that God had sent him some help just when he needed it. Putting his hand into his pocket, he pulled out a small handful of coins and smiled at Joseph.

"Here lad, take a shilling for your efforts this afternoon. I am only sorry I can't give you more, but you have worked hard and I cannot let you go without something for your labours. Come back tomorrow and we can talk about your employment. I need to go home and think about it before I make any firm decisions."

Happiness and gratitude washed through Joseph's heart. He shook Jacob's hand and agreed to return the next day. Whatever the old man was willing to pay would help and Joseph knew that he would take the job. The market was just about to close so he hurriedly bought half a pound of bacon, a cabbage, a few potatoes and some apples and set off back home. Today had been a satisfactory day in all respects and he knew that Esther would be pleased.

Esther paced the floor. Joseph had been gone all day and she was worried. She had expected him to return for dinner, but the soup she had made for him had long since gone cold. It was now tea-time and there was still no sign of him. Her imagination was playing games with her emotions and she was unable to think straight. Thoughts of him lying beaten in the street plagued her and by the time he eventually arrived, she had almost planned his funeral. When the door opened and Joseph walked in, she ran to him and hugged him tightly.

"Where have you been? I have been so worried about you being so long!" she shrieked.

Joseph held her tightly and began to explain what had happened that day. He gave her the bag of shopping and she relaxed.

"I have to return tomorrow and Mr Ashworth will discuss the terms of my employment. He says he cannot pay a lot, but at the moment, anything is better than nothing and perhaps it will be the start of a new business."

The evening meal was almost a feast and they enjoyed the bacon, potatoes and cabbage that Joseph had brought from the market. Sweet, stewed apples completed the meal and the family were at last able to think optimistically about the future. The money they had left in the tin could be hidden away and kept safe for a 'rainy day'.

Joseph was up early the next morning and ready to go to the market before anyone else was awake. He walked the short distance up the incline along the main road and into Bacup, whistling as he went. Jacob Ashworth was just setting up the stall when Joseph arrived and he was impressed with the enthusiasm he showed. It was agreed that Joseph would work for three days a week for a sum of six shillings. Joseph could not hide his disappointment at not being employed for the whole week, but gladly accepted Jacob's offer of employment. It was possible that if the amount of work increased, then Joseph would be offered a couple of extra days. He would work hard and make a good name for himself, and sometime in the future he might be able to set up his own business. Joseph knew that there was a waiting list for stall holders in the market and put his name down on the list immediately. When people got to know his work was reliable, he was certain that they would come back time after time.

Esther had her own plans and decided that she should also go and find work. There were plenty of vacancies in the local mills, and often not enough people to do the jobs; so within days of Joseph starting work in the market, Esther had been offered a job as a weaver in Stacksteads mill. Mary too was given the opportunity of working alongside her mother carrying bobbins. Between them, Esther and Mary would bring home a total of £1 each week. Joseph however was not pleased by the prospect of both his wife and daughter working if they didn't need to. Esther was quick to argue that he was not yet employed full time and so the extra money would be very useful.

"What about Mary?" Joseph asked. "Have you forgotten so quickly why we had to leave Hyde? There are people who will poke fun at her and she will be unable to work if this happens. You know how she will react if names are called and the overlookers will not put up with anyone who is unable to work properly."

Esther was adamant. "It is fortunate for us that Mary has been employed by the mill. She is too big to do many of the jobs which the children normally do and would not be able to carry out a responsible weaving or spinning job. If she works with me, then I can keep a watchful eye on her. The mills around here need workers and are willing to take on anyone who can do the job."

With this curt reply, she turned away from her husband dismissing any further arguments. Only time would tell whether they would manage and she was determined to make things work. She had stayed at home whilst they lived in Hyde and Mary still managed to get into difficulties. Working each day might just help to keep her occupied and at the end of each day she would be too tired to do anything else.

Chapter 8

As the knocker-upper woke them the next morning, rattling his cane against the window, Mary struggled to get out of bed. Esther had to coax her gently whilst making sure that they were at the mill gates for six o'clock. Once the whistle had gone for the men and women to enter the yard, the gates would be closed after them and anyone arriving late would be fined. Esther did not want to be late on their first day. After a quick breakfast of tea and bread, the two women set off. The clattering sound of clogs and boots on the cobbled streets could be heard everywhere as mill workers all over the town made their way to work. The mill whistle sounded and Esther and Mary were enveloped in the flood of all the other men and women, who were being swept along to the mill gates. All around them women with shawls covering their heads and men with their cloth caps, and a multitude of children of all ages, were greeting each other good morning with a cheery smile and enquiries about each other's families.

Once inside, the noise did not seem to abate either. The looms chattered loudly, but the workers did not. They had to learn to communicate with each other by lip-reading as the deafening noise of the machinery blocked out any other sound. Esther and Mary made their way to the weaving sheds where they were to work, and were soon involved in the hot, exhausting work which was to become their daily routine. Mary was unaccustomed to the excessive noise she could hear and felt scared. The overlooker showed her what to do and she began to carry the full bobbins to the weavers who needed them. She could see her mother and this gave her the courage she needed to continue, but many times during the day, she made mistakes and was constantly scolded for carrying empty bobbins back to the weavers instead of full ones. This, as far as the overlooker was concerned, was wasting valuable time and would not be tolerated. By the end of her first day, Mary was exhausted and could hardly summon the strength to walk home. However, this was only one day, and she knew because her mother had told her; that she had to do the same thing each day until the weekend when she would be given some time off. During the next few months, Esther and Mary fell into the same routine and eventually, the monotonous repetition of Mary's routine job was imprinted on her mind and she began to cope better.

By the end of the year, Joseph had managed to secure full time work with Jacob and his prospects were looking up. Poor Jacob had not the strength he once had and had decided that Joseph would be a good person to take over his business eventually. He had no sons, only daughters and badly wanted to leave his business to someone he could trust. Meeting Joseph had been the luckiest thing to happen to him in a long while and he had developed a great respect for him during the year he had worked with him. Jacob's bones were weary now and he found it more and more difficult to hold the tools he had once used to fashion beautiful furniture with.

Joseph had big plans. Jacob had already spoken to him about taking over the business and he longed for the day when he could be his own boss. The market hall was a good place to start out, but he wanted a shop where he could make and sell furniture and perhaps employ other joiners. He could take a risk now that Esther and Mary were bringing in wages to add to the family finances. By the summer of 1875, he was to get his wish. Jacob died suddenly and Joseph was left with the sole responsibility of looking after the stall in the market. What Joseph hadn't considered, was the fact that although Jacob had taught him about running his business, and even suggested that Joseph might sometime take over as manager, he had not made a will to that effect and so the stall was left in the hands of Jacob's daughters. It was decided that they would continue to run the money side of things whilst he received a wage in return for doing the work. Joseph was not happy about the situation, but in spite of the many arguments he had trying to persuade the women that the business had been intended for him, nothing changed. It was time for him to find a small shop and start out on his own. He reasoned with himself that he had customers who knew him now and had built up a large trade of people who wanted not only repairs, but custom made furniture. It wasn't long before he had found the ideal premises situated on Newchurch Road and only a ten minute walk from his own home. The shop was tiny, being a converted terraced cottage, and so had two small rooms downstairs and the same upstairs. His plan was to use the front room downstairs as the shop, the back downstairs room as his workroom and the upstairs rooms as storage for the furniture he would make. The rent of this small property was just within his reach, especially if he used some of their savings in the tin as payment for the first couple of months. All he needed now was to buy a few more tools and put an advertisement in the Bacup Times.

Esther was delighted with the way in which Joseph had worked so hard to help the old man Jacob, and was disappointed for the way Joseph had been treated by his daughters. She was even more thrilled when he told her that he had decided to rent the small shop on Newchurch Road. The day before the grand opening of the shop, both Esther and Mary spent several hours cleaning the dusty rooms and helping Joseph to polish the items of furniture which he had ready for display. It wasn't long before 'Freemans Furniture' was ready for business. Joseph had been to the Market Hall telling all the men and women he knew about his shop and had put an advertisement in the newspaper explaining that the first ten customers would be given half price repairs; and that the first customer to buy a piece of furniture would get a big reduction in the price. He hoped that this would get his first customers through the shop doors and that he would soon build up his trade.

The first day of business came and went in a blur of activity. He had several sales of new furniture and his first ten repairs had been left to have the work done. Joseph had promised that the repairs would be ready within two days and he worked late into the evening on that first day to make sure that he could fulfil his promises. Esther saw little of her husband at this time: he left for work almost as early as she did for the mill and didn't arrive home until late evening. She knew that it would be a small sacrifice to make to ensure their security and also the furtherance of his business.

Christmas in 1875 was a happy time for the whole family. Esther and Joseph were able to afford a plump goose to celebrate Christmas Day as well as an array of juicy vegetables and crisp roasted potatoes. Esther had made a pudding full of fruit which was served with a creamy custard sauce. It was an especially happy day for them because Joseph's father and their son Charles Frederick had travelled from Halifax to see them. Fred had just celebrated his nineteenth birthday and it had been a long while since they had seen him. He was still working on the farm with his grandfather, but was not really happy with farm work. James was close to retirement and it had been agreed that when the time came, he would find lodgings somewhere, leaving Fred free to find employment elsewhere and the farm would be worked by Joseph's cousin and his family.

"My, you have grown lad!" said Joseph to his son. "It's been such a long time since we were together and it's nice to see you again."

Fred smiled an embarrassed smile and glanced down at his hands. Such a long time had passed since he had been in the company of his parents that he felt awkward. He looked upon his grandfather as his guardian now, but did not want to upset his mother. He knew that she had been through a very tough time when they had all lived together in Scout and looking at her face now, he was aware of her age. Esther looked tired and although she was not quite forty years of age, she looked older. Her hair was greying quickly and the lines on her face spoke of a hard life. Today though, she looked happy. Her family was around her and she felt complete. After their hearty Christmas meal, they sat down together to play dominoes and cards. Laughter filled the small cottage as they teased each other about the obvious cheating that was taking place and Mary struggled to remember the rules of each game. Before long, the day was over and they settled down for the night. James and Fred both slept on mattresses in the front room and in spite of the cold of the night, were as snug as could be.

James and Fred set off the following morning, the carter taking them as far as Todmorden, where they would meet up with another carrier who would take them to Halifax. The road was straight and uncomplicated except for the undulating nature of the countryside. The land between Bacup and Todmorden was steep, hilly moorland and often blocked by snow in the winter months. The way to Halifax from Todmorden was less steep; the valley becoming more apparent with trees in abundance on either side. They passed through Hebden Bridge where the canal, river and railway all converged and three storey houses lined the steep hillsides; and then onto Halifax where the last part of their journey began. From Halifax, they travelled along steep pathways out of the town and into the lush green countryside surrounding it until their farm at Scout Hall was in view. They were lucky as the weather was dry but cold; and no snow had fallen for several days. When at last they glanced down from the top of the hill looking over Scout, they were tired and grateful to be in sight of home.

"Just smell the air lad," said James softly looking at the tree covered valley. "This is home."

When Esther waved her son goodbye on that cold crisp morning in December, she realised just how much she had missed him and vowed not to leave it too long again before they met. She watched his slight figure as he walked down the road away from them and out of view and sighed. Joseph closed the front door behind them once his father and son were out of sight and the house felt empty. Sadness washed over them leaving the jollity of Christmas behind. Feelings of guilt hung onto Esther knowing that she had abandoned him when perhaps they could have managed quite well living together in Hyde. It was too late now and she silently promised him that she would see him soon. Unfortunately, she was unaware that she would not be able to keep this promise.

Chapter 9

The air in the weaving shed was hot and humid. All around them cotton fibres flew like miniature snowflakes, often making breathing difficult. Esther felt hot – hotter than she had ever felt before and the perspiration ran down her back in little trickles making damp patches on her dress. There was still at least an hour to go before she was able to finish for the day and every minute seemed like an eternity. Mary was unaware that her mother was feeling ill and continued to fetch and carry for the weavers, smiling as she went. She had learned to lip read and could tell what all the weavers were saying, but because of her own difficulties in expressing herself, she hardly ever spoke. The noise seemed excessive and as the shuttles flew along the looms, Esther began to lose concentration. All at once, one of the shuttles flew off the end of her loom and shot like a bullet across the weaving shed. Esther felt faint and tried to hang on to the edge of the loom which had lost its shuttle. Mary watched with horror as she saw her mother slide to the floor and she raced to be by her side. In the middle of this pandemonium, the shuttle had landed on the floor, fortunately missing one of the other weavers by inches.

"Get back to your looms!" bawled the overlooker to the concerned weavers who by this time had surrounded Esther. Mary held on to her mother, cradling her head on her lap and ignoring the pleas of the overlooker to return to work. She glanced up at him with tears beginning to fall down her cheeks.

"Sick," she whispered quietly, but her voice was not heard among the clatter of the machines.

Jed Barnes, the overlooker for the looms concerned, took one glance at Esther and saw for himself that she was ill. He helped her up and carried her to the doorway where she could breathe easier.

"The master will want you to go home lass," he said. "You have a fever and are no use to us if you faint at the loom. Mary can go with you, but make sure she is back at work tomorrow. There are plenty of folks waiting for your jobs so take a couple of days to recover; then if you have not returned, I will find someone else to take your place."

Mary helped her mother onto her feet and out of the mill yard. It was not a long walk home and they managed to get there before Esther collapsed again. It was obvious that she had a fever, but Mary did not know how to help her mother. She had gained such confidence since she had started work, but panic took over and all she could think of was fetching her father. Esther lay on the couch, her head tossing from side to side, almost delirious with the fever that by now had a strong hold on her. Her hair was wet and lying in tendrils around her scarlet cheeks. Mary paced the room trying to think of what she should do. Perhaps her mother might like a drink of water? Racing to the pump in the yard outside, she filled a jug and carried it indoors to her mother. Mary tipped the jug carefully allowing a trickle of water to drip into her mouth. Esther coughed as the shock of the cold water entered her body and she choked with the effort of trying to drink.

Mary decided to find her father and bring him home; but where was his shop? She had only been there once when she had helped her mother to clean the day before the grand opening, and was unsure if she could manage to find her way back there again. The spring air was chilly and Mary did not stop long enough to collect her cloak. She shivered and rubbed her arms to try to keep warm. As Newchurch Road came into view, her mind raced. The shop was along here somewhere, she was sure. After walking for several minutes, Mary became disorientated and was unsure now as to her own whereabouts. She leaned against a wall and began to cry. Now she really was lost! She must be brave and help her mother. Just as she was about to walk on, she was approached by a young man who had seen her predicament and was about to offer his help. On seeing his face, all Mary could remember was the episode with the young man in the park in Hyde and she began to scream. The poor man did not understand what he had done and tried to calm her.

"Please," he began, "I don't want to hurt you. You seemed upset and I thought I might be able to help."

Mary cowered against the wall still sobbing and by this time, people from the shops nearby had come out of their doorways to see what all the commotion was about. A few doors down, Joseph was dealing with a customer when he heard the noise and wondered what had caused the shouting. He finished his transaction and walked with the customer to the doorway. He shook hands with him and bid him good day. It was almost time to close the shop and as he glanced up the street he saw Mary paralysed with fear with the young man standing next to her. Fearing the worst, he raced up to them and almost knocked the man to the ground.

"What have you done to her?" he bellowed, whilst putting his arms in a protective vice around her shoulders.

Before the young man had time to answer, Mary looked into Joseph's eyes and feeling the fatherly refuge his arms were offering, she held on to him tightly.

"It's mother," she said. "Sick."

The young man boldly interrupted them to try to explain what he had been trying to do, and Joseph allowed him a few seconds to explain before he took

Mary into the sanctuary of the shop. The young man followed them, opening the door into the back room where they could have some privacy. By this time Joseph had calmed down and realised that the young man had been trying to help. He quickly explained that his wife was ill, and that he needed to return home as quickly as possible.

"I am sorry for the way I treated you Mr..?"

"John, John Booth," he replied. "I have a sister of a similar age and was only trying to help. I see now that your daughter has some difficulties and apologise for any fright I might have given her."

Joseph thanked him again and bade him goodbye, then after quickly locking the shop, hurried home with Mary by his side.

Esther was lying on the floor by the time Joseph and Mary arrived home. Mary had been gone almost an hour and Esther was very hot. Joseph immediately took her upstairs to their bed chamber and stripping her of her wet clothes, he put on her night gown and began to bathe her head.

"We must try to cool her to get rid of the fever Mary," he told his daughter, "but I think we had better get the doctor to see to her."

Joseph did not want to leave Esther alone again and knew that Mary would not know where to go to find the doctor; so he asked his neighbour's son if he would run and get Mr Wilson the doctor. Esther had influenza and was ill for several days. Mary would not return to work without her mother at her side and so it was likely that when Esther was well enough to return to work, they would not have jobs to go to. Mary however, was a good help to her mother, which assisted her recovery. A week after Esther had become ill, she decided that it was time to see whether or not their jobs were still available and so the pair walked the familiar route to the mill in time for the six o'clock whistle the next day. Jed Barnes was surprised to see them, having told them that their jobs would go after a couple of days if they did not return.

"Mr Barnes," pleaded Esther, we have come to see whether you will allow us back to work. I do not see anyone else taking our place at the loom, so believe that the jobs are still here." She was not fully recovered and had an agonising cough. Jed Barnes realised that she had come back to work as soon as she could and felt sorry for her. She had been lucky though, as he had been about to give her job to someone else.

"The job is still yours Mrs Freeman, and Mary may continue with hers, but there will be no allowances made for you. If you are not well, go home. If you stay, I will expect a full day's work from you." With that, he turned and returned to his own looms and the two women got on with their work.

Joseph was not happy about his wife working in the hot dusty conditions in the mill after she had been ill and had told her so. The money that they all brought in was very useful, but he knew that somehow they would manage without if they had to. His shop was making money, but not the amount he had imagined it would. The daughters of Jacob Ashworth had continued to keep the stall on the market and were employing another joiner to do the work. They were concentrating mainly on repairs and so some of Joseph's customers had returned there. Still, he was making and selling furniture and he was enjoying his work.

Spring disappeared into summer and the evenings grew longer. Esther had not felt really well since her return to work, having developed a weakness in her lungs which meant that she was left with an almost unending cough. After returning from the mill each evening, she helped Mary to cook the evening meal and then retired to bed. The house became untidy and washing was left dirty. Mary did her best to help her mother and eventually learned how to use the copper in the yard to heat the water for the weekly washing. Mrs Barton who lived next door, showed Mary how to use the mangle to get rid of the water left behind and before long, Mary was completing the whole washing process by herself. Mrs Barton was a round, kindly woman who was used to Mary's quiet ways and kept an eye on her when she was in the yard doing the washing. The privies and copper were shared by several families and the women often got together in the yard to chat whilst they were washing.

"Eh lass," she said to Mary one day, "you will make your mother proud the way you have learned to do all the chores on your own."

Mary smiled and felt a warm glow of happiness inside. She loved her mother and would do anything to make her happy. Gradually, by the beginning of August, Mary was in total command of the household tasks. What Mary was unable to do however, was venture out of the house alone. She still had nightmares about the attack at the park in Hyde and the awful episodes of name calling she had endured and could not bring herself to go out without her mother or father. Going to fetch her father when Esther had fallen ill had been traumatic for her and had been a reminder of these past events which had until then been buried in the back of her mind.

Within a couple of weeks, Esther was ill again. She had a blinding headache and could not focus on her work at the loom and knew from her previous illness that she must not work in this condition as she could be a danger to herself and others. The looms were dangerous machines, ready to take off an arm or scalp a child when left unattended. Many weavers had suffered injuries from flying shuttles and some were serious leading to the death of the victim. Esther resigned herself to staying in bed where she could be looked after by Mary. Her headache worsened and she rapidly developed a fever which Mary tried to calm with cool compresses. Nothing seemed to work and Esther tossed and turned, delirious and babbling. She mentioned her dead children many times during this fever and it was obvious to Joseph that she was suffering greatly. After a couple of days, the fever seemed to abate and Esther became more lucid, but this brief recovery was short lived and Esther's cough became more acute.

Joseph returned from work one day to find his wife being tended by his daughter and in obvious pain. Esther's chest felt heavy, pain coursing through her side each time she tried to cough. In the chamber pot beside the bed was the awful outcome of each coughing spasm. Whenever she coughed, it left her breathless; and with each passing hour her lungs filled with more fluid and she found it more and more difficult to breathe. Doctor Wilson had attended her again explaining that she had pneumonia. He had prescribed a pain killer and a poultice for her chest, but nothing seemed to have helped to ease Ether's pain. Joseph sat by his wife's bedside, holding her hand and stroking her forehead. He knew that she could die, as many people did with this illness; but prayed that she would recover. He talked to her of the good times they had experienced together and of their children. He apologised for not looking after her in the way that he could have, and promised to love her forever. Joseph sat with his wife all through the evening and then the night, sending Mary to bed with an assurance that he would look after her mother; but in the early hours of August the 19th 1876, at the age of forty, Esther lost her will to live and died in the arms of her husband. Joseph was distraught. When Mary opened the door to their bed chamber that same morning, she saw her father sat on the bed holding her mother tightly in his arms. Instinctively, she realised that her mother had died in the night and knelt down beside the bed to pray for her.

Esther had been gravely ill for only two weeks when she died of pneumonia and Joseph felt that this was more than he could bear. He had already buried three of his children in their infancy and now he had lost his wife. She had only been forty when she died and her death had been a shock. The fever soon became a severe infection on her chest and although she was not a strong woman he had expected her to survive. It was unthinkable that he would be left alone with Mary.

Joseph could not bear to talk to his daughter. He knew that she would also be grieving, but could offer her no comfort. His emotions were confused; feeling wretched about the loss of his dear wife, and at the same time hating her for leaving him to cope with Mary on his own. How he wished it had been Mary who had died and not Esther. Joseph did not know how to cope with this confusion of feelings, desperation finding its way into his whole being. When the undertaker had been to lay out his wife's body and see to the funeral arrangements; he sat, head in hands in the rocking chair by the range which Esther had loved so much. His last gift to her was to arrange for her burial to take place alongside her dead children at All Souls, Haley Hill in Halifax. The church was magnificent and he knew she would have been proud to have been buried there.

Mary was confused. Her father seemed to be cross with her and she didn't understand why. Was it her fault that her mother had died? She sat in the quiet of her bed chamber and cried until she could cry no more. Her eyes were red and swollen and she had no one to confide in. Her mother always understood how she was feeling and Mary never felt self-conscious when she was talking to her. Now she was gone and somehow she had displeased her father. The worry that he would make her go back to the mill on her own was making her feel sick. She was unable to eat or talk to him; and talking to God had not helped her either. He had allowed her mother to die, so why would he help her?

The day of the funeral was hot. Mary sat with her father on the carriers cart behind the coffin that held her mother's body. She was dressed in a black mourning dress that Joseph had bought and it was stifling her. The high neck and tight bodice made it difficult to breathe and she experienced an overwhelming feeling of suffocation. The journey took several hours so they had set off very early in the morning and by noon the sun was beating down on them relentlessly. When the church eventually came into view, the two silent mourners who were sat by the coffin of their wife and mother breathed a sigh of relief.

As they alighted from the cart, they were met by Fred and Joseph's father James. For the first time since Esther had died, Joseph showed his daughter some consideration and held out his hand to assist her from the cart. Esther's own family were also there to mourn their dead sister. She had many brothers and sisters who were still living in Halifax and although they had not seen her for many years, they wanted to pay their respects to a sister who had suffered so much.

Before the burial got underway, Joseph wandered around the churchyard looking for the graves of his children among the grassy banks. He recognised the location within minutes, the site having been opened already to receive the body of his wife; and silently moved over to the side of the grave. The words were difficult and he knew in his heart what he wanted to say, but struggled to say them.

"I am sorry we have not been to tend to your grave," he whispered; "but your mother is with you now and she will once more look after you."

As Joseph walked back to the small crowd of mourners, he watched as Esther's sister put her arms around Mary's shoulders in sympathy. Mary looked at her aunt, desperate for some love, but could only see pity, not true affection. Pangs of guilt came over Joseph and he held on to Mary's arm as they followed Rev Charles Holmes the vicar, into the church. The air inside the church was much cooler and Mary began to feel less restricted in her movements and once outside again, she saw that black clouds had appeared and the breeze had increased, chasing leaves around the churchyard and moving the branches of the trees nearby. As her mother's coffin was lowered into the ground, the sobs of her fellow mourners were heard above the sound of the wind; but Mary could not cry. She held on to her father's arm as the earth was dropped onto the wooden box below her; and she said her own silent goodbyes. Joseph too was dry-eyed. What good were tears now when he had been abandoned to bring up his only daughter; an adult herself and an imbecile? His worries were for the future and no amount of emotional outbursts would help him now.

Chapter 10

Joseph was deep in thought as he made the return journey with Mary to their home in Stacksteads. A deep frown furrowed his brow and he hardly spoke at all. Mary could tell by the solemn expression on his face that he was concerned, but had no inkling that his worry was about her. What were they going to do now without Esther's wage? He did not think that Mary would be able to work without her mother by her side and so her small addition to the family income was also gone. His main concern was whether or not Mary would be able to cope on her own while he was at the shop. What would he do if she couldn't manage? Should he take her to the shop? No, she might actually discourage customers if she became over-friendly, which she often did when she was nervous. All of these thoughts raced through his mind, but he could find no solution. He would have to wait and see what the next few days would bring.

It was late into the night when they finally arrived home and Joseph sent Mary to bed. She was an adult at the age of twenty two; an age when she should have been thinking of marriage and children of her own; but at heart she was still an immature teenager who needed reminding about the routine things in life, such as washing and going to bed. Esther had always looked after Mary, and Joseph was beginning to find this new responsibility tedious and irritating. He sat by the range, now cold as it had not been lit for some time, being the end of summer and the weather still mild. His mind was still racing and he knew that he would not be able to sleep. Eventually, the tears came and he allowed himself to cry relentlessly. Upstairs in her bed, Mary heard her father's tears and got out of bed. She crept back down the stairs to see him holding on to Esther's shawl which had been hanging on the back of the door, the sobs wracking his body with the anguish that he felt. Instinctively, she tip-toed over to him and put her arms around his neck, shushing him in the way that her mother often did when she had been upset. He glanced at her forlorn face and the tears stopped. Mary gently sat on his knee, as a small child would when being comforted by her father, and they clutched each other in a tender embrace. She was such an affectionate girl and Joseph knew that he must try and cope for both their sakes. After all, it would have been what Esther wanted him to do.

Although very tired, Joseph decided to return to the shop early the next morning. He told Mary that he would be back at dinner time, planning to close the shop for an hour each day at that time. He found it very difficult to concentrate on his work, all the time wondering whether Mary was managing alone. When he finally arrived at dinner time, he found that Mary had started the washing as she had done whilst Esther was ill and that she was in relatively good spirits. She had not been able to cook for them, but he cut several thick slices of bread and they ate this with a dollop of jam on top. Although not a lavish meal, it filled their stomachs and was enough to keep them going until later. The afternoon passed quickly and after closing the shop for the day, Joseph bought enough food from the market to last them a few days. He was no cook himself and until he could find someone to help with the meals, they would have to live on the things he could manage to make. A large piece of ham had been purchased along with vegetables and he put all of this into a large pan on the range. Suddenly realising that the range was still not lit, he set about this task quickly, knowing it could take some time to heat before cooking his meal. By the time the meal was cooked, it was very late and Mary had fallen asleep. He woke her and they ate the unappetising meal which Joseph had made, neither one making any comment about his culinary expertise. Exhausted, he finally went to bed determined to be more organised in the future.

The following weeks did not get any easier for Joseph although he had managed to light the range and keep it lit so that there was always heat for cooking and hot water. Mary seemed to cope although Joseph did not know what she did when he was at the shop. She was always there when he returned and that was what mattered at the moment.

Mary watched her father from the window. He set off to work each morning, leaving her behind to do the chores. She could manage to do the washing as there was always someone about in the yard to lend a hand when she struggled, but pressing the clothes was a different matter altogether. Twice she had burnt her hands on the flat iron as she had left it to heat up on the top of the range, and she had singed more shirts than she could remember. Mrs Barton had her own family with eight children in all, and could not help Mary with the ironing, but had suggested folding the clothes as neatly as she could and then leaving them. Joseph would have to press his own shirts if he was fussy about them! Mary was bored at home on her own, and longed for someone to talk to. She sat and sewed her samplers until she had sore fingers and although she had tried to keep the house tidy, it never seemed to look any different. The winter was almost upon them and Mary began to feel that she was suffocating. The house became an oppressive place and she longed for an escape.

Snow began to fall like the downy feathers from a tiny white chick, signalling that winter had indeed taken a hold. Mary watched as the flakes stuck to the window sill and was fascinated by the magical patterns she could see. Opening the door, she stepped out into this magical world, holding out her hands to catch the flakes. Squeals of delight erupted from her throat and she held her head up towards the sky, watching in ecstasy as they fell onto her face. Within minutes, the cobbled street was covered in a fine layer of white, and not a soul was to be seen. Mary was soaked to the skin as she had not even stopped to put on her shawl, but at this moment, was completely oblivious to the cold and wet. Loving every second of this encounter with the snow, she danced about in front of the cottage, kicking and tossing its flakes into the air. From inside the house next door, Alice Barton watched in dismay as Mary became more and more drenched by the snow.

"Get in lass!" she cried. "You will catch your death! The snow will soak you and you have no cloak on to keep you warm."

Her mind firmly on the snow, and not on anything else, Mary did not hear her, and Alice was forced to dash out of her own house to persuade her to return inside. Once in the warm of her own home, Mary realised that she was cold and glancing at her dress, she was horrified to see just how wet it was. Alice made her a hot cup of tea and sat her by the range to dry off. It was fortunate that she had seen Mary otherwise the young woman would have frozen to death in no time.

The snow continued to fall gently, but in no time the cobbled streets were thick with a cushiony layer. Joseph had few customers during the afternoon and decided to close the shop early. He trudged along Newchurch Road, his feet making a double line of deep footprints following his path, and as he turned along and up the slight incline towards his house, the snow fell faster, making visibility more difficult. Very few people were braving the weather unless it was urgent and he was delighted to be in sight of his warm cottage. Alice was keeping an eye out for Joseph. She wanted to catch him before he actually got inside his house so that she could talk to him, but the snow was making it difficult for her to see more than a few feet from the front of the house. As Joseph approached the house, he paused for a moment to look at the beautiful scene the snow had created. It was breath-taking, how weather as dramatic as this, could create such beauty. Snow had formed little mounds where children had obviously been playing, enjoying the opportunity whilst it was available. From a nearby door he heard his name being called and turned to see who it was. His neighbour was stood in her doorway, urgently beckoning to him and he wondered what the importance was. Betty quickly told him of Mary's escapade in the snow and of her worry about her being left alone in the house.

"Well what else can I do woman?" he yelled at her, displeased at the way she seemed to be poking her nose into his business. "You look after her if you think you can do a better job!"

He stormed into his house feeling embarrassed by the way in which he had been almost reprimanded for not looking after his own daughter properly. She was an adult now for heaven's sake, not a child needing constant supervision!

"What have you been up to young woman!" he shouted at Mary as soon as he set foot through the door. "Have you no sense, playing out in the snow without your cloak like a small child!"

Mary began to cry. She did not understand why everyone was cross with her and hated her father at that moment. He was always bad tempered, never smiling like he used to. Perhaps it was her fault, but she didn't realise what she had done to make him feel like that. Dashing towards him, she lashed out at his face and chest, pummelling him with her fists, her nails clawing at him like an unleashed tiger.

"Bad father!" she screamed. "Bad father!"

Joseph was taken aback by the sudden ferocity of her onslaught and instinct made him push her away towards the range. Mary tripped and fell backwards, banging her head on the corner of the rocking chair. She sat on the floor in a dishevelled heap, holding her head in her hands and sobbing. She was right after all. Her father did not like her any more, or he would not have pushed her. Joseph tried to comfort her, realising that he had been too rough with her; a reaction to the guilt he felt at his overpowering urge to lash back, instead of making the effort to keep Mary calm. For several minutes Mary would not allow her father to come near her and she eventually went to bed having not eaten since breakfast.

Worry about his daughter played on Joseph's mind all night. He could not see any other way but to leave her at home whilst he worked, or to put her in the workhouse. This was his only other choice, but one which he knew Esther would never have allowed. He decided to leave things be for the time being, but if business was not too hectic, he would come home early or close the shop at dinner time to allow him time to come home and check on things.

The following morning, the snow had almost disappeared and Mary watched as her father walked down the street on his way to work. He had told her that he was coming home at dinner time, but she would show him that she was big enough to look after herself. Mary knew where the savings tin was kept and was determined to go shopping for something for them to have for tea. She was hungry and although there was bread in the pantry, she hungered for something else – a taste of freedom!

Her cloak fastened tightly around her head and shoulders, Mary set off to find the market. The streets were wet with melting snow and her boots were soon soggy, but Mary was determined to behave like an adult. The walk along Newchurch Road was straightforward, and as she sauntered by her father's shop, he was not aware of her passing. The market was unfamiliar to Mary as she had only ever been there once or twice before, and then with her mother. Her mouth felt dry and she could feel the intensity of her heartbeat as she wondered which stall to go to. Seeing her dilemma, a young man at a nearby fruit stall called over to her.

"Hey, Miss! What are you looking for? Lots of nice fruit and veg here on my stall, and I'm a bit tasty even though I say so myself!"

Mary smiled at him, not really understanding his flippant manner of speech. She stood at his stall deliberating for some time about what to buy and laughing with the young man who owned it. Her flirtatious behaviour was the opportunity he had been waiting for and he put his arm around her waist squeezing gently and bent his head to kiss her neck.

At the next stall, John Booth was watching the proceedings with some concern. He thought that he recognised the young woman, but was unsure where he had seen her before. He did not like the way in which the young stall holder was taking advantage of his even younger customer, so was keeping a close eye on her. Mary was enjoying the attention the young man was giving her and beginning to relax in his company. He did not seem to threaten her as others had done and she liked the way that he smiled at her. Mary was not sure whether or not he should have his arm about her, but it made her feel secure and so she did not discourage this familiarity. However, as she gazed around her, she could see another man staring at her from the side of the next stall. He had been buying candles and tapers and as his goods were being wrapped in brown paper and tied with string, she recognised him as the man who had come to her assistance when she was lost and trying to find her father's shop. At the time she had thought that he was going to hurt her until eventually her father reassured her that he was only trying to help.

"Mr Booth!" she shouted. "Mr Booth!"

As soon as she spoke, he remembered her even though it had been some months since they had met. She was the young lady that almost got him into trouble when he had only been trying to come to her assistance. He knew from her father that she was a vulnerable young woman and was alarmed at the thought that the young stall-holder who was behaving in an inappropriate way, would take advantage of her.

His purchases held firmly in his hands, he stepped over to where she was standing.

"Hello Miss Freeman, I hope you are better than the last time we met?"

Mary did not know what to do. She felt suddenly anxious about this new situation. Who should she engage with – Mr Booth or the young man who was paying her such attention? Feeling unable to converse properly with either one, she said nothing and tried to smile. John could see that she was becoming alarmed and was just about to suggest to the stall-holder that he release his grip on her, when he did just that. The young man in charge of the stall suddenly realised that he could well get into trouble if the young lady was to take fright and scream. He released her from the firm grip he had around her waist, took off his cap and smiled cheekily as he spoke to her.

"I bid you good-day Miss, and hope to see you here again soon." He turned back to his fruit and vegetables where, by that time, he had a small crowd of people waiting to be served. John took hold of Mary's arm and led her out of the market.

"I will walk with you towards your father's shop if you will allow me," he said quietly so as not to alarm her, but he was unaware that the last thing she wanted to do was to see her father. Mary suddenly pulled her arm from his, and set off running towards home. She did not want her father to know that she had been out and hoped that Mr Booth would not tell him. He would be very angry and shout at her again when all she had been trying to do was get some shopping. By the time she reached the house, she was tired and out of breath and wondered whether it had all been worth the effort. However, she had loved the feeling that someone was interested in her and knew that she would visit the market again soon.

John Booth considered the situation and decided that he might pop into the furniture shop as he was passing that way, and tell Mr Freeman that he had seen his daughter in case something happened to her on her way home. However, as he approached the shop, he could see that the sign on the door said 'closed' and so the decision was taken from him. He wondered why the shop was shut at dinner time as he had never known this to be the case before. Perhaps Mary had called in anyway and Mr Freeman had taken her home. Hoping this to be the case, he went on his way and thought no more about it.

Joseph had hardly any customers all morning and business had seemed slack all week. He was concerned that his usual customers were being persuaded to go back to the market shop with offers of even cheaper repairs. Times were hard and fewer customers were willing to pay a good price for quality furniture. Still, he would not worry too much as if he could still get the repairs, then he would be able to make a living. What he needed to do soon was to advertise his quality bespoke furniture in the newspapers which would reach the well-off; who would then be willing to travel to see it and pay a decent price for the privilege of owning it. These thoughts turned through his mind as he walked home, hoping at the same time that Mary had behaved herself. Little did he know that she had only been in the house a few minutes when he too arrived!

As her father entered the door, she could see that he was concerned, but his smile on seeing her gave her the reassurance that she needed and she knew that he was happy to see her. Mr Booth had obviously not spoken to him, or she was sure that he would have been very angry. Joseph returned to work after making dinner for them and told her that as they did not seem to have much in the pantry, he would bring food home with him. She would have to go to the market another day and so carefully put back the money she had borrowed from the savings tin, ready for the next time.

John Booth sauntered back towards his home in Coupe. The walk was a long one, taking him almost an hour, but it gave him time to think. He was worried about the vulnerable young woman he had just witnessed making a fool of herself in Bacup market. He realised from what her father had implied, that she had some difficulties and did not fully understand the implications of what she had done. He felt guilty at not having warned Mr Freeman of his daughter's predicament and by the time he got home, he was determined to return the following day and explain what had happened.

The following day dawned bright and clear, but by the time John had put on his boots and coat to go out, the clouds had gathered and snow had begun to fall. It would probably be a light shower, he thought, and set off towards Bacup once more. When the familiar sight of Newchurch Road came into view, he felt relieved as the snow was becoming thicker underfoot and the cobbles very slippery.

Mary Freeman was also out in the snow and had just set off on her journey once more to the market. As she walked along Newchurch Road, she decided to cross over onto the opposite side of the road to her father's shop, to avoid accidentally bumping into him. The snow was falling heavier now and she pulled her shawl up over her head to keep warm. As she walked, the snow crunched beneath her feet and she delighted in the noise it made, purposefully placing her feet to gain maximum impact from the sound and feel of the crunching snow. Unaware that she had been seen, she carried on towards the market, basket in hand and money from the tin in her pocket.

From a short distance behind, John could see her vague figure ahead and felt almost certain that it was her. Joseph's shop was in sight and John made for the doorway, determined this time to go and explain Mary's intention to her father. The shop was empty and Joseph was gazing out of the window at the snow. He watched as the hazy figures of men and women hurried along trying to complete their daily business swiftly in order to get home without any further delay. When John Booth entered his shop, he was pleased to see someone and was hoping for some business.

"Good morning Mr Freeman," said John. "Do you remember me? I was the man who assisted your daughter when she came to find you. I seem to remember that your wife was poorly at the time. May I enquire after her health now? I hope that she is much recovered."

The expression on Joseph's face was enough to tell him that all was definitely not well and he realised straight away that he had spoken out of turn.

"I do remember you Mr Booth, but I have to tell you that my wife passed away soon after we met. Mary is proving to be difficult since her mother died and I am at my wit's end trying to manage the shop and ensure that she is kept safe."

John paused before he spoke again, worrying in case the news he had come to tell him would upset him even more. But he needed to be made aware of the situation his daughter had begun to get herself into, so tried to be diplomatic.

"It is Mary I have come to speak to you about. I saw her yesterday at the market and I am afraid you would not have approved of her behaviour." As John continued to talk, Joseph felt embarrassed by his daughter's behaviour and when John finally told him that he had just seen Mary heading once more for the market, the pair set off immediately to find her. Mary was stood at the fruit stall where John had seen her the previous day. The young stall holder once again had his arm around her waist and she was leaning against his shoulder and flirting in a most provocative manner. Joseph knew that she did not realise the seriousness of her actions, nor the consequences they might bring, but his immediate reaction was anger: anger directed at his daughter for bringing shame onto his family and even more anger at the young man who was leading his innocent daughter astray.

The aggression he had not felt since dealing with Barney Smith rose in him and in one swift movement, he pulled Mary from the arms of her suitor then aimed and levelled a punch on his cheek catching him completely unawares.

"You bastard! You should know better than to lead an innocent girl on!" he bawled. "She doesn't understand what she is doing. Leave her be immediately!" He pulled Mary away from the stall and she began to cry. What had she done that was so bad? To Joseph's surprise, she hit out at him, scratching his face with her nails and screaming at him to let her be. Passing shoppers looked on in amazement at the scene before them and a small crowd had begun to gather. Joseph was alarmed by the way his daughter had reacted and was afraid that the constable would soon be on the scene, ready to make arrests for rowdy behaviour.

It was John who eventually persuaded Mary to return to the shop which her father owned and the three of them took time to warm themselves before the range in the back room before returning to their own homes. Joseph thanked John profusely, offering to do his next furniture repair for no payment and after John had left the shop, he sat with his head in his hands for quite a while, trying to decide what to do next. Mary could not understand why her father was so angry. She had only been shopping, something her mother did almost daily and wasn't the man at the stall just being friendly?

Joseph locked the shop door and put up a notice which told customers that it would be closed until further notice. He had to do something with Mary before he could work all day in the shop again. There were few people about now and the snow had taken a grip on the landscape. Joseph had not known such a bad winter for many years and he was relieved to see the door of his cottage. Once inside, he helped Mary out of her wet things and put more fuel on the range. They had enough food to last a couple of days and then he would take Mary with him when he went shopping. The shop would have to remain closed until he could find a way to manage with his wayward daughter. Meanwhile, they had their savings. Thank heavens for the money in the tin!

Chapter 11

Spring turned into summer and Joseph had to accept the fact that if he stayed at home to look after Mary, he would not be able to work. His business had failed because he had been unable to keep regular shop hours and he blamed Mary. Resentment built up in him like a canker – growing and festering inside him until he had to get rid of it or die. As long as Mary was occupied in the home, or escorted when she went out, she was no trouble. She just had to be watched over, especially when she fraternised with young men. Mary had grown from a very nervous young woman who felt threatened each time a new person spoke to her, to a gregarious character who gave her unreserved attention to any man who gave the impression he was interested in her. She was unable to differentiate between friendship and love – they were the same to her and she rejoiced in any affection shown to her. This part of her personality had become the major difficulty for Joseph and he realised that he needed help. What he needed, was a woman to see to the things which his wife Esther had done so well, including taking care of his daughter. He did not want to pay anyone to do this, indeed he could no longer afford to do so. The savings he had kept in the little tin had dwindled to a few pence now and he could no longer afford to pay the rent on his house *and* the shop, so his shop had now been let to someone else and the small items of furniture he had left were stored in his own home.

After having persuaded Mrs Barton his neighbour to keep an eye on Mary, Joseph set off to see if he could find any casual work mending furniture or doing odd jobs. The day was fine and with a spring in his step, he made his way into Waterfoot. Although he had lived in the area now for three years, he was more acquainted with the town of Bacup and had become a familiar figure there. The small villages of Waterfoot and Newchurch would, he hoped, offer him something new. He suddenly felt young and free again and realised that this was how he could feel again without Mary to hinder him and so was determined to resolve his predicament without delay.

The small shops in Waterfoot were welcoming and it seemed that the area had its own furniture emporium, so he began to walk up the hill towards Newchurch, knocking on doors as he went and chatting in his friendly manner to the housewives who opened the doors. He could be a charmer, there was no doubt, and he enjoyed himself flirting with the women whose husbands were out at work. There was purpose in his flirting though, and that was to advertise his services as an odd job man who could complete even the smallest or most complicated household task.

He had reached the top of the hill by the early afternoon, and was on his way back down again having earned himself a few shillings, when he realised that he had not eaten or had a proper drink in all that time. He was hungry and extremely thirsty and thought that he might just pop into the next pub he came to. He felt sure that he had passed one near Glen Bottoms earlier on in the day. His mind set firmly on the refreshment he needed, he turned the corner heading swiftly towards the pub. He glanced up and saw a woman who he guessed to be about his own age or perhaps a few years younger. She was pulling at the handle of her door which did not seem to budge. The window panes rattled in the casement as she tried with all her strength to open the door, but still nothing would give.

"Good morning missus, is there anything I can do to help you?" He asked.

She was close to tears, her face reddening with temper, and completely unaware of the man standing behind her. As she turned to meet his gaze, he was captivated by the fragility of her features. Her eyes were the brightest of blues, surrounded by a mass of dark brown hair, tied back in a knot which had become tousled in her efforts to open the door. The anger in her features only served to enhance her appeal and Joseph tried not to smile at the situation she had got herself into.

"I am sorry if I scared you," he continued, "I could see that you were having difficulty with your door and thought I might be able to help you. I mean no ill towards you."

The woman in front of him paused for a moment before answering. She was obviously wary of him and studied his face slowly, trying to assess his character.

"Who are you sir?" she asked him in reply. "I have not seen you around these parts before."

"Mr Joseph Freeman at your service," he said jovially. "I am a joiner by trade and have lived for the past three years in Stacksteads. I am out today looking for work, but am happy to help a lady like you who is in distress."

The woman regarded him carefully. She needed help and he had offered it, so she could see no other way to get back into her home than to accept this stranger's offer. She grudgingly accepted and stood to one side whilst he rummaged in his bag for the tools he would need. Within minutes, he had the door open and his tools put away.

"Your lock is broken and you will need a new one to make sure that this does not happen again," he smiled. "If you will allow me to, I can fix it for you."

The woman agreed to his suggestion and he was soon working hard fixing the lock. It was fortunate that he carried one or two spare parts like this, or he would have had to come back. As he worked he saw her cautiously glancing at him and once or twice their eyes met. She was quick to turn away, obviously embarrassed by the fact that he had seen her looking at him. He too was not slow to take in what he saw. She was a comely woman of slight build who was obviously in need of money. Her home although neat and clean, was furnished with the minimum of furniture and her clothes had seen better days. She too was clean and tidy and he was unsure whether or not she was married. He assumed that she was, because there were signs that the house was also occupied by children – a few wooden toys and children's clothes airing over the range.

The door fixed, he made to leave.

"What do I owe you Mr Freeman? She asked him quietly.

Knowing that she would not be possessed of much money he was reluctant to take payment.

"If I could just pray upon your hospitality for a moment and ask for a drink of water to quench my thirst on this warm afternoon, that will be enough," he answered. "And perhaps you can tell your friends that you know of a good joiner who can do all their odd jobs around the house. It is work I need and a recommendation will be of great help."

The woman went to get him a large mug of water and returned with a smile.

"I would be only too pleased to do that for you Mr Freeman," she said as she gave him the water. Joseph sat down briefly on the door step and knew that he must learn her name before he left.

"Would you do me the honour of telling me who I have been working for this morning," he asked.

"Mrs Booth, widow of the late William Booth and I am most grateful that you have managed to solve my problem," she told him. "I don't know what I would have done if you hadn't come along when you did. I am sure that it must have been fate."

Joseph finished his drink and handed back the mug. His thirst quenched, he knew he must continue on his way. All thoughts of visiting the pub were now a distant memory.

"I will call on you again when I am in this area in a week's time, if you will permit me, to see whether or not you have had the chance to speak to any of your neighbours," he added; knowing that this was his excuse to see the young widow again. *Ideas were already forming in his mind.* He turned away from her taking the chance to glance back once more. She too was looking his way and he swiftly gave her a wink of the eye and a cheeky grin before setting off home.

His day had been very fruitful in more ways than one. He had made a few shillings and met a comely young woman as well! The sun had most certainly been shining on him that day, and he pranced along like a young colt, his hat set at a jaunty angle and whistling a cheery tune. As he opened the door to the cottage, Mary stared at him in utter amazement. She had not seen her father so jolly in a very long time, and she too was overjoyed that today at least, he would not be making disapproving remarks about her.

"I have made some money today Mary," he laughed. "I hope that you have been good!"

Mary responded with a nod of the head, somewhat unsure of what he might do next. Had her father been drinking? She had vague memories of him being drunk when they had lived in the place where the nasty men lived, but she couldn't remember him being like that here. She only knew that she felt nervous when she was in the company of drunken men. There was thankfully nothing to worry about, for her father was only drunk on happiness, and as they ate their evening meal he put his arms around her and gave her a fatherly hug.

"Things will be fine Mary, I have a plan."

Of course, he didn't tell Mary of his plan, as he felt slightly guilty about the part he would have to play in putting her in the workhouse, for that is what his scheme was for her. He had heard that the workhouse in Haslingden was a good one with a fine reputation as far as workhouses went. But first, he must woo the widow!

During the next few days, he left Mary several times, always asking his neighbour to keep an eye on her. He made enough money to keep them fed and pay the rent, but Mrs Barton had made it quite plain that she did not want to be responsible for Mary's actions and so Joseph knew that he must visit the workhouse soon to make enquiries. The day came when he had promised the widow that he would return to see her. He put on his best jacket and made sure that he was clean and tidy and not wanting to seem too insistent, he waited until mid-morning before he set out, telling Mary that he had an appointment and would be back later in the afternoon.

Just before midday, he knocked sharply on the door which he had carefully repaired the previous week and waited. After what seemed like ages, the door was opened by the woman whose face he had memorised. She was more beautiful than he had remembered; her twinkling blue eyes smiling out at him and her face framed by a sleek coiled plait on the top of her head.

"Good day to you Mrs Booth," he said. "I just thought I would call again to see whether or not you had managed to speak to any of your neighbours. I have had some work in the district and could fit in any repairs in the next few days." The lies seemed to trip so easily off his tongue, sowing the seeds for what he hoped might be his future.

Mrs Booth invited Joseph in for a cup of tea and as he looked around at this small house once more, he already felt at home. It was spotless and Mrs Booth had obviously taken time to make sure the house was ready for his visit.

"There are one or two neighbours who have small jobs which need doing, and I have some chairs which need mending," she said, "but I don't think I can afford to have them done just yet."

"There is no need to worry Mrs Booth," Joseph replied. "I am sure we can sort something out." The widow seemed to relax a little and Joseph took his chance.

"I have lived around these parts for the last few years in a little house which I shared with my late wife," he said. "I too am finding it very hard to pay my way in the house alone when work is so short and so I thought I might look for somewhere to lodge for the moment. Paying the rent on a room will be much less than the rent for my house. Perhaps I could be bold and make a suggestion to you?"

The widow looked taken a back and Joseph thought that he had spoken too soon. She obviously thought that he had improper intentions towards her and had begun to panic.

"I realise that I am still a stranger, but you seem such a kind, gentle lady who could do with some friendly support. I just thought that I might enquire whether or not you had a room to let. If so, I would be happy to take it and pay whatever you ask. I would be able to help you around the house, but keep to my room when I am not needed."

Mrs Booth did not speak and although she had begun to relax a little, Joseph was still unsure whether or not she would think favourably of him.

"You do not need to answer me just now," he

continued, "and I will not be offended if you decide not to, but please think about it."

The atmosphere between them had become cooler and so Joseph hurriedly made his goodbyes explaining that he would return again in a few days to see if she had made her mind up, wishing he could have handled the situation with more tact. He had rushed her and now she would more than likely turn his proposal down. Still, he was getting desperate and she was a comely looking woman who would be ideal for his needs. If she was happy to rent him a room, he would eventually charm his way into her bed, or so he thought.

The journey from Newchurch to Rawtenstall would take him too long to walk and then return in time for tea, so he spent some of his money on the tram which would get him into the centre of Rawtenstall in no time. It was only a short walk up to the workhouse from there. His mind was made up now and he must see what the place was like for himself. He had heard good things about it from articles in the Bacup Times which he read every so often. It was with purpose then that he walked up the long driveway to the main entrance, passing what he presumed were inmates sitting on the benches outside. The workhouse was a relatively new building, made of stone with two conspicuous domes telling the neighbouring towns of its existence.

As he entered the huge doors and walked up the stone steps to the main aisle, he was met by the porter who enquired about his business. Joseph simply told him that he had come to make enquiries about the possibility of the workhouse taking his daughter. The porter silently indicated that Joseph should follow him and he was shown into the reception rooms used by the master and his wife. The matron was a stern looking woman who wore a grey starched dress covered by a white apron. Her cap hid most of her hair and what could be seen of it, was drawn back severely. Her presence was intimidating as she was also a big woman who showed no signs of femininity. He had wanted to have a glance at the place which was to become his daughter's home for the foreseeable future, but the conversation which passed between them left no room for niceties. On entering the room, he could see that a man was also seated behind a big desk who the matron introduced to him as her husband, master of Haslingden workhouse.

Joseph simply explained that his daughter was what some people would call an idiot. He did not like using the term himself, but knew that he had to paint a bleak picture to secure a place in this establishment. The fact that she was an adult and had no means to support herself, being in reality a pauper, meant that Joseph was in a reasonable position to make his plea heard.

"Well Mr Freeman," the master demanded. "Why can you not support your daughter yourself?"

Joseph was ready for this question, deciding that he would not tell them the complete truth. "I am soon to marry again, but Mary does not like my new bride. She was very fond of her mother and sees this new lady as a threat to her. In the past few months, Mary has been very aggressive towards her, scratching her face quite brutally. After my marriage I am to move away and will not be able to see to her needs myself. Of course I intend to visit her as often as I can, but I am sure that Mary will be much better off here with you."

"The fact that you may visit, is of no consequence to us Mr Freeman," replied the master. "Your application would normally need to go before the board of Guardians, but I see no reason for it to be refused. An idiot child is a blight on our society and she is better away from those of us who are decent people, especially if she can be a danger to those around her. It is a pity that you did not bring her with you for us to interview and examine as to the state of her medical condition. Nonetheless, we can do this on her arrival."

Paperwork was filled in and it was decided that Mary should be brought as soon as possible. She would be set to work doing one of the menial tasks that the inmates were asked to do to earn their keep. It was quite possible that Mary would be kept busy in the laundry or in the workhouse weaving sheds. Generally speaking, Mary was not violent, only becoming agitated if she saw an injustice being done and so the matron was fairly happy that she would be fine once settled. This would be her life and she would need to get used to it.

Joseph left the intimidating presence of the master and felt as if a mighty load had been shifted off his shoulders. He was glad to leave the place, but left in a more positive frame of mind. He would not tell Mary where she was going until they had arrived there, and even then, he had no intention of letting her know that he may not visit her for a long time, if at all. He did not arrive back home until quite late and was aware immediately of the fact that Mary had once more been out on her own. Mrs Barton did not even wait until he had taken off his jacket and boots, before she was hammering at the door, complaining bitterly about having to go and bring Mary back from town.

"She was off again on one of her jaunts to who knows where! It will not do Mr Freeman. I have a family to look after of my own and cannot keep chasing after your looney daughter!"

On hearing the word 'looney', something in Mary immediately snapped and she launched herself at Mrs Barton pulling at her hair.

"Not a looney! Not a looney!" she screamed.

Joseph was forced to restrain his daughter

apologising profusely to his neighbour whilst trying to reassure her that she would not need to look out for her any more. Tomorrow could not come soon enough!

Chapter 12

It was with a slight tremor of doubt that Joseph went to see the widow Mrs Booth again, just over a week after his last visit. Mary had been left at the workhouse as planned, and although she was obviously distressed at being torn from the security of her father and the life she had always known, Joseph had by now almost forgotten the event. He had promised to return and visit her whenever he could, but knew that if his plans were to bear fruit, this might never happen. He fervently hoped that Mrs Booth would give him the answer he wanted.

He had no need to worry. Hannah Booth had really decided the day he had asked her, that the idea of taking on a lodger was a good one. She had discussed it with her children, making sure that they were happy with the proposal, explaining that the extra money would mean a few treats for them occasionally and that their new lodger would be able to keep on top of all the odd jobs, and mend all their bits of broken furniture for them. So when Joseph arrived on her doorstep, nervous and praying that she would accept his idea, she smiled as she let him in and Joseph knew that luck had also smiled on him.

Joseph settled in well to his new way of life at Glen Bottom, having brought with him some of his own furniture from his home in Stacksteads. His room was clean and he always had a good meal on the table when he got in from work. The only disappointment to him was that he was no longer able to keep up the shop. However, with his friendly smile and winning ways, it wasn't long before he had built up a set of regular customers who were ready to call on his services as a good joiner and odd job man. He worked hard to make sure he could always pay the rent and was happy. His relationships with the family were mostly formal, not yet being on first name terms with each other; but the children with the exception of John had accepted him into their home. John was a surly child who was not yet ready to accept another man into his home, even though it had been several years since his father had died.

Joseph found that he was attracted to Hannah from the very first day he walked into the house, but knew that it was too soon to set about courting her properly. His plan had always been to marry her, but it was a happy accident that he experienced a physical attraction to her. He must make himself invaluable and at the same time, be the perfect lodger. Hannah's broken chairs were mended by the end of his first month in the house and wherever he saw a job that needed doing, he didn't wait to be asked, but set about the task immediately. Joseph became the perfect gentleman and it wasn't long before he was addressing her by her Christian name and being called Joseph, not Mr Freeman, in return. The children were a different matter. Hannah had four children by her former husband, the eldest of whom was a girl also named Mary Ellen. She was a constant reminder of his own daughter, but in name only. Hannah's daughter was slightly built like her mother, unlike his daughter who was quite plump. Her other three children were all boys and Joseph enjoyed playing with the younger two; Arthur being only four years old, and who enjoyed the rough and tumble games which Joseph encouraged. The eldest of Hannah's sons was John. He was a surly ten year old whose resentment of Joseph was plainly seen. John had been close to his father and was probably the worst affected by his father's death. John saw himself as 'the man' of the house and Joseph's presence made him feel belittled.

Hannah was confused by her feelings for this man,

who had been allowed into her home primarily as a lodger. She tried not to admit it to herself, but she too was beginning to develop an attraction for him. He always knew when she needed something mending and before she knew it, the job was done. Whenever she felt in need of a friend, he was always there and each Friday, he paid her the rent that was due without any quibble, often giving her extra; 'for a few treats' he would tell her. As the Christmas of 1877 came close, and although William had been dead these last four years, she was apprehensive of the first Christmas she would have with another man, not her beloved William, in her home. She need not have worried; the day passed in a flurry of activity. Joseph accompanied the family to church, realising that she was quite a religious woman, and they sat together almost as a family would and for the first time in several years, Hannah felt as if her family was complete. In the church were John and Naomi Booth, Hannah's former in-laws, with their son John. As Joseph gazed across to look at the seated congregation, he saw this familiar young man several pews in front of him, and his face suddenly went ashen. He had no idea that these people were related to his landlady, as so far she had not introduced them; but he did not want to be seen in the company of another woman and her family, by the man who had helped him with his daughter,

Making his excuses to Hannah before the end of the service, and head bowed with his jacket collar turned up to keep out the cold, Joseph left the church as quietly as he could, but not before the Booths along with several others of the congregation, turned in time to see him disappear around the screen at the back of the church. Hannah smiled almost apologetically at those who turned around and after the service explained that her lodger was feeling unwell and had left the church to avoid disturbing the congregation. Naomi had already expressed her disapproval at Hannah's decision to take in a lodger, but understood the reasons for her decision. John however was more tolerant and keen to meet the man who had become so indispensable.

"You must bring your lodger to meet us soon Hannah. Don't hide him away. He must be a good man to work so hard for you," smiled John. "We would love to meet him, wouldn't we Naomi?"

Naomi did not speak, but hurried her husband down the path as quickly as she could. She had no desire to meet this man. The only man in her daughter-in-law's house should be her husband, and he had been dead for four years! Naomi too had never got over the death of her son William, having helped Hannah to nurse him through typhoid for many weeks. It was not something you forgot too easily.

When Hannah got home, she was a little annoyed by Joseph's disappearance from the church as he looked quite well now; but said nothing, not wanting to spoil the Christmas festivities. Joseph had helped Hannah to buy a plump goose and she was able to give him the tastiest dinner he had eaten in many years. Even when Esther had been alive, they had rarely splashed out on a goose! To make up for his behaviour at the church, Joseph spent hours playing with the children, showing them how to play dominoes and chess. He had made a beautiful chess set during the last few months and it had been a present for Hannah. He had wrapped it in brown paper and tied it with red ribbon and given it to her after church that very morning. She had been overwhelmed by his generosity and rather embarrassed by the fact that she had no gift for him. That day was a turning point in their relationship and they spent more time in each other's company, Joseph rarely staying in his room now after the evening meal. But Joseph seldom went to church with Hannah, always excusing himself with some explanation or other. He did not want to risk meeting up with the Booths if he could avoid it.

Spring made its appearance early, and although the weather was still quite cold, by the end of March the lambs were dancing in the fields and the spring flowers were budding through the grass. Both Mary and John were out at work part time, and learning their letters at school for a few hours each day. The two youngest children, James and Arthur, also spent part of the day at school and so she was able to enjoy her time alone in the house. With the small wages that the children brought in and Joseph's rent, Hannah was just about able to stay at home. Hannah relied on his money now and realised that if he left, she would need to go out and find work herself. She thanked God every day for bringing Joseph to her in her hour of need. Each time she looked at his handsome rugged face, she felt a familiar warm glow of attraction and realised that she was falling in love with him.

"Hannah?" said Joseph taking hold of her hand. "Would you like to take the children for a walk this Sunday after church?" The children were all out at school or work and he took advantage of the times they had alone together. "It would be enjoyable for the children and a relaxing day for you."

Hannah's own thoughts returned to the days when she and William had walked in the fields above Coupe and could not bear the thought of going there with someone else.

"Where would we go?" she asked him.

"There are many lovely places we could go to, but I thought perhaps we could walk in the fields above Newchurch and see where it takes us." He squeezed her hand and was tempted to kiss her. She looked so vulnerable as if, in asking her to walk with him he had touched a nerve and perhaps released a hidden memory. He gave her hand a little reassuring squeeze and brought her fingers to his lips, gently kissing them.

"We will have a wonderful day, just wait and see."

The following Sunday, when the sun shone and the air was crisp and dry, the whole family set off for their walk in the early afternoon. Hannah had been to church with the children and when she arrived home, Joseph helped her to make the dinner before they made tracks for the empty fields above Newchurch. There was an old quarry and the land around it had been left to grow wild, but it had a beauty all of its own – bleak and untamed, with views across the valley which made the heart feel free. By the time they had reached the top of the moor, their hearts were pounding with the exertion, Joseph having carried young Arthur for some of the way. Hannah's cheeks were rosy with the glow of the exhilaration that she felt, and Joseph looked at her knowing that he had made the right decision to ask her to marry him. He fervently hoped that she would accept him today and not make him wait. The boys ran off in all directions hiding in the tussocky grass which was all around them and a good place to have fun. Mary wandered over to a patch of wild daffodils which she could see sprouting through the earth and Joseph saw his opportunity. Hannah looked relaxed as she watched her children enjoying the fresh air and sat, legs outstretched in front of her, smiling at Joseph.

"You were right," she said. "This was just what we all needed; some fresh air and exercise, and on such a beautiful day too."

Joseph walked over to her, took off his jacket and sat by her side. "You are the most beautiful thing here," he told her. "I think that you know I have begun to develop deeper affections for you than that of a lodger, and I have also dared to hope that you might also return those feelings." Hannah opened her mouth to speak, but Joseph put his finger to her lips.

"Please, let me continue. You have taken me into your family and allowed me to feel needed. Before I came to stay with you, I was lonely and you have given me a new beginning. Please say that you return my feelings!"

Joseph took hold of her hand and it took all of his strength to resist the temptation to kiss her. He could see that Hannah was flattered, but he could only hope that she would admit to having an affection of some kind for him. Eventually after what seemed like hours, she gave him his answer.

"I loved my husband dearly and when he died, I was left a lonely woman with four young children to bring up alone. I managed because I was forced to, but I missed my dearest William dearly. He will always be the father of my children and I will never forget him. But, I have enjoyed having company again in the house as well as someone to help with the jobs that I find difficult to do, and in the last few months, I have allowed myself to become quite fond of you. I will always put my children first, but you have shown me that I could find happiness once more."

Hannah glanced down at her hands, almost embarrassed by the words she had spoken and afraid to admit that she too needed a man in her life. Joseph leaned forward and placed his hand in the middle of her back, encouraging her to move towards him. It had been a long time since she had been kissed in this way and she instinctively wanted to move away, but Joseph smelt of soap, not tobacco or beer like so many of the men she had met. As she glanced up again, he tenderly kissed her lips and she returned the kiss. He was keeping his emotions in check and she respected him for that, knowing that there would be plenty of time for the physical side of their relationship to grow.

During the following months, their relationship developed slowly, maintaining an air of respectability for the sake of the children and allowing them to become fonder of the man who came to their home as a lodger. By the time the autumn leaves were falling, Hannah knew that she was in love with Joseph and he with her. The children went off to work and school as usual and Joseph prepared his tools for another day of trudging the streets looking for work, but as soon as the children had left the house, he put down his tools and went into the yard to find Hannah. She was stood by the copper, her face pink with the effort of possing the clothes. Her hair was tied in a loose knot and she was constantly trying to keep the stray strands away from her face. He thought that she looked more beautiful than he had ever seen and as he approached her, she was putting more washing into the tub. He took the clothes from her and in spite of her protestations, led her back into the scullery away from other prying eyes and listening ears. Once in the scullery, her got down on one knee and asked her the question he had been waiting to ask for so long.

"Hannah, you know how I feel about you and I think that you like me well enough. I have loved you for many months and want to ask you something."

Hannah held on tightly to his hands, only guessing what the question might be, but knowing what her reply would be if she was right.

"Will you marry me Hannah? I will be a good husband to you and will always think of your children as my own. Who knows, one day we might have children of our own."

As Joseph waited anxiously for her reply, he felt uncomfortable with the thought of having more children. He did not know whether he could cope with the anxiety they brought, having lost three of his children already. Hannah had not been told much about the family he had once had with Esther. It was something that he still found painful to discuss and did not think that she needed to know about it. However, he had all but promised her that she could have a new family with him. Perhaps that was what she wanted and if it meant that she would marry him, it was worth putting the germ of an idea into her head. After all, it might never happen!

Hannah's reply brought him from his musings.

"Yes Joseph," she replied. "I will."

The wedding was set for December. There was no reason to wait, but there were people that Hannah felt she had to tell. Naomi, she knew would not be happy about the idea that her daughter-in-law was going to remarry. In many ways, Naomi behaved as though her son William was still alive and Hannah knew that she had a difficult conversation ahead of her.

As Hannah returned from her visit to the Booths, Joseph could tell that all was not well. Hannah looked upset, her eyes damp with the tears she had obviously shed on her way back home. She pushed past him not wanting to speak and he left her to reflect on the harsh words which had obviously been spoken. He did not really care that the Booths had not received her news with the same pleasure that she had felt; secretly feeling glad that he would not need to explain himself to John Booth if he had eventually met him. The prospect of telling more lies was not one he relished, but he would have done if the need had arisen. However, for Hannah's sake he needed to show some sympathy and when she was ready to talk about her visit to the family he listened to her story with consternation. Her father-in-law was unwell and it would seem that Naomi was less than receptive to the news that her daughter-in-law was to marry for a second time. The fact that another man was to become responsible for her grandchildren was more than she could bear and she was shocked, not delighted at Hannah's news, warning her that if she went ahead with the union, she would not attend the wedding or visit Hannah in her home with her new husband.

Joseph's spirits rose, reassured now that the small threat posed by the Booth family to the secret of his wayward daughter, was no longer a problem to him. Aware that he must continue to show Hannah the sympathy she needed, he spoke soothing words, held her hand and tried to reassure her that all would be well. Thoughts of his daughter Mary had been far from his mind and he knew that sometime soon he must go and visit her, an ordeal he did not relish.

Chapter 13

"Where are we father?" Mary was confused. She did not like the look of the tall iron gates they had just passed through and as they closed behind them she felt a shudder of bleak anticipation. Her father had not spoken since they had left home that morning and she was unsure of his reasons for bringing her to this unfamiliar place. As they approached the large foreboding building, Mary felt suddenly afraid.

"Where are we father?" She asked again. But as soon as they had climbed the steps up to the main entrance, a man approached them. He was the porter and showed them into one of the receiving rooms set aside for interviewing new inmates and their relatives. The master and matron were there waiting for them as well as the relieving officer. It was their job to decide whether or not the intended inmate was a suitable candidate for the workhouse. Joseph's previous visit had already alerted them to his daughter's mental condition and he had no doubt that she would be accepted. The matron looked at Mary, unsmiling and spoke with a firmness that left Mary in no doubt of her intentions.

"Good morning Mr Freeman. You can leave Mary with us now. It is best to leave straight away."

Without turning back to speak to her at all, Joseph left Mary with the matron. Mary was distraught, crying out after him, pleading for him not to go. She did not understand why he had brought her here and even less why he was about to leave her. The woman they had met took hold of Mary by the arm, her vice-like grip leaving a vivid bruise; and tried to lead her away, but Mary struggled with all her might. She did not want to stay here without her father and could not see why she should. It took all the strength that Mrs Hay, the matron, had to keep hold of her and Mary kicked and screamed in her efforts to escape. Within minutes however, a man had appeared from a small room close by and assisted the matron in restraining the hysterical young woman. He took hold of Mary's hand and within seconds, she had sunk her teeth into his arm leaving a trickle of dark red blood to ooze onto the floor. Mary had no other way of showing her displeasure at the rough handling she was being submitted to. The master; for that was who she had bitten, immediately took hold of a stick he was carrying and beat her on the back until she was quiet. His wife brought him a piece of cloth to bind his bleeding arm and tried to calm the hysterical young woman who was doing her best to escape.

"We do not put up with that sort of behaviour here and if it continues you will be held in a cell until you calm down!" bellowed the master.

At this point, Mary realised that she was not going to escape and could no longer see her father, so fell to the ground in utter despair. Why had he brought her here? What had she done to deserve this? Mary was immediately taken to the bathhouse to be stripped and scrubbed clean. This procedure was common to all inmates on entry to the workhouse, but Mary did not understand this and the degrading action of being stripped by a person she did not know made her feel both unclean and worthless. A rough calico shift over a grey dress, woollen stockings and a cap was given to her to put on and she was taken to the weaving shed and put to work immediately. Tears were never far away and although Mary remembered the times when she worked in the mill with her mother, this was just not the same. The rooms were different and she did not know her way about. The overseer shouted at her to get on with the winding of the bobbins and she tried to remember what she had done when she had her mother to remind her. It was such a long time since and Mary made many mistakes that first day – a day she would remember for many years to come.

Supper that night was announced by a booming bell which was a signal to all inmates to prepare themselves and attend the dining hall. The meal was sparse – a large mug of tea with bread and cheese. Mary devoured the meal instantly, not having eaten that day at all. By the time she had been scrubbed from head to toe on her arrival, she had missed her dinner time meal, and Joseph had given her but a small piece of bread and scrape for her breakfast. Prayers were chanted thanking God for their bounty, and thinking of the minute amount she had just eaten, she found it difficult to think of it as bountiful. The same booming voice she had heard earlier that day coming from the mouth of the master, reminded them all of the rules they had to live by. Dissention was in many cases punishable by the withholding of a meal, or even worse, a whipping. She sat in the dining hall along with many other inmates; the women being separated from the men at different sides of the room. She dared not speak and was terrorised by the thought of meeting the master or matron face to face again.

Once the meal was finished, she was ushered by another inmate towards a large room which contained about twenty iron bedsteads, all neatly arranged in rows along each side of the room. This was obviously a place where people slept, but Mary was still expecting her father to reappear and take her home, so it was a devastating blow to her when she realised that she was expected to sleep there too. The mattress was hard and lumpy and the covering which was meant to keep her warm was simply a grey woollen blanket. The woman, who had shown her where to go, had a small child by her side and the pair soon curled up on the bed next to

Mary. Several of the other inmates sat on their beds and pulled a book or magazine from under the mattress. These were their prized possessions and they guarded them carefully. Mary could read a little, having been taught by her father and wished with all her might that she had something to read too. The woman had told her that another bell would sound at bedtime – round about eight o'clock, but Mary was exhausted and lay on her bed. The icy chill in the room made her shiver and she pulled the blanket up over her shoulders and within minutes was fast asleep.

Mary was startled into wakefulness by the sound of a bell and rough hands pushing her about. "Get out of your day clothes lass or you will be in matron's bad books!" Mary looked up at the source of the rough handling to see the woman from the next bed standing over her. She had been asleep for over an hour and now it really was bedtime. She watched as others slowly undressed for bed, leaving on their shifts and putting their day clothes on the bed for extra warmth. Mary shivered again as she did the same, feeling acutely embarrassed as others looked on. Mary was the new girl in the house and she was of some interest. The woman next to her walked over to the other side of the room and picked up a blanket from an empty bed. She returned to Mary and gave the blanket to her.

"Here, you might as well have Owd Jenny's blanket. She has no use of it where she has gone."

When Mary gave the kind woman a puzzled glance, she sniggered, "She's dead girl. Dead and buried, and better off she is too!"

The callousness with which she spoke of a dead inmate shocked Mary, but she was soon to realise that fending for herself was more important than worrying about someone who was dead.

The following morning after a poor night's sleep,

she was woken yet again by the sound of the bell. This time she needed no one else to tell her to get dressed. She hurriedly put on her clothes and followed the other women to the wash house where they all had a quick wash in cold water. Beds were to be made and she was desperately in need of relieving herself, but where? To her relief, she saw the friendly face of the woman in the next bed to her and tried to ask her where the privy was. The woman, who by now had introduced herself as Annie Law, took her to the privy which they all had to share.

"You are going to have to get used to finding where things are and not bothering me all the time," said Annie. "I have my own children to look after." Nonetheless, it was to Annie that she would turn time and time again when she was unsure during those first few weeks, and it was Annie who became her one and only real friend; friendship and love being the things which Mary so desperately needed.

Breakfast was a bowl of what was supposed to be broth, but the contents were greasy and not very filling. Many inmates helped themselves to more than one bowl, it being the only food they were going to eat until dinner time, but Mary could not stomach the idea of eating the greasy contents of her bowl. Annie and Mary both worked in the weaving shed and it was there that Mary began to nurture her obsession for someone to love. Acceptance and respect were things that rarely came into Mary's life and when she was given either, she clung onto them. Taunts and name calling had been commonplace wherever she had lived and she was used to it. So when some of the other inmates began to call her 'idiot' and 'dummy', she tried her best to ignore the taunts. Annie had already realised that her new friend was different, being unable to express herself properly and before she realised it she was looking out for

Mary's interests. James Dobbin, the overseer in the weaving shed was an inmate himself, and although it was not usual for the two sexes to be put together, he was trusted by the master to do his job without interfering with the female patients.

Annie worked on her loom and Mary fetched and carried the bobbins for her – full ones for her to weave with and empty ones to take away and be refilled. It was a monotonous task, but one which Mary could just about manage, but after the day's work was finished, she had little energy for anything but sleep. The food was not palatable and she had little appetite, so her weight began to plummet and she had not the same energy she once had.

"You must eat," Annie said to her during the dinner time meal. "If you don't, you will not survive. Just eat and don't think about the taste."

With Annie's encouragement, Mary made the most of the dinner she was given. It was usually the best meal of the day, sometimes with meat and potatoes as well as bread, and although it was tasteless, there was usually plenty of it. As the weeks passed, Mary became accustomed to the daily routine of eat, work and sleep; all interrupted by the clanging of the bell, and had realised that there were others in the house who were like her – shy, and not very bright; but also that there were others who were in fact lunatics and some of them quite strange. She often watched them, but made sure that they never saw her, as they were prone to shout abuse at those who had the gall to stare. It was at times like this that she wondered why her father had left her there and wondered if she would ever see him again.

Summer flashed by, the only difference to Mary being the fact that she now only needed one blanket on her bed; and she constantly wished that her father would come and collect her. By the time the autumn had set in, she had resigned herself to the fact that she would probably be in the workhouse for the rest of her life and tried to make the most of it. But as December, and Christmas approached, she was unaware of the events which were about to change her life.

Chapter 14

Once Joseph had left Mary with the master and matron of the workhouse, he walked briskly out of the main door, down the steps and along the wide drive back to the main road. He looked back once, and then not until he had got right down to the road where he knew that Mary would not have been able to see him. This was the start of his new life and she was not going to spoil things any more. He had given her little thought until now; the day before he was due to marry Hannah!

The approach of Christmas brought excitement in the household, not just because the festive season was almost upon them, but because Hannah and Joseph were to marry on the 22nd of December. Hannah had made all her children new clothes for the event and Mary could not wait to wear her new dress. The boys had new breeches, shirts and jackets and although not as bothered as Mary about their appearance, they were quite proud of their new attire. Hannah's neighbour and best friend Betty, had also made Hannah's dress. As this was not her first marriage, she was to be married in the Register Office, not a church; and convention did not really allow for her to wear one of the more specially designed dresses. However, the two women had gone to great pains to make a tasteful dress which would be suitable for the event and be used again perhaps for another family occasion. The dress was blue with a tight fitting bodice, showing off Hannah's slight figure perfectly. The bodice and skirt were trimmed with cream lace and the three quarter sleeves frilled with several inches of cream lace. The same lace was used to edge a beautiful blue bonnet which would complement the outfit exactly.

The house had been prepared in advance and the children would now sleep in the bigger bedroom which she had shared with her husband William and she would share the smaller room with her new husband Joseph. There was to be no special party afterwards other than a family celebration at their tiny cottage and so the children decorated the house with ribbons and holly. By the time December had made its appearance, the children had become used to the idea that their mother was to remarry and were resigned to it. Only John made his disapproval known, being openly hostile to Joseph whenever he had the chance. His thoughts were with his *real* father and he was of the opinion that his mother should never have considered marrying Joseph. In spite of his tender years, John was intuitive and there was something about this man that he did not like – he was too charming. John was waiting for the time when Joseph would show a different edge to his personality. He only hoped that he would not be the sort who would beat his mother or waste his money on drink. He had seen far too many examples of that already in his short life and witnessed what the consequences could bring.

The day of the wedding dawned and the family dressed for the occasion. Hannah looked radiant in her new dress and in spite of the cold day, she had a warm glow which seemed to keep out the frost. Joseph had been made to stay next door at John and Betty's house so that he could meet his new bride for the first time at the Register Office and he too looked a picture in his best suit. The ceremony went without a hitch and Joseph could not believe his luck when he finally came out of the stately building that housed the Register Office, a married man again. Naomi and John had not attended the wedding and the only people present besides the happy couple, were Hannah's children and their friends and neighbours, John and Betty. Hannah knew she had made the right decision in marrying

Joseph when she saw the happiness on his face as they left the Register Office a married couple. It had hurt her feelings when she realised that Naomi would not after all forgive her and attend the wedding, but Joseph's love for her would make up for that. Joseph also knew that he had made the right choice in taking Hannah as his new bride. He was not sure whether or not he actually loved her, but he was very fond of her and had high hopes that their marriage would be successful; but for now, his anticipation of their wedding night was uppermost in his mind.

It seemed as though he had been waiting for this moment for such a long time, and so when Joseph guided his new bride up the stairs to the bedroom for the first time as man and wife, he was already aroused. He could not wait to get her into bed and was the first to undress. As his clothes fell to the floor, he could see that Hannah was still dressed and that she was acutely embarrassed. Her face was flushed pink and she tried to look away from his naked body, but Joseph slowly undressed her and without thinking of her needs, he took her in his arms and began to make love to her. The night was cold and Joseph did not give Hannah any time to put on the new nightdress she had been given by her friend Betty. The windows were frosty even on the inside and their steamy breaths made little clouds of condensation. She shivered as Joseph placed her on the bed, partly because of the cold and partly because she too was becoming aroused; but because of the intense cold she was relieved when their lovemaking was over and she could snuggle down under the blankets. It had all been over too quickly for Hannah, not what she had expected at all. When she and William had made love, he was always mindful of her desires; being a thoughtful and tender lover.

Joseph however, seemed only concerned with his

own needs and as soon as they had finished making love, he turned over in bed and instantly went to sleep. He was completely satisfied with his evening's work and Hannah had seemed receptive to his advances after she had got over her initial embarrassment. As he drifted off into a peaceful sleep, his thoughts were of a positive future. At last he had a woman to share his bed. What more could he want?

When morning broke, the ground outside was covered with snow and the children were excited. The thought of making snowballs was uppermost in their minds and only John gave any thought to his new step-father at breakfast that morning. When the children had gone off to work or school, Hannah set about the daily routines, almost forgetting the previous day's excitement. Christmas was almost upon them and she wanted this one to be special, it being the first Christmas she and Joseph would spend together as man and wife. Joseph gave his new wife a hug as he also set off to find work and was confident that his new family was going to make him happy. He put all thoughts of his previous life away in a locked up corner of his mind and threw away the key.

When finally Christmas Day dawned, the expectations of the day were realised and both Joseph and Hannah were happy. Joseph watched his wife as she prepared the dinner, and he played with his step-children. Even John was more relaxed and Joseph felt content. The house was filled with laughter and excitement as they ate, drank and had fun. Joseph could not remember a time when he felt happier, until for a moment when he allowed himself to think of his daughter Mary, who would be spending this Christmas in the workhouse.

Chapter 15

There was a great flurry of excitement in the workhouse. The following day it would be Christmas Day, one of the few days in the year when there was no work to be done except the essential jobs of housework and cooking. Mary did not know what to expect, but those who had been there for several years told stories of decent food and some entertainment. On Christmas Eve, after work was over and supper eaten, the inmates were given the task of decorating the Great Hall where they ate their meals and worshipped. Since Queen Victoria had married Prince Albert, the idea of decorating the home for Christmas had developed and the Queen had set a new tradition in the use of a Fir tree and decorations to mark the occasion. The new workhouse in Rawtenstall prided itself on being one of the most modern in outlook in the whole country, and liked to give the outside world the impression that its inmates were well looked after. The hall, a vast room which usually only echoed to the sounds of plates being scraped, and not to the sound of voices; began to liven up.

Mary, along with many others, pinned sprigs of holly and other greenery to the walls in the hall and even used paper streamers to hang from the gas fittings which adorned the room; their voices, so usually hushed slowly began to show signs of excitement. Already hung on the walls were numerous paintings of past and present guardians of the establishment, whose faces were always there to remind them of 'how fortunate they were' to be in the care of such men and women. Interspersed between these portraits were religious tracts, hung there to prompt any sinner of their responsibilities to God and each other. Mary was constantly drawn to one which said 'God is Good', and wondered why 'He' had sent her there in the first place if 'He' was so good. Annie guided her children and Mary; whom she now considered to be her child; to the hall and they set to with the decorating. It was late when they finished and the exhaustion of the day's work and the 'treat' of putting up the Christmas decorations, made them fall into a deep sleep.

The following morning whilst breakfast was being eaten and the inmates were admiring the festive decorations, the Master gave a speech. Silence suddenly reigned as his voice bellowed above the hushed murmurings.

"Attention! It is with God's good grace that we are able to celebrate His day with each other, and by the grace of the guardians of this establishment that we have this magnificent building to live and work in! The Guardians will be visiting you during the midday meal and some may well take it upon themselves to serve you at table. This is a most holy day and one on which we should say our thanks to those who have helped us. We all work hard to ensure your good health and it will sadden me greatly if, when asked about your treatment here, you complain. These good people give up their time on this family day to visit and talk to you; so please show your respect and thanks accordingly."

Many of the fancy words which the Master used were misunderstood by Mary, but she understood the gist – that they were to have important visitors. Only the kitchen staff needed to work and so Mary and Annie went with the other families to play games and spend some time outside in the grounds. The workhouse had extensive gardens, some of which were given over to growing vegetables; and a maze of footpaths led in and around the building. The weather was bitterly cold and there had been a blizzard in the few days before, so the ground was covered with a thick blanket of crunchy glistening snow. Mary was reminded of the previous winter when she had enjoyed playing outside her home in Stacksteads. That time was different however. Even though she had been soundly scolded by her father, at least then she had a father to keep her company. As Mary absently wandered along the pathways, thoughts of her father entered her mind. Before she knew it, she was by the main gate; a place which she had not seen since she passed through its iron grip all those months ago. Anticipating freedom, she pushed at the gate hoping for a miracle and that it would open, but she was disappointed. Gazing out of the confines of the institution which she now called home, Mary hoped that her father would come and visit her. After all, it was Christmas.

Christmas dinner was at two o'clock and they enjoyed beef, potatoes, vegetables and gravy. This was followed by plum pudding and the meal was enjoyed by all. The Guardians made their visit and spoke to many of the inmates; all of whom showed complete humility and gratitude as promised. Mary was glad that no one spoke to her, but was surprised by the attention given to her by Mr Dobbin, the overseer who looked after the weaving shed.

"Merry Christmas Mary," he said with a smile. "Have you had an enjoyable day?"

Mary was slightly embarrassed and did not answer, but smiled in return. When no one was looking, James winked at her and blew her a kiss from the side of the hall. Mary was thrilled more by this simple action, than by the presence of the Guardians who had taken very little notice of her. It stayed in her mind for the rest of the day, and the picture of the kiss blown to her dominated her thoughts throughout the day. It could only mean one thing – that James Dobbin actually liked her and the excitement that she felt thrilled her and her heart felt the glow of a first love.

Entertainment was provided for the inmates during the afternoon – a magic lantern show which one of the Guardians had set up. They were summoned back to the hall again where they gazed in wonder at the pictures before them and they all agreed that it was a marvellous thing. Supper consisted of tea and cake with a sing-song before bedtime. Mary went to bed thinking of the day's activities, especially the kiss blown to her by Mr Dobbin and in contrast, the fact that her father had not been to see her, even today – Christmas Day.

The days passed and the drudgery that was everyday life in the workhouse continued as normal. Mary had become accustomed to the routines and knew what to expect for the most part of each day. Her main abhorrence was the weekly bath. During this procedure, she had to suffer the indignity of the presence of a workhouse officer at all times. The officer would see that she washed herself properly and although the officer was a woman, she felt acutely embarrassed by the process.

The weaving shed was a hot place whatever the weather and in spite of the cold and frost outside, Mary felt uncomfortably warm. She had no other symptoms of illness and could not understand why she felt so bad. Her mouth was dry and the fibres ever present in the air made her cough. Her head was pounding and her dress was soaked with sweat. Annie had just given her an empty bobbin to replace with a full one, when the room began to spin and blackness appeared all around her. When she opened her eyes again some moments later, she saw the concerned figure of James Dobbin peering down at her and raised voices ringing in her ears.

"Back to your machines, the lass is not harmed, she has just fainted!" shouted the overseer. He could not afford for the weaving shed to become idle; it was more than his job was worth. He picked Mary up and guided her to a wooden chair at the back of the room and gave her a drink of water. Mary was both embarrassed by what had happened and happy, that James had actually picked her up and carried her in his arms. His concern was mistaken for much more and Mary had no doubt in her mind, that James Dobbin had more than just a passing fancy for her.

Unaware of what was going through Mary's mind; James smiled at her as soon as she opened her eyes, relieved that she was not hurt. He did not want any accidents in *his* weaving shed!

"Are you ill?" he asked.

"Just my head," Mary replied quietly, returning his smile with a hug.

James was startled by her inappropriate behaviour and quickly looked round to see if anyone had witnessed the sudden outburst of affection she had shown him.

"You must not do that!" he whispered hoarsely, pulling her arms from around his neck. "That sort of behaviour will get you in front of the master for a whipping if you are not careful!"

Upset by James' curt response, Mary sulked and after a short rest was soon back at work. She had to carry on in spite of the fact that she felt unwell. By the evening, Mary had a fever and for the first, but not the last time, she was taken to the workhouse infirmary to recover. Her stay in the infirmary was unpleasant, surrounded by the acutely sick inmates who were there. She was suffering from a nasty chest infection which seemed to linger, making it hard to breathe and difficult to swallow. Her recovery was slow, and she had plenty of time to reflect on the events of the day she had given James Dobbin his first sign of *her* admiration. James Dobbin however, had given her no more thought after she had left the weaving shed that day.

Chapter 16

The pub was busy and Joseph had sat down by himself to contemplate the events of the day. He had a large glass of beer and slowly drank from its depths, soaking up its calming effect like a sponge and relaxing in the warmth of the cosy atmosphere. Tramping around the streets looking for work had become an onerous task and he did not relish the thought of doing it for much longer. What he really needed was a steady job that paid well where he didn't have to put in much effort. The shop had been better than this, but it was too late to go back. Joseph's savings were paltry and he knew that if he was to earn any money he would need to find good work soon. So far, he had managed to keep Hannah happy and pay her a small amount each week with the excuse that work had been hard to come by. In truth, he only spent a part of his day working and the other part was spent sitting in the pub like this contemplating his future.

Whilst he had been in Rawtenstall that day he had walked up to the gates of the Union Workhouse seriously trying to decide if he should go and visit Mary. As he stood there, he managed to persuade himself that it was better for both of them if he went away without seeing her. She would become upset and want to go away with him, which was out of the question. How could he explain her to Hannah? Burying his head in his hands, he closed his eyes for a minute to try and compose himself. It was no good; he needed another glass of beer.

By the time he had drunk several more beers, Joseph felt much better and decided it was probably time he went home. Hannah should have made the supper by now and then he would go to bed and try to get things out of his mind. He might even make love to Hannah tonight if she was lucky! When he finally staggered through the front door, he was faced with a stern glance from Hannah who obviously realised that he had been drinking. He had never come home in such a bad state during the time they had been married and Hannah was surprised. Drunkenly, Joseph sat at the small table which he had to share with Hannah and her children and ate his meal in silence. John, who was sitting next to him, spoke up.

"Have you been to the pub? You smell of beer!"

"Mind your own business!" barked Joseph in reply, and carried on eating his supper. When he had finished the meal, he sat by the fire for a few minutes and got out his pipe. This was something else that he rarely did at home, knowing that Hannah disapproved, but he did not care. The younger children, oblivious to his mood wanted him to play.

"Go away, can't you see I'm tired and need to rest!"

The children immediately quietened, not being used to outbursts like this from their step-father. Hannah shoo-ed them away and sent them up to bed. She needed time alone with Joseph.

"What is the matter?" she asked when the children were out of the way. "It is unlike you to shout at the children and John *was* right; you *have* been drinking beer!"

Her face was puce and Joseph could tell that she was angry. Getting up from his chair, he staggered over to her and put his arm around her shoulders breathing his beery breath all over her.

"Nothing is wrong. I am just tired like I said."

But Hannah knew that something was amiss otherwise why would he behave so much out of character. She had watched her uncle William when he had been 'in his cups' and it hadn't been pleasant. Beer took its toll and William had gone off the rails and ended up in prison. Joseph eventually went to sleep in the chair and Hannah left him there, going up to a lonely bed for the first time since she had married him.

When morning came, bright and clear, Hannah made her way down the stairs hoping that Joseph would be in a better frame of mind. He was jovial and made no reference to the events of the previous evening. Giving her a kiss on the cheek, he set off as normal to find work, leaving Hannah and the children to get on with the morning's schedule. However, Joseph had no intention of working and instead walked into Bacup where he bought a newspaper. He took his paper and went into a small café where he ordered a large mug of tea and browsed through the paper. The Bacup Times contained news from around the world as well as local news; and it was there that he saw advertisements for jobs both in Rossendale and further afield. The newspaper read; he looked in at the market hoping that there would be work for him at Jacob Ashworth's old place. He had no such luck, and was on his way out of the market Hall, when he bumped into his old neighbour Mrs Barton who enquired after his daughter Mary.

"I am afraid that Mary came down with a bad chest infection like her mother and had since died," he told her.

Mrs Barton was shocked, and offered her condolences. After a few minutes of banter, Joseph took his leave of the woman and went on his way. He had not enjoyed lying to her, but did not want her to know where Mary really was.

By the time Joseph returned home that evening, he had not earned a penny and was searching his mind for a convincing excuse. Reluctantly, he had not been to the pub, deciding that after the previous day's antics, he would certainly be 'in the dog house' if he came home drunk again. Opening the door to the house, he fully expected Hannah to be in making the supper for the family, so when the house was empty, it came as a surprise and he was a little bit annoyed. Where was she? He didn't need to wait long however before she arrived with the children by her side. She had been to see Naomi and John Booth having received a message to say that John was quite ill. Naomi had not been pleased to see her, but had welcomed the children and it seemed that their visit had cheered their grandfather.

That night, their lovemaking was passionate and lengthy for once and as Hannah lay in his arms, he explained that he was finding work more difficult to come by.

"I may need to go and find work elsewhere. I have been reading some advertisements for jobs in the Bacup Times and it appears that I might actually get work now back in Halifax. If I can't, then it is possible that my cousin may employ me on his farm for a while to get some money. I don't want to leave you alone just yet, but there may come a time when I have to."

He had done it and finally sown the seed of an idea which he might have to use. Sleep that night came slowly for Joseph as he thought over his new idea. Hannah would not stand for laziness he knew, and until some form of employment turned up which did not require too much effort, then he would have to carry on pretending that he was doing odd jobs.

The following morning, he was up early and took a few shillings from his own savings which he intended to gamble. During the last few weeks, he had become a good card player and knew of a card game which he could join that evening. When he eventually got to the pub, after wasting time in the pursuit of employment, he was delighted to see that the game had not started yet. He put some of his coins on the table and the game began. Within a couple of hours, he had won a considerable amount of money which he pocketed and returned home, making sure that he was not too drunk.

The lateness of the hour had worried Hannah. Joseph was always home just about supper time and she wondered where he was. When he finally arrived, he explained that he had found some work and gave her a couple of shillings.

"I think you should buy yourself a treat," he said. "You deserve it for putting up with me!"

Hannah gratefully accepted the coins although she had no intention of spending it just yet and was relieved that he had found work. Giving him a kiss for the money, doubt crept into her mind. His breath smelled of beer and his clothes of smoke. Had he been to the pub again? Keeping her thoughts to herself, she got on with the task of dishing out his supper and making sure the children were in bed. Joseph was as attentive as he could be, helping with the chores and later on a thoughtful lover. Hannah seemed to relish his attentions and Joseph was content for now at least. He had found a way to earn some cash *and* enjoy himself.

Slamming the cards on the table, Joseph grinned with glee. He had won again and a considerable amount of money at that. The other players sat around the table had all lost money to him during the past few weeks and they had begun to suspect him of cheating. It all seemed too much of a coincidence. It was possible of course that he just had beginner's luck, but only time would tell. To show he was a generous man, Joseph bought all who had played cards with him a beer and one drink led to another, and another. By the time the pub closed for the evening, there were several men who staggered their way back home; all thinking that Joseph was a fine fellow. Joseph however, had been canny. He had drunk slowly and so not partaken of as many beers as his friends. He had spent quite a bit of his winnings, but he thought that it was worth it just to get the other men on his side. It was still late and pitch-black when he finally arrived home to his concerned wife who had kept his supper warm for several hours. As he opened the door, Hannah said nothing, but slammed his dried up stew which had lain congealing on a plate since supper time, down on the table.

"That is your meal. I hope you enjoy it!" she muttered sarcastically.

Joseph knew that she was annoyed with him and was not pleased to be eating the mess that lay on his plate. He put a few forkfuls of the food into his mouth and tried to swallow them. It was dry as a bone and so he was glad when Hannah made him a large mug of tea to wash it down with. He could see that she was watching him from out of the corner of his eye and did his best to eat the food. When he had eaten as much as he could, he turned to her and spoke the one word which he thought might get him out of trouble.

"Sorry!"

Hannah looked at the remorseful expression on his face and smiled. Joseph put his arms around her and as usual won her around with promises of changing his ways and bringing in more money. He had, of course not informed her of his whereabouts that evening. Nor did he intend to. She had guessed from the smell on his breath that he had been at the pub, but the thought that he had been gambling had never entered her mind.

The money that he had won was put away with his own savings, not in the tin which they kept in the pantry, which actually contained the few shillings the family had saved. When he had won a bit more, he would give her a good amount to keep her happy! When they made love that evening, it was with a passion that Hannah had not experienced before with

Joseph and she was content. At least, she thought, he still loved her.

The next few days followed a similar pattern, and Joseph won again. His fellow card players had upped the stakes and given in to the temptation to beat him fair and square. In reality, Joseph could not understand his luck, for he had no strategy and was not cheating. He knew that his luck must come to end sometime, but for now he continued to win. By this time he had amassed the sum of at least fifty pounds and decided to give Hannah some extra money. He told her that he had been working hard and that the money had been earned in this way. She had no reason to disbelieve him and accepted the cash gratefully. There was now enough money in the family tin to pay the rent for the next couple of months and to keep them fed without needing to worry.

Within days of winning a large amount of money, Joseph had finally started to lose his lucky streak and his gambling pals had begun to get their own back. It became obvious to him that he would now need to either start winning again or find another, more normal way of earning his wages. The fact that he was now losing made him extremely bad tempered and he had begun to snap at the children. This was something which Hannah could not tolerate and led to greater friction between them.

Their disagreements were put on hold for a while when Hannah was sent the news that her father-in-law, John Booth, had succumbed to the bronchitis he had endured, and died. The funeral was held at St Nicholas in Newchurch, where her beloved husband William had been laid to rest and it brought back many memories for Hannah. She remembered the happy times they had spent together, hardly ever falling out; but she also remembered the devastating events surrounding his illness and subsequent death. As the whole family sat in the cold damp atmosphere of the church, Joseph held her hand. His presence at this sad family occasion had been tolerated by Naomi, but she had made it quite clear that she did not want to speak to him. Whilst he had no feelings for John Booth, Joseph did understand Hannah's feelings of melancholy, and wanted to give her his support through the ordeal ahead. When the service had ended, and the family had trudged outside to the freshly dug grave, Joseph watched with trepidation as the familiar figure of John and Naomi's youngest son John, approached him.

"Your face is familiar, Sir. Do you own a shop in Stacksteads?"……..

Joseph, anxious to be away from the graveyard and the accusing glances he was being given, gave a curt reply, cutting off any further questions.

"You are mistaken, young man! I live in Waterfoot as you well know, and have never had the good fortune to be the owner of a shop."

Ignoring any further prompts to continue their conversation, he guided a confused Hannah to the edge of the grave, which already held her first husband, and turned his attention to the burial. Immediately the concluding words had been spoken, he took hold of Hannah's hand and guided her towards the iron gates of the churchyard.

"Come, my darling," he whispered. "This is not a happy place for you, and it is better that we return home now, to save you any further distress."

Hannah was a little surprised at Joseph's sympathy and felt strangely unsettled by the conversation which she had heard earlier. However, she did feel the need to return home and so she allowed herself to be ushered through the gates and then home to Glen Bottom. John Booth, however, knew that he was right; he did know the man who was now married to his sister-in-law, but would bide his time until the right moment came, to question him again.

As Hannah lay in Joseph's arms again that night; and in spite of the unsettling events of the day, she thought hard about their relationship and realised that she must try to make it work. What she wanted was another baby, a son or daughter with Joseph to make their little family complete, but conceiving this child had not been as easy as it had with her other children.

After John's burial, Joseph tried to continue to find work again. The spring weather had made his mood more jovial and he did not visit the pub for a few days. Work however continued to elude him. He did not want to walk the streets looking for employment and so the draw of the smell of beer and a game of cards did not escape him for long. He loved Hannah in his own way, but he was feeling tied down and knowing that she wanted to have another baby had not made him feel better. So far, he had been careful in their lovemaking not to get her pregnant, but did not know how much longer this approach to his own population control would work.

Spring and summer passed in relative harmony. Joseph had been given work in the local mill, mending machines and generally doing odd jobs. It had kept him busy and out of trouble for a while and he had become more settled, even though he was bored with the same old routine. Hannah though was far from well. She had a fever and lay in her bed for several days until the worst of it had subsided. Mary had been a great help to her, calming the fever with compresses and generally keeping the family fed. Joseph was hardly ever in the home, working during the day and often not getting home until late. His visits to the pub had been less frequent whilst Hannah was ill; a guilty conscience keeping him at her bedside when he was at home. Hannah's recovery was slow as she was still very tired and often had feelings of sickness, but she slowly returned to her role as mother and wife.

By the Christmas of 1880, she was almost herself again and her relationship with Joseph appeared to be improving; the children were happy and for the first time in ages, they were a content family again. Not long after Christmas, Hannah realised that she had not seen her monthly bleeding for some time and the sickness she had experienced while she was ill had returned. Suspicions played on her mind, knowing that her body should have returned to normal by now. It could only mean one thing: she must be pregnant! Her happiness was there for all to see and even though she continued to suffer from feelings of sickness, the secret knowledge of the unborn baby gave her strength and a new serenity.

Hannah had decided not to tell Joseph about the baby until she was really sure, and her son James was about to start work soon at the woollen printing works. James was nervous, for it would be hard physical work, but Hannah knew that his wages would come in useful if as she suspected, there was soon to be another mouth to feed. Hannah's boundless supply of energy gave her a new contentment and she too had made enquiries about employment in the local cotton factory, where there was a vacancy for a warehouse woman. She could try and work up till the birth of the baby and perhaps return to work afterwards if she could find a woman to look after the child during the day. The other children would all be at school or in employment and so if her plans worked, they should be more financially secure.

Within a few weeks, she was sure she was pregnant and decided to tell Joseph first, then the children. Whilst they lay in bed that night, Hannah whispered her secret.

"Something wonderful has happened Joseph. Can you guess what it is?"

Joseph had noticed a change in Hannah's behaviour in the weeks before, and had his own suspicions, so was immediately put on his guard when she spoke. He tried not to show his emotions and made light of the question.

"Can it be that we have been left some money by a hitherto unknown benefactor?" He replied.

Hannah sat up and looked straight into his eyes. Joseph thought that she looked radiant at that moment; her hair tousled, her eyes bright and her face smiling. Instantly he was aroused and before she had time to tell her secret he put his lips on hers in a passionate kiss. Joseph made love to her with an animal instinct that he had not felt for so long; then he laid on his side, his energy rapidly waning. Hannah faced him and with the glow of a woman who has just made love she told him her secret.

"It's not money," she told him, "but a gift from God. We are to have our very own baby by the summer."

Joseph was struck dumb. This was definitely not what he wanted. Feelings of sickness overwhelmed him and his stomach churned. Another child would tie him down for good and would add to the burden put upon him already to feed and clothe the family. What if this child died as his poor little ones had all those years ago? He felt sure that he couldn't go through all of that suffering again. However, he had heard of ways that an unborn child could be got rid of before it was actually born, and he also knew that not all pregnancies were followed by a live birth; so perhaps he was worrying too soon. Hannah would never agree to kill her unborn child and so realistically that was out of the question.

He was suddenly brought from his thoughts by Hannah's insistence.

"Well, speak to me Joseph. Are you happy? Isn't this what we have wanted for many months now? Just think; our family will be complete when you and I have this new baby to love." She gazed at him, not understanding his reluctance to answer and trying to find an answer written in the emotions in his face.

Trying to keep his feelings hidden, he replied. "Of course I'm happy, just a bit surprised, that's all."

Sleep did not come easy that night for either of them: for Hannah because she could not shake off the concern that Joseph was none too happy about her news, and Joseph because he was now panicking. He did not want another child.

Chapter 17

Looking back at the house he had shared with Hannah for the last few years, Joseph felt only a tiny pang of remorse that he was leaving her for a while. He did not know how long he would be away, but had told his wife that it was necessary in order to find work. That she would believe him was almost certain, and he knew that she was a strong woman who would cope whatever life sent her way. His intention was to go and stay with his uncle who lived on a farm near Halifax. What he needed more than anything else was to get away and time to think. Once more he was in a predicament that he had not intended to be in. The truth was that Joseph was selfish and lazy. He was bitter about the blows he had been dealt in life and could not cope with anything else and often suffered a melancholy that would not leave him. He wanted to be looked after, but in reality was not prepared to give much in return so his only answer to a problem was to escape from it.

The long road from Bacup to Todmorden was steep and rough, not fit for trams and the only way he could travel that way was to ride with the carrier unless he was prepared to walk. Once in Todmorden, it was easier to either; continue with the carrier who would in all probability be going to Halifax, or get a tram which would take him a good part of the way. Halifax was a busy town, full of woollen mills and places to trade. Sheep grazed on the many farms which covered the hills and surrounded the town, and the soft water was ideal for finishing and dyeing woollen cloth. Piece Hall, famous for so long for its links with the woollen trade was now a busy market place, but the colonnaded grandeur of its architecture still stood out as one of the finest buildings ever seen.

A great sadness overwhelmed him as he travelled

the journey to his Uncle Joe's farm just outside Halifax, reminding him of the same journey he had undertaken with his daughter Mary to bury his wife Esther; so it was with a heavy heart that he finally arrived late in the evening. Joe Freeman was his father's only brother and also farmed the hills around Halifax. He had many sheep and although Joseph had been used to working with cattle, he knew that he would have to throw himself into the job of shepherd quite quickly or be sent away.

"Does your father know you have come here?" asked his uncle after he had got over the shock of seeing his nephew for the first time in many years. "It is good to see you lad, but I wonder what brings you here, and not to your father's farm."

Joseph tried to explain as best he could without giving too much detail away. His own father was getting older now and had decided to retire from farming. There was nothing left to farm at Scout now except sheep, and Joseph really did not want his father to question him about his motives for leaving his wife. He had given his family very few details about his new marriage, or indeed of the whereabouts of his daughter Mary. His shameful behaviour in leaving Mary at the workhouse was not something he was proud of, and he tried his utmost to forget that she was there. He knew that his father and his uncle would probably disown him if they had been aware of Mary's predicament, and so in his view it was a case of 'least said, soonest mended'. The assumption that Mary was still living with him and his new wife was left unchallenged. Joseph's excuse for the visit was much the same as the excuse he had given to Hannah. He convinced his uncle that work was hard to come by in Waterfoot, and so he had thought that perhaps trying to find employment in his home town might be a good idea. As a child, Joseph had developed a close bond with his uncle; having been named after him, and so it was soon agreed that as there were no prospects of being employed with his father, Joseph could stay for a short while as long as he helped out on the farm.

Winter was lingering and the weather around Halifax could be extremely cold at this time of year, but walking the fields with his cousin James helped to clear his head and for a while he threw himself into the farming jobs he was given. When he had been there for a few days, Joseph found brief employment at the nearest woollen mill as a carpenter and odd job man, but it was not to his liking. The fresh air and hard physical work gave him a renewed strength and he was starting to feel more relaxed. But thoughts of Hannah and the forthcoming arrival drew him back down to earth and he knew he had to make a decision. Once more he had run away from his problems, but the distance he had put between his new family and himself, had cleared his head. His choices were obvious to him now: go back to Hannah and face up to his responsibilities, stay near his family and find employment here or move further away where he would not be known. What he did about Mary was another decision to be made, but for now he could only think about his immediate future and his mind was in turmoil.

More and more, questions were being asked of him about his life back in Lancashire and Joseph did not want to answer them. What he knew now for certain was that he could not face having the responsibilities of fatherhood thrust upon him again, and so his decision had been made. He said his goodbyes to his uncle with a promise to let them know of any developments in his job situation. Joseph's uncle was uneasy and he had the impression that all was not well with his nephew.

The last few yards of the journey home gave Joseph feelings of anxiety that he had not felt for a long time, for he knew what he must do. The little house was empty when he finally reached home, and to his surprise, it was six o'clock before anyone else arrived. He felt somewhat perturbed by the fact that there was no one at home to welcome him, expecting to be greeted with open arms. The house was cold and there was no warming meal ready or cheery welcome. When the door finally opened, Hannah was chattering loudly to Mary, the pair being dressed in their warm woollen dresses and stockings, with shawls covering their heads to keep out the cold. The chill February air followed them in and for a moment the atmosphere was icy. Hannah stopped talking mid-sentence when she saw her husband sitting in the chair by the range and for a moment she was struck dumb.

"Joseph!" she cried. "It's lovely to see you again. You have no idea how much I have missed you!" She ran over to him, expecting to feel the embrace which she had longed to feel for many weeks now, but Joseph coldly turned away from her.

Muttering under his breath he snarled, "I don't think that you can have missed me all that much, or you would have been here to greet me." Then raising his voice so that she could hear him, he continued. "Where have you been? I was worried when I came home and found an empty house!"

Hannah was a little hurt by this sudden attack, but realised that Joseph had been genuinely worried. "I had to go and find work Joseph. Money was getting short and you weren't here, so I have a job as a warehouse woman at the mill where Mary works. I am well and so is our baby. See, touch my stomach and feel how it has grown."

Joseph did not care about the baby, but all the same,

177

he was secretly pleased that his wife now had a job. The pressure would be off him now to earn as much and so feigning consideration, he helped Hannah make the supper and fussed around her. It wasn't long before the subject of money arose, Hannah prodding Joseph to tell her that he had been successful in making money whilst he had been away. He was evasive in his reply, telling her only what he felt she needed to know, and exaggerating his bad luck in finding suitable employment. There seemed no end to the lies he could tell her. Hannah was disappointed when Joseph only gave her a few shillings, but was relieved to have her husband back home. She would need his support in the months to come and did not want to antagonise him now about money, knowing that it would make him more bad tempered. His coldness towards her though was mystifying and she could see no reason for it. As sleep claimed her that night, she was unaware that Joseph was downstairs and counting the money in the family savings tin. His mind was busy and by the time dawn broke, he had finally made up his mind what he was going to do.

In the days that followed, Joseph's routine fell into almost the same pattern as before. He would go out at the same time as the rest of the family in the morning and return at tea time; the one difference being that Hannah was also going out to work which gave him the opportunity to return to the empty house during the day whenever he liked. He rarely sought work, but neither did he spend a lot of time in the pub. At this time, he did not want to antagonise Hannah, or indeed, make her suspicious of his future plans. The café in Bacup market became a favourite haunt for the next couple of weeks and Joseph often sat in the café drinking tea and reading the Bacup Times. As he was engrossed in the newspaper, he was jolted from his study by a familiar voice.

"Good morning Mr Freeman. I thought it was you." The speaker sat down across the table from Joseph and took great delight in the discomfort he appeared to be causing. As Joseph looked up from his newspaper, he was irritated to see Hannah's brother-in-law, John Booth seated opposite him.

"What do you want!" growled Joseph. He did not want to become involved in a conversation with this man.

"I think that it was in this very market that I first saw your daughter," replied John calmly. "She was getting herself in a bit of a predicament, if you remember and I had to rescue her."

Joseph was temporarily lost for words, not knowing whether to deny that he knew him; as he had done when quizzed at the funeral, or just admit that he knew him and make an excuse about Mary. John did not look the sort of man who would let the subject drop and so he decided to make his excuses; after all, if all went to plan, he would not be in Waterfoot for much longer.

"I am sorry, Mr Booth, it had completely slipped my mind. Yes, I have you to thank for Mary's wellbeing on that day. If she was here now, I am sure that she would thank you again herself." Joseph kept his calm exterior, waiting for John to assume that Mary was dead.

"Is Mary unwell? Has she gone to live somewhere else?" asked John. He was not entirely sure what Joseph meant by the fact that Mary 'was not here'.

"Mary died shortly after your rescue I am afraid. You know that she spent a lot of her time wandering and often talked to anyone she met. Sadly, she went out without her cloak and then caught pneumonia. She was dead within a couple of weeks and I was left without both my wife and daughter in the space of a couple of months." Joseph's lies tripped off his tongue and he felt

179

no remorse, only the compelling need to get rid of John Booth and satisfy his curiosity.

John Booth left the market under the impression that Joseph had been regrettably robbed of the love of his first wife and his daughter, until the moment he met Hannah. He did not often visit his parents these days, having recently married himself, but the uneasiness he still felt made him make a mental note to mention the information he had just received about Joseph Freeman, the next time he visited.

Joseph watched John Booth disappear from view and knew that he must act fast. He was thankful that Hannah did not see her previous in-laws very often and so it was unlikely that she would find out about Mary within the next few weeks. He settled down once again to read the advertisements for employment. It was one such announcement that caught his eye.

Wanted~
Boarding-house keeper for respectable house
Male or Female, but must be clean and of good character
And able to carry out repairs to the
Property when needed.
Reduced rent for suitable applicant.
Applicant must be available for interview on March 25th.
Apply in writing to:
Mr JS Bowker (agent of the owner)
46 Bennet St,
Buxton.
Derbyshire.

Buxton featured in several articles which Joseph had read, promoting the health-giving properties of its waters and the bracing countryside air which surr-ounded the town. Buxton was fast becoming famous as a Spa town and as a result, there was an increase of new building taking place; hotels, shops and housing were all in demand. The newspaper also featured several advertisements for building workers such as joiners, plumbers and general labourers. Although he would not earn a living from this, he would be able to find a job in the building trade there.

This was just what he needed! March 25th was not long away and so he must hurry. Without delay, he spent a few coins on decent writing paper and took the newspaper article home. Before Hannah or the rest of the family had time to return from work, he had written his application taking the unusual decision to ask that any reply be delayed, explaining that he was visiting the area soon and would call to the house for his reply. He fervently hoped that he would be interviewed and employed straight away.

The following Sunday, he walked with the family again taking the opportunity to calm any suspicions that Hannah might have had. He need not have worried, for Hannah was completely unaware of her husband's plans. The children played happily and Hannah talked of her plans for the new baby, trying to draw Joseph into conversation, but his mind was elsewhere.

As the door closed behind them the next day, and the family all set off to work or school, Joseph said his normal goodbyes to Hannah. She set off with Mary to the mill after leaving Arthur with a neighbour until it was time for him to go to school, and Joseph walked off around the corner, all the time watching to see when the family were well on their way. Leaning against a wall for a few minutes to maintain his composure, Joseph smoked a cigarette. Once finished, he turned and retraced his steps to the house, quickly looking around to make sure that no one had seen him. The house seemed strangely empty as he glanced around for the last time. He had packed his few belongings into a small leather bag and made sure his tools were in his tool bag, then emptied the savings tin from the larder shelf. When he looked around the small bedroom he had shared with Hannah he remembered the good times and felt a pang of remorse. These feelings did not last long and he persuaded himself that he should never have married Hannah. That had been his biggest mistake. If he had just remained as a lodger then he might still have been happy here. Still, he needed the comforts of a woman's love warming his bed at night and Hannah would never have agreed to sleep with him if he had not married her. If she hadn't got pregnant, he might have stayed longer but that had been the final straw.

Taking a last look around to make sure he taken all his money, he opened the door and without looking back, set off on his journey. He had money in his pocket and the hopes of an easier life in Derbyshire and so he felt good. His spirits raised and hopefully his problems over, he could look forward to a new life.

The tram rattled its way into Rawtenstall where Joseph planned to take the train to Manchester and then on to Buxton. As he watched the buildings go by, his thoughts returned to his daughter Mary Ellen and he wondered whether or not he should collect her before he actually went to Buxton. Almost as soon as the thought had entered his head, he dismissed it reminding himself of the trouble she had caused him whilst they lived in Stacksteads. No, once he was settled, and then if the time was right, he would go and collect her; after all, she was probably better off where she was!

Chapter 18

In the few short years since Mary had entered the workhouse, her obsession with James Dobbin had not lessened. She sought out his attentions whenever she could even though she had on one occasion been punished for making improper advances. Men and women were actively discouraged from fraternising with one another, having separate dormitories and day rooms. But even though they still sat apart at meal times in the large dining hall, Mary could see him and she always smiled. He thought nothing of it initially, but if he did not smile back, Mary would loudly speak his name to try and get his attention. In spite of her difficulties, she was not an ugly young woman although she was of stockier build and had a round face with chubby cheeks which always seemed to glow.

James tried to keep his distance whilst they worked in the weaving shed, but by the summer of 1880, he was finding this difficult and discovered that he also had a fondness for the strange young woman. It had been a long time since he had lain with a woman and began to dream of what it would be like to be with Mary. That she was still a virgin he was almost certain. She had never married; society assuming that 'idiots' did not have the same feelings as 'normal' people and would in all probability not be able to make a marriage work. James knew that Mary liked him; how could he not? She was always smiling at him and pretending to be coy when in the weaving shed. His own imposed sexual abstinence had made him frustrated and he thought that if he could find a way to be with Mary, she would be a willing partner.

Mary's advances towards James had not gone unnoticed though. Annie watched over Mary like a mother as she had done since Mary's arrival in the workhouse and knew that Mary had a fancy for the only man in the whole of the workhouse who had shown her some attention in the time she had been there.

"Mary," she whispered quietly. "You must not make advances to any man in here! You will be punished and might even get taken away by the magistrate if you are caught in an improper situation! The least they will do is take away some of your food, but the chances are you will be put in a cell for a few days then brought before the Guardians who will turn you out to walk the streets!"

Mary did not really understand the implications of what Annie was trying to tell her and had totally forgotten how scared she had been all those years ago when she had thought that a man was going to hurt her. Mary lived for the moment and was unable to plan ahead; and what she wanted right now was to get a cuddle from James.

The heat was stifling in the weaving shed, and the heat was stifling outside. Most of the women were in their summer uniforms and wore fewer petticoats than normal. Mary was dreadfully hot and was finding it difficult to work. She continued to wind the bobbins and to make her body feel a little bit cooler she wafted her skirts around trying to encourage cooler air around her legs. A sudden dizziness came over her and she staggered towards the door where James was standing.

"Hot," she croaked seconds before she fainted right into his arms once again. James carried her to a cooler spot in the shade just outside the shed and sat her against a wall. Her skirts were lifted above her knees and he could see that she wore no drawers. If he lifted her skirt a little bit more, he would be able to see the darkness beyond, wherein lay the gateway to such pleasure. His arousal was obvious, but the bell rang to signal the end of the working day and he knew he must restrain himself. The other women from the weaving shed, with the exception of Annie, went about their business leaving Mary in James' care. Knowing that he must be very careful not to show any interest in *any* woman, he persuaded Annie that Mary would be fine and soon be back in the day room ready for the supper bell. Reluctantly, Annie left Mary in his care and went back alone.

Mary had indeed recovered and was sitting up against the wall, smiling at James, her saviour. He held out his hand to her and gently drew her towards him, catching a tiny glimpse of the top of her legs, enticing her into a passionate embrace. Mary clung to his shoulders with a vice-like grip and was reluctant to let him go. She had not experienced anything like this before and strange new emotions overwhelmed her. Realising that he had overstepped the bounds of decency and the rules of the workhouse, James apologised.

"I am sorry Mary. I should never have kissed you. It was not a gentlemanly action and will not happen again!"

Mary, who was distraught by the thought that this could be the end of their liaison started to weep loudly. Looking round, James tried to calm her, for he did not want her distress to draw attention to their situation. The only way he was able to do this was to put his arms around her again and to promise that if she did not tell anyone, he would try to meet her again. The supper bell sounded and for now Mary accepted this, returning to the dining hall to eat her supper.

Summer sped by and before long the winter of 1880 had settled in. The Christmas festivities gave way to a slight relaxation in the rules, especially when the guardians came on their annual visit to give out small gifts and show what good benefactors they were. After the Christmas morning service, Mary had searched for James, needing his affection but not understanding the implications of what she was about to do. The workhouse was designed to make it difficult for the two sexes to meet, each having their own exercise yards and sleeping arrangements, but Mary saw her chance when she left the dining hall. As usual, they had all been bombarded with righteous scriptures during the meal and as it was Christmas Day, the only day apart from a Sunday on which work was not done, they had also to endure over an hour of preaching from the rector who came to see them each week. The Ten Commandments were recited and great emphasis put on 'Thou shalt not commit adultery', 'Thou shalt not steal' and 'Thou shalt not bear false witness.' Punishment for breaking these rules which everyone was expected to live by; was of course severe. The rector preached hellfire and brimstone for all who dared to think otherwise. Mary sat through these sermons each week not really understanding the ideology within them and when she saw James Dobbin leaving the dining room after dinner, she followed him.

The long corridor which stretched down the centre of the building separated the dormitories and day rooms. On either side were several smaller rooms used for interviewing patients, some cells and the bathrooms which contained the tin baths used each week for the inmates' ablutions. It was into one of these rooms, normally kept locked, that Mary enticed James. Once inside, they were completely alone and although James knew he was doing wrong, he took advantage of Mary's vulnerability and need for love. Pulling her skirts up around her waist he gently probed between her legs searching for the warmth which he knew awaited him. Feelings of arousal overcame Mary as she let loose her natural feminine instincts; at the same time her innocence made her a passive partner as she was really unsure what she should do. It was he who took the lead and laid her on the cold stone floor, and kneeling astride her he began to stroke her breasts through the bodice of her dress. His passion, held in check for so long took over from his common sense and he quickly untied the laces which bound her bodice together. Her firm white breasts revealed, James began to caress and kiss them making Mary squeal with delight. Within minutes, he had entered her and she cried out in pain. It was too late, James could not stop and when he finally climaxed, Mary was clinging on to him, not knowing what had happened to her. The pounding sensation she had felt had been unpleasant at first, but a strange sensation of excitement had followed and she found that she had actually enjoyed this encounter.

James was disgusted with himself, although he had not expected to enjoy it and the sexual relief he had felt had been tremendous. However, he knew that if Mary told anyone, they would both be severely punished, probably being brought before the guardians and he at least would be thrown out of the workhouse with nowhere to go. Although he did not want to be an inmate in this place, he had no money and no relatives to help him out, so in spite of the shame he felt at needing to be in there, at least he was fed and had a roof over his head. Mary must be made to keep quiet about what had happened.

"Mary, I want you to keep this as our little secret," he whispered to her with a smile. He knew that if he played on her child-like mind, she just might react in the way he wanted her to. Mary returned her smile and giggled.

"Our secret," she said and squeezed his hand. James

silently left the room, making sure that no one was around to see him and Mary followed his lead, tiptoeing into the corridor where she walked slowly back to her dormitory.

"Where have you been?" Quizzed Annie, as Mary approached her bed.

"Nowhere," replied Mary trying to contain her secret as James had told her. She was happy though and it was difficult not to show this, so she pretended to feel unwell, explaining to Annie that she had a headache and lay on her bed. Annie was suspicious. She had seen the way that Mary looked at James Dobbin and hoped that she had not spent the last hour in his company. When Mary got up, she would have a chat to her, warning her of the dangers of getting too close to James, for Mary was very naive and easily manipulated, making her an easy target for any man.

As the weeks passed, the signs of Mary's clandestine liaison with James were becoming more obvious. Queasiness overwhelmed Mary and she was violently sick into the chamber pot. This feeling of nausea had been present now for some days and Mary could not understand why. During the day she was well enough to work and her appetite was as it should be, but when she arose in the morning, she could not wash away this awful sick feeling. Aware that Annie was watching her, Mary wiped her mouth and smiled, trying to persuade her that all was well. At breakfast, Mary ate her portion of bread, but could not face the gruel. This was the first time she had felt unable to finish her breakfast. Even though the food was not appetising, Mary normally ate what she was given, having no alternative unless she wanted to go hungry. Annie eyed her carefully, aware that she had already been sick, but said nothing. Time would tell if her suspicions were well founded.

By the time the spring sunshine was beginning to make the plants grow again, Annie was sure that Mary was pregnant. Mary herself knew that something was happening to her body, but it wasn't until Annie spoke to her that she fully understood.

"Have your courses stopped Mary?" Mary looked at her with bewilderment on her face.

"Your monthly bleeding, has it disappeared?"

Mary looked down at the floor and replied, "Yes," then tears started to flow. Annie put her arms around Mary and hugged her tightly. When Mary had finally recovered, Annie spoke to her again.

"Tell me truthfully, have you lain with James Dobbin? Did you let him touch your private parts?"

Mary nodded her head and whispered, "He loves me. It is our secret, so don't tell."

Annie groaned. "You are going to have a baby Mary. That is what happens when you let a man do that to you, but you must keep that a secret for now and not see James again or he will get into trouble. Do you understand?"

Again Mary nodded, and grinned broadly. "A baby! My baby! I will love it!" Immediately she began to rock an imaginary baby and sing quietly to the child she would eventually have. Annie tried to quieten her, "Shhh you must not let anyone know until it is too late or they will make you get rid of it." Annie gently put her hands on Mary's stomach. "Your belly will grow until the baby is ready to be born. Then I will help you."

Mary's pregnancy was miraculously kept quiet until the beginning of the summer months when most women were beginning to wear thinner garments and she was unable to keep her growing waistline covered by a thick skirt and shawl. It was however, matron who spotted the bulge beneath Mary's dress and hauled her into the office for questioning.

"You are with child girl! Who is the father?" she demanded.

No amount of threatening and screaming could persuade Mary to talk as she was terrified. Her mouth tightly clamped shut, she was taken to one of the cells where she awaited an examination by the doctor. Meanwhile, the matron marched off to the dormitory where Mary slept. Pushing open the door with a force which almost knocked another inmate off her feet, she stood in the doorway and bellowed at the top of her voice.

"Right! Who knew that Freeman was with child? Why did no one report this to me earlier?" A sea of blank faces looked right back at her, all amazed that the 'idiot' Freeman had managed to get herself in this condition. When no one answered the matron, she threatened; "If no one comes forward to tell me what is going on, then you will all miss your supper!" and then she marched out. Annie was in turmoil. Should she admit to knowing about Mary's condition and risk being punished even further, or should she keep quiet and let the whole dormitory miss one meal. If she told matron what she knew, then James Dobbin would be taken before the magistrates and in all probability thrown onto the streets. She had no sympathy for James, but she had grown to love Mary and understood the distress this would cause her. The decision was made: she must keep her peace and say nothing, after all, what was one meal when they were hungry already?

Mary's examination was humiliating for her. The doctor took great delight in the intimate examination he made Mary endure. Callously she was prodded and poked and asked more questions about when she had lain with the baby's father. Eventually, after a sleepless night in the cell, she was taken back to matron's office.

"The doctor tells me that your baby will be born in a couple of months. You will have the baby here and then I am afraid you will have to leave. This is a very serious situation. Fraternisation with the opposite sex is absolutely forbidden and **you know that!**" You have schemed and behaved in an improper way and as a result you will bear a bastard child. You have become the lowest of the low – a slut!"

Mary was sent back to her dormitory where she was shunned by all except Annie. It had been made clear to her that she would receive no special treatment and would still be required to work daily in the weaving shed as before. When word finally got round that the 'idiot' was pregnant, Mary arrived one day in the weaving shed only to find that James was no longer there. He had signed himself out the previous day on the pretext that he was going to live with a relative in Bury. Mary was distraught, but only Annie knew the reason why.

**

Midsummer brought an abundance of new life. Trees and flowers were at the peak of their beauty and in a small cottage in Newchurch, the lusty cries of a new-born baby could be heard. When Jenny Althorpe had finally washed the infant and placed him in the arms of his mother, she looked down at his tiny face with concern. The birth had been a difficult one and the tiny baby had been born with his foot twisted at an unusual angle. Hannah had been alone, only asking for the help of the midwife when the pain had become too much. Her other children had been kept away from their mother until the baby had been born, the distressing sounds of their mother trying to deliver a healthy child too much for their ears. After the baby had been placed in Hannah's arms, she looked at him and cried. Tears flowed in rivers down her cheeks until she could cry no more. What should have been a joyful time, had been a time overshadowed by the grief experienced by an abandoned woman. Joseph should have been here to see his son, but he was gone. Hannah had to count her blessings though; that she was warm and safe, her new baby was in good health in spite of his twisted foot, and her family were around her. She had little money, but her earnings paid the rent man and the family were fed.

Loud cries and footsteps bounding up the stairs brought her from her melancholy. It wouldn't do to let her other children see her so sad. John was the first through the door to see his mother, shortly followed by Mary and her younger brothers.

"What shall we call your tiny brother?" asked Hannah. After much discussion, John suggested 'Ernest' and so the new baby was named.

"Why has he got a funny foot" asked Arthur, "will it be better soon?" Silently worrying whether or not her new son would ever walk properly, Hannah answered.

"I am sure it will be fine, now we must let him sleep and say our prayers for him." Hannah looked down at the infant and saw the likeness to his father. His hair was dark and his features reminded her in so many ways of Joseph, but she knew that he would not have his stature.

**

A few miles away, a similar scene was taking place in the workhouse, but the outcome would be very different. Mary Freeman's baby was about to be born in the bleak surroundings of the infirmary ward. Unlike Hannah, Mary had no family to comfort her or soothe away her worries; her needs being met by the cold-hearted approach of the nurse in charge. Mary's pains had been excruciating and she was frightened. Annie had tried her best to explain what was going to happen to her, but she was not prepared for the assault on her body made by the labour pains. Mary cried out in agony as wave after wave of pain coursed through her body and she thought that she was going to die. She was shown no sympathy by the nurse and Annie had not been allowed to visit her at all, so when her daughter finally arrived, Mary was exhausted and sore. The baby did not cry and when she was placed into her mother's arms, her face blue and her body still, Mary somehow knew that she was dead. She rocked the tiny dead infant, singing to her and hoping that she would somehow move, but it was not to be.

The nurse finally prised the dead baby from her arms saying, "It's your own fault. People like you were never meant to have babies."

Mary's cries could be heard echoing through the corridors of the infirmary wing and into the main building. After a few days confinement, she was deemed fit enough to resume her normal work and returned to her place in the dormitory and to Annie's sympathetic ears. The tiny doll-like infant was wrapped in a cloth and taken to the mortuary where arrangements would be made for her burial in an unmarked pauper's grave.

Mary would never know her daughter.

Chapter 19

Buxton, Derbyshire 1881

Sunlight streamed through the window of 46 Bennett Street and caught the myriad of tiny dust particles that floated in the air. As Joseph glanced out of the window, he watched the busy street filling with people going about their daily business. He too would be off to work in a few minutes and he felt lucky to be alive. Buxton was a thriving town, made famous by the spa waters which many people thought contained healing properties. Everywhere you looked, new houses, shops and hotels were being constructed and this building boom had given him the opportunity he needed to find work. Joiners were one of the tradespeople who were much sought after, and he had easily managed to find work. In his own home, he had lodgers who were painters, and many other people involved in the building trade lived in the houses close by. His role as a lodging-house keeper had been easy; being accepted after a short interview to ascertain his good character, by the agent of the owner, Dr Bennett. A local physician, Dr Bennett owned the land and had started to build the houses upon it in response to the ever growing demand for housing, and naming the street after him. Joseph's house had been one of the first to have been built only a few years earlier and so the house was almost new, having three bedrooms, a kitchen, a parlour and a sitting room. Joseph was a proud man.

The summer months had sped by in a flurry of activity and he had little time to think about the life he had left behind him. Not once did he wonder if his son or daughter had been born or consider Mary who was still incarcerated in the workhouse. Autumn came and the leaves began to change into their many wonderful shades of crimson and gold, which Joseph observed as he walked through the Pavillion Gardens on his way to work each day. The cold crisp air reminded him of his birthplace in Halifax and it was then that he began to wonder about Hannah and their child. Christmas would not be long in coming and many of the shops in the centre of Buxton had taken up the tradition of decorating their windows with bright, merry ribbons and a fir tree festooned with ornaments and candles. His lodgers, especially young Jane Brennan, had tried to persuade him to decorate the house for the festive season as unlike the rest of them, she would not be going home to visit family. The excitement and anticipation of a joyful occasion like Christmas was evocative of Christmases past and Joseph suddenly felt lonely in spite of the fact that he was surrounded by other people. The more he thought about Mary, the more he began to feel sorry for his actions in sending her to live in a place like the workhouse and decided it was time for him to go and bring her home. He would go before Christmas and Mary would have her next Christmas with her father in their new home. He was earning good money now and had room enough in the house, even though she would have to share with Jane and Hetty his female lodgers. After all, he now had enough help in the house if things were to go wrong with Mary and he hoped that she might actually help him to look after the lodgers.

His mind made up, Joseph set off early one Saturday morning, taking the train again to Manchester and from there on to Rawtenstall. The clickety–clack of the wheels on the railway lines made him nod off to sleep and it seemed no time at all before he was changing trains in Manchester. As the familiar sight of the workhouse building came into view from the trees surrounding it, Joseph began to worry. What if he met someone he knew? Even worse, what if it was someone who knew Hannah? Alighting from the train, he hurried along the main road going towards Haslingden and turned off onto Union Street along the approach to the workhouse itself. The drive to the workhouse seemed longer than it had been before, and Joseph almost turned back without fulfilling his intention of collecting Mary. Once inside the gates though, he was more positive about the job he had come to do and walked assertively into the main door. The porter immediately came out of his office and enquired what business Joseph had in coming to the workhouse.

"I would like to see the master please on private business," replied Joseph in a haughty manner. Who did he think he was, this porter? Joseph did not want to divulge his private business to such a lowly person.

Within minutes, Joseph was standing in the master's office expressing his wish to take Mary home, but was more than surprised by the reaction of the master.

"Mr Freeman, it is usual to give a small amount of notice in order to ensure that all belongings of the inmate have been gathered together, but if you would be willing to wait an hour or so, I am sure that this can be arranged quickly."

Joseph agreed that this would be acceptable and was shown to a seat to await his daughter. The master however, wanted to continue the conversation.

"We have wanted to speak to you Mr Freeman, on a very delicate matter, but have had not had a forwarding address to write to you." Joseph frowned, wondering what was to come.

"What I have to report is of a very unpleasant nature, and I am sure it will come as a great shock to you as it did to us. Miss Freeman was discovered earlier on this year to have been consorting with a man in a most inappropriate manner, the results of which concluded in a pregnancy. It did not come to our attention until it was too late and your daughter was already with child. The father is unknown to us as she has repeatedly refused to divulge his name. I believe he may have already left our protection and so it is impossible to bring him to justice!"

Joseph paled at the significance of this revelation. A child! God help him, how could he bring up a child with his daughter Mary. As he was trying to digest this information, the master looked on almost pitying the man before him. Recovering enough to speak, Joseph enquired about the baby.

"The child? Where is the child?"

"I am afraid that the child was stillborn, which is probably a good thing considering your daughter's mental state. It was a daughter and would more than likely grown up like her mother."

Although Joseph was also relieved that the child did not survive, he did not like the suggestion that his daughter was a lunatic. His sense of justice aroused, Joseph looked for someone to blame for the whole incident.

"I left my daughter in your care and you allowed her to behave in this way!" he bellowed. "I have a good mind to take this before the guardians of the workhouse and see what they have to say about your failure to protect a vulnerable girl!"

"Mr Freeman," replied the master, "your daughter behaved in an immoral way as only a woman of the night might act. Believe me, the guardians have already been informed and as I said earlier, we tried to contact you to come and collect her sooner, but had no means of finding your whereabouts. It is normal in such circumstances to imprison such a person and then send them out to find their own way in the world. The only reason your daughter has avoided such treatment was because of her defenceless nature."

At this moment, Mary was ushered into the room and the conversation ended. On seeing her father for the first time in over two years, Mary was unsure how to react. Did this mean that she would go with him? Joseph smiled at her and she went straight to the security of his arms. She was confused, feeling angry at him for not coming earlier; but overjoyed that at last he seemed to want to take her back with him. Joseph could not find the words to ask his daughter about her child, and knew that it would wait until they had the privacy of their own home or until Mary decided that she needed to talk to him about it.

Dismissed from the workhouse in a brusque manner, Joseph and Mary walked briskly down the path towards the main gates, almost fearing that if they did not hurry, the gates would close and lock them inside forever. Mary held onto her father's arm whilst he carried her bag in the other, and the pair made once more for the train station; no real conversation passing between them. Mary did not know where they were going; she was content that she was with her father. The main road was busy with carriages, carts and people passing the time of day and when a voice was heard from behind them shouting Joseph's name, Mary was surprised.

"Joseph! Joseph! It is you, isn't it!"

Joseph turned round not knowing who to expect, but wanting very badly to disappear and saw what he knew to be one of Hannah's acquaintances.

"I haven't seen you for a long time," she continued. "How are your wife and new baby? He must be a few months old now!"

Joseph growled at her in a very rude manner. "I am sorry, you are mistaken. I have no idea who you are and

I have no wife and baby!"

As he turned back to face Mary, she looked puzzled.

"Who is that lady? Mother is dead, so why did she ask about your wife?" Joseph put his arm around his daughter in an effort to shield her from any further revelations.

"Don't worry my dear," he whispered. "She does not know what she is talking about." He turned smartly away from the woman and ushered Mary quickly away. He had recognised her and did not want to give her time to talk further.

The train journey gave Joseph time to explain his actions to Mary. She must not be told of his marriage to Hannah or of the baby he had never met. This would be his secret and one he would hold until the day he died. For now, his explanation to his daughter contained a story of hardship; a man without work, until he moved to Buxton where he was now living happily. Mary would never understand his motives for the choices he had made whilst she had been in the workhouse, nor indeed his reason for taking her there in the first place, so he did not try to justify himself. Sadly, he could not find the right words to question Mary about the birth of her dead daughter and this was a discussion which would wait for many months.

Deep in thought, Mary looked out of the carriage window at the outside world. It seemed a beautiful place and one which she had never thought to see again. The fields, still white with frost gave way to the bustle of the town and Mary arrived in yet another new place which she was soon to call home. Joseph held her hand as she stepped down from the carriage, taking her small valise which contained all her possessions. Mary watched as other passengers did the same and it wasn't long before the station master had slammed all the doors and was blowing his whistle ready for the return journey to Manchester. The station was thick with clouds of steam from the engines and the acrid smoke made Mary cough, so once more she held on to her father's arm for security. They hurried out of the grand station entrance and found a horse cab which would take them to Bennett Street.

Mary's heart was beating so fast that she thought it would burst. As the house came into view and she caught her first glimpse of Bennett Street, she was pleasantly surprised and what she saw made her heart sing. What she had expected was a dirty little cottage, but what she actually saw was a row of fine stone terraced houses with tiny gardens at the front. Walking up the tiny path to the door, she turned to her father.

"Is this our home father?" she asked.

"Yes Mary," he promised. "This is your new home and you will never need to return to the workhouse as long as we are living here."

Joseph opened the shiny painted door and welcomed Mary into the parlour of their new home. In spite of the tedium of the journey and the exhausting hours travelling, Mary's face was a picture of happiness. She believed her father's words completely and his promise would remain with her for the rest of her life.

The house was cosy and although not massive, it was certainly bigger than their house in Stacksteads. The parlour had a large fireplace and in it was a welcoming fire burning brightly, giving the room its homely atmosphere. A dresser stood along one wall; and on it were a selection of plates of all sizes and dishes, which she supposed could be used for serving food. A large clock ticked loudly as it sat on the mantle and as the hour approached, it chimed a beautiful melody. Mary was escorted to the chair by the fireside and her cloak taken from her. She felt like a princess who had been whisked away to a magic castle and the enormity of what had happened to her during the last day, began to dawn on her. She was suddenly brought round from her reveries by the sound of a voice behind her. As she turned around, she saw a young woman, probably about her own age who was smiling as she spoke.

"Hello Mary. I am Jane Brennan and I am a lodger here where your father lives. He has told me a little bit about you and I am longing to get to know you better. It will be wonderful to have someone nearer my own age to talk to. I think I am just a few years younger that you are and I know that we will get on famously."

In reality, Joseph had hardly spoken to anyone about Mary except to tell the rest of his lodgers that his daughter was coming to stay with them and that she was not quite like other girls of her own age. He left out any details about her mental state, leaving them to make their own minds up about that. In his opinion, the less they knew the better. Jane was a bright young woman from Liverpool who was working as a servant in a big house close to the park and walked each day to her job. She was not required to live in and had some Sundays off which she generally used to socialise with other servant girls she knew, walking in the park or seeing the sights in Buxton. As she talked to Mary, she was aware that she was extremely shy, not wanting to answer any of her questions so she did not press her for a reply. In the few months that she had known Joseph, she found that he was a very private person, giving away little about his past or revealing his feelings. Jane did not know whether she liked him or not, but felt a little uneasy in his presence. He spoke of religion, but never went to church and when he finally revealed that he was going to bring his daughter to live with them; Jane was astounded, having always thought that he was a bachelor.

The week before Christmas passed by in a flurry of activity. Jane took Mary to look at the brightly decorated shop windows in the centre of Buxton. Bright lights twinkled and they gazed in wonder at the multitude of gifts on offer. Mary was mesmerised by the beautiful dolls she could see which had come from faraway places like Germany, Austria and Switzerland and could not take her eyes off the glittering window displays.

"Do you like the dolls, Mary?" asked Jane as she saw the wonderment in the young woman's eyes.

"They are beautiful," replied Mary quietly. "I never had a doll like that. It looks just like a baby."

Taking Mary's arm, Jane turned her away from the shop window. "I'm afraid that the likes of us will never be able to afford dolls like them," she said. "They cost more money than I earn in a month, so all we can do is dream."

Mary was distracted by thoughts of the perfect doll she had seen and Jane could sense the sadness in her, so trying to take her thoughts away from the doll, she wandered over to one of the street vendors nearby.

"These chestnuts smell delicious, don't you think Mary? Shall we buy some?"

They were soon tucking in to their chestnuts, wrapped in small paper parcels, so hot that they had to quickly transfer them from hand to hand to stop them from burning their fingers. They sat for a moment or two on a bench by the edge of the park, and peeled the tiny, fragrant brown nuts; the crisp skins flaking off to reveal the creamy white centre which they ate with glee. Mary smiled at Jane and the doll was forgotten for the time being. They each held on to a couple of the warm chestnuts and put them inside their mittens to keep their hands warm. Standing on the corner of the park, was a group of carollers who were assembling a small crowd of people around them. As the carollers sang to the strains of 'Good King Wenceslas' and 'Silent Night'; Mary and Jane watched in awe as the violinist expertly fiddled the tunes and the singers raised their voices in harmony in praise of the baby Jesus. Spirits raised, they set off back home dawdling past the bigger houses which lay on either side of the park. Startlingly visible through the large bow windows, were the Christmas trees lit by candles and laden with decorations of angels and cherubic children, tinsel and ribbon, and home-made cookies which more than likely had been made by the children. It would not be long now until Christmas Eve when they would be able to put up their own greenery inside the house, and a wreath made from holly and ivy would be fastened to the front door. Joseph was not an extravagant man and he did not want a Fir tree, but since Mary had settled so well during her first few weeks in Buxton, he had felt more relaxed and so happily encouraged Mary and Jane to decorate the house with greenery.

The welcoming smell of a home cooked stew greeted Mary and Jane as they opened the door; cold, but cheery after their trip to the shops. Hetty had made a warming stew with potatoes and dumplings to fill them and amidst the chatter which took place during the meal, there was talk of the wonderful dolls, chestnuts, brilliantly decorated trees and home-made cookies. After the meal, Hetty showed Mary how to make their own cookies using apple and cinnamon and the sweet aroma of the spices filled the house. Christmas in Bennett Street was well on its way!

"Did you enjoy looking in the shop windows?" Joseph asked Mary when at last they had settled down for the evening.

I saw beautiful dolls, like a baby," replied Mary smiling and rocking her arms as if cradling an infant.

Jane explained what they had seen and she quietly told Joseph of the faraway look in Mary's eyes as she had gazed at the dolls.

"She just seemed so sad," whispered Jane, "like they reminded her of something."

Joseph instinctively knew why Mary longed for one of the dolls, but remained quiet. It was Mary's secret and what was her secret, was also his.

Christmas in 1881 was the happiest Mary had known for many years and Joseph had already noticed a change in her since he had brought her home. Whether it had been the influence of the workhouse or not he wasn't sure; but Mary appeared more confident and better able to join in a conversation. Jane and Joseph's other female lodger Hetty Mycock shared a room with Mary and they seemed content in each other's company. Hetty was also a servant and although she said she was married, her husband did not lodge with them.

By Christmas Eve, the only people residing at number 44 Bennett Street were Joseph, Mary and Jane. The other lodgers had left the night before, to travel to see their families for the festive season, as was the custom. Jane and Mary giggled as sprigs of mistletoe were hung from the doorways to catch an unsuspecting person and claim a kiss. The sprigs with the most berries on were saved for this purpose as after each kiss, a berry had to be taken off. Jane did not know if they were to have visitors during the next few days, but she was going to make sure that if any young men came to the house, there was always enough mistletoe to be kissed under. In the evening, they sat and sang carols around the fire after giving each other a small gift. Mary had not had enough time to make her father a large gift, but presented him with a small embroidered bookmark which she had made whilst in the workhouse, and wrapped in bright red tissue tied with green ribbons. Joseph gave Jane a set of embroidered handkerchiefs and she gave him a grey muffler which she had spent some time knitting. Mary had not received a present from her father and when she looked at him expectantly, he smiled and disappeared into the other room. He was gone only seconds and when he returned, he was carrying a large box wrapped in blue and silver paper and tied with an intricate silver coloured ribbon.

"Merry Christmas Mary," he said as he passed her the box. For quite a few minutes, Mary was unable to open the wrapping to see what was inside, but when she did, she tore at the paper frantically trying to get to its contents. Two blue eyes gazed up at her from the inside of the box and a mop of curly brown hair covered the head of the baby doll inside. Mary was speechless, but she tenderly took the doll from the box and held it close.

"My baby," was all she said as she rocked it back and forth. The doll could not be prised from her grasp and as the evening drew to a close with a glass of spiced wine, Mary went up the stairs to bed content. Jane thought it was a strange present for a man to buy his grown up daughter, but yet again, Mary was strange and she did not question Joseph about his motives for giving this unusual present.

On the morning of Christmas Day, Jane and Mary were up bright and early to start the preparations for Christmas dinner. The doll stayed upstairs on Mary's bed and was not spoken about. Christmas decorations rustled and twinkled in every corner of the parlour; with a set of wax figures depicting the nativity scene being the centre piece. Mary was astonished by the amount of food they had to eat – a plump, juicy goose was the star of the show, with golden roasted potatoes and a mountain of vegetables. The Christmas pudding had been made some weeks earlier and great anticipation was felt as it was brought from the kitchen, hot and fragrant, covered in brandy and set alight. As they tucked into it, each found a tiny silver sixpence, which they held tightly making a wish and then kept it for good luck. Mary couldn't help being reminded of the Christmases she had spent in the workhouse where the food had been fairly plentiful on that day, but nowhere near as tasty; and she wondered what Annie and her daughter would be doing now. Peals of laughter filled the house and the afternoon was spent playing silly games. Joseph gazed in contentment at the scene which surrounded him; his belly was full, he had wine in his glass and happiness enveloped his family. It was difficult to imagine a merrier occasion.

Chapter 20

Having three bedrooms, Joseph decided that he could easily take in another three lodgers now that Mary was here to help with the meals and housework. She seemed content to do that and so after the rush of the Christmas break when most people were allowed at least one day's holiday; he set about advertising for more lodgers. What he wanted was either a family who could share the room, or three other boarders of the same sex. By the end of January in the New Year, his house was full and although each boarder paid only a small amount of rent, he was earning more money than he had in years.

The new family who moved into the house arrived on a Sunday afternoon and Mary was delighted to see that they had a newly born baby girl. Patrick and Sarah Murphy had two children; the eldest being a boy named Peter who was seven years old and their new baby Moira who was only a month old. Their story was the same as for many; having moved from Ireland as newly-weds to escape famine and poverty, they arrived in Liverpool only to find that the situation was not much better. After spending several years as a navvy, Patrick brought his family to Buxton to find work as a labourer. In spite of his hard life, Patrick was a gentle man, very quietly spoken and he loved his family dearly. He was welcomed into the Freeman household and quickly settled in. Mary immediately focussed her attentions onto baby Moira and whenever she could, would nurse her.

Watching Mary from a distance, Jane was surprised at the confidence with which she held and cuddled baby Moira; but somehow felt ill at ease with the way in which she treated the baby. It felt almost as if Mary thought the child was hers. The attention which Mary had lavished upon her doll had now been transferred to Moira. Sarah and Patrick were content to allow Mary to nurse the child and before long, Sarah had asked Mary if she would be willing to look after baby Moira so she could be employed to wash all the clothes for the household, for which she would be paid a few shillings. Mary's happiness at this request showed no bounds, her face was full of smiles and her eyes twinkled. She sang as she held onto Moira and although she had to hand her back to Sarah for a feed, she was content to take on the role asked of her.

Mary scrutinised her reflection in the mirror. Was she really so ugly? Her large eyes stared back at her, desperate to find a reason why no one loved her. Her father liked her, or so she thought, but the one man she had loved had abandoned her and their baby. Thoughts of that day had plagued her for some months now and she was unable to get the picture of her dead baby out of her mind. She knew that the passionate moments she had shared with James had led to the baby's birth; Annie had explained all that, but it didn't explain why James had not wanted to stay at the workhouse. Her father would not allow her out of the house unless she had a companion and she was bored. What he hadn't realised was that in the workhouse, at least she had been occupied; having no opportunity to be bored. When most of the household were out at work and she was alone with Sarah and baby Moira, she tried to help with the daily chores. Mary didn't mind sweeping or cleaning dishes or even washing clothes. In this house, they had their own back yard which housed the privy and a large copper, but Sarah did all the washing and she looked after baby Moira.

"Can I take Moira out in her baby carriage?" she asked Sarah.

Her arms elbow deep in water, and all her energy

put into the posser, Sarah was not listening.

"Sarah, can I take Moira out?" repeated Mary in a more urgent tone. Still Sarah did not hear and so did not answer. Frustration welling up in Mary's chest, she gasped loudly, turned on her heels and went back to the baby. The day was bright and clear and Mary longed to go outside. She knew that she shouldn't, but within minutes, she had Moira dressed in her bonnet and coat and tucked warmly into her baby carriage with a layer of snug blankets. The spring day beckoned and Mary put on her own bonnet and coat, tied her new muffler around her neck and set off to the park with Moira in the carriage. As she walked along the pathways which crossed the beautiful park, Mary smiled and chatted quietly to the baby sitting prettily in front of her. Moira was about six months old and taking notice of the world around her, babbling in her own way at the passers-by and accepting the admiring glances she brought. Mary sat on a bench for a while also smiling at the other women who were out with their babies that day. They looked like a normal mother and daughter and Mary suddenly realised how much she had missed her own child. She hadn't even had the time to give her a name, but she had had the time to love her. In the minutes and seconds before the infant was roughly taken from her, the inseparable bond between a mother and child was formed. Her daughter would have been just a few weeks older that Moira and in her mind during the next few seconds, Moira became that baby. As they continued their walk around the park, Moira fell asleep so Mary laid her down, pulling up the hood of the baby carriage to shelter her from the chill breeze and continued to walk.

Mary strolled past the ducks on the pond and through the gardens just beginning to burst forth with new life, and into the main streets of the town. A large curved street with very grand houses came into view and across from it was one of the town's spring water wells. There were people filling containers and glasses with the water from the well and suddenly Mary felt very thirsty. After taking her turn in the queue of people waiting to take the waters, Mary cupped her own hands below the trickle of water and drank greedily. Her own thirst abated, she turned her attention to the sleeping baby. It would not be long before she awoke needing her own drink and so she would need her mother for that. Mary knew that she must go home soon before Moira became distressed and so turned and made for Bennett Street. The distance to their home was much further than Mary had remembered, and by the time the house came into view, Moira was exercising her lungs to capacity and drawing the unwanted attention of people on the street. Mary became flustered and other than hurry home, she did not know what to do.

When Sarah had finished with the washing, she put the posser into the outside shed and went back indoors. She was cold, because although the day was bright and sunny, there was still a chill wind in the spring air. Expecting to find Mary looking after Moira's needs, she sauntered into the parlour only to find the room empty.

"Mary!" she bellowed at the top of her voice. When there was no reply, Sarah climbed the steep stairs to the room she shared with her husband and family, to see whether or not Moira had been taken up there for a nap. It was almost time for her dinner and Sarah knew that she would be getting hungry. Her engorged breasts also told her that it was time to feed her baby and she felt uncomfortable.

When there was no sign of either Moira or Mary in the house, Sarah began to feel concerned. She had seen the way that Mary looked at her daughter recently and had felt uneasy about it. Where could they be? Without waiting to put on a coat or bonnet, Sarah dashed out into the street, looking up and down to see if there was any sign of them. The baby carriage was gone and Sarah feared the worst.

"Have you seen a young woman pushing a baby in a baby carriage?" she asked a woman who was bustling by.

"Eh, there's many a young lady out with her baby today. The park's only a spit away and the day is bright, so why wouldn't they?"

Without waiting for any further reply, Sarah dashed off in the direction of the park. The woman was right! That was the most likely place for her to have taken the baby. Gasping for breath, Sarah turned the corner into the Pavillion gardens, urgently glancing about her for any sign of Mary, but saw none. She felt sick with worry and sat for a second or two on the very bench on which Mary had sat earlier. Tears began to trickle down her cheeks and she was convinced that she would never see her daughter again. Of one thing she was certain, if Moira was returned to her safe and sound, she would never again allow her out of her sight! As Sarah sat on the bench, a tall policeman with a long moustache approached her. He had seen her distress and wanted to help.

"Good morning ma'am. Why are you so distressed? Is there any way I can help you?" he asked.

Panic beginning to increase, Sarah told him about her missing daughter.

"It's my daughter, officer. I think that she might have been stolen!" She continued to relate the story of her daughter's disappearance as they walked rapidly back towards the house. When they were in sight of Bennett Street, Sarah could hear quite clearly, the sound of a baby's cry.

"That's her! I can hear her crying!"

Then, at the other end of the street, the baby carriage came into view with Mary urgently pushing the wailing infant. As they approached each other, Mary saw the policeman and wondered what had happened, unaware of Sarah's distress at finding her daughter gone.

"I think she is hungry," smiled Mary. "I quite forgot the time and we have had such a nice walk."

Sarah ignored Mary's chatter, grabbed the infant and ran inside the house, the door banging on its hinges as she went. Wondering why Sarah was so upset, Mary followed her into the house, and close on her heels was the policeman. He needed to find out whether or not there had been any criminal intention in this incident. Sarah was too angry and upset to speak to Mary and she had Moira to feed, so she took herself up to her room and closed the door. Meanwhile, the policeman gently talked to Mary about her walk to the park. He had realised on seeing her that she was probably backward and it was obvious that she had not done the child any harm. He found it difficult to get any sense out of her as she too had become upset when she realised that Sarah was angry with her for taking baby Moira out to the park. Deciding to return later to talk to Mary's father, the policeman took his leave and left the women to sort out their differences.

When Joseph opened the door sometime later, he was surprised to see a policeman staring at him and for a moment he thought it was PC Walford again. Dismayed and initially very frightened, he showed the policeman into the parlour, all the while worrying about the purpose of his visit. Was it possible that the man he had attacked all those years ago had died and he was being hunted down for murder? The inside of his mouth went dry and he felt the colour drain from his face. He had thought that past events had been left in the past and the thought of going to prison made him feel sick. The policeman's voice brought him from his morbid thoughts.

"Mr Freeman. Are you ill? Please sit down whilst I talk to you. It is no serious matter that I have come to discuss but simply one which relates to an incident earlier on in the day. Did Mrs Murphy not explain what had happened?"

Slowly Joseph began to realise that he had not come to arrest him and as the policeman told him of the scare that Mary had given Sarah when she took baby Moira into the park; he began to relax a little. The policeman was satisfied that no criminal action had been intended and soon took his leave. Joseph realised that he must talk to Mary about the birth of her baby and try to help her come to terms with the traumatic event.

Mary was sitting by the range in the kitchen with a mug of tea in her hand. Her eyes were glazed and she stared into emptiness hardly noticing her father enter the room. Joseph asked the other lodgers for the privacy of the room, and he went to sit next to her. Taking her mug from her and holding onto her hand, he began to talk.

"Mary, a policeman has been to see me tonight about the scare you gave Sarah. You are not in trouble lass, but you need to understand that Sarah did not know what had happened to her baby and that she was very worried. That is why she feels angry with you." He paused for a minute to allow his words to sink in. "Why did you take baby Moira without asking Sarah?" he continued.

Mary looked at him and simply said, "My baby."

Tears threatening to come, Joseph knew that it was the right time to mention her baby and try to find out what had happened at the workhouse.

"I know about your baby Mary. You had a beautiful daughter, but she died as soon as she was born. God has taken her and she will be looked after in heaven." Again pausing to give Mary the chance to reply, he put his arms around her shoulders for the first time in many years and hugged her. They sat like that for a few minutes and slowly tears began to dampen his shoulders and he could feel Mary's agonizing sobs as she let out the sadness she had felt for so long. Eventually as the tears subsided, Mary looked back at her father and knew that he was not angry with her.

"Who was the baby's father Mary? Who did you lie with?" He needed to know the answer to this question even though he was aware that there was nothing he could do about it. The man would be long gone by now and the chance of Joseph being able to confront him was highly unlikely.

"James," she replied quietly. "He loved me."

The anger that he felt towards this man knew no bounds. If he ever saw him, he knew that he would be unable to keep his hands to himself. His rage intensified and he clenched his fists tightly. He had already almost killed one man by accident. He would definitely kill this man if he had the opportunity. How many times had he heard people make comments like, 'girls like this shouldn't be allowed to do such and such', or 'people like them should be locked away!' Girls like *his* daughter had feelings too, and this bastard by the name of James should be locked away!

Joseph left Mary alone to recover and she was found later, sat in the rocking chair cradling her doll. The following morning, the Murphy family took their belongings and left. Joseph never rented a room to a family with a baby again. He did not want to put Mary through the torment she had already endured again, nor did he want to chance another incident like the last one.

Chapter 21

Buxton 1883

The words in the letter made Joseph's heart sink. It was not really unexpected news, but nonetheless the revelation of his father's death was a shock. Yet again he would have to make the journey to Yorkshire for a funeral, bringing with it the memories of previous unhappy events. Still, he thought, it would give him the chance to see Fred again after all these years. The last time he had seen his son was at Esther's funeral seven years before and so much had happened since then. Fred had no idea that his father had indeed remarried or that somewhere, he had a new brother or sister. Joseph seemed to think that the baby had been a boy, but he was not sure. That was his secret and he was unlikely to tell Fred about Hannah or the baby. The trip to Yorkshire had only served as an untimely reminder that they had in fact ever existed. He had not given them a thought for many months, but now he could not get them out of his mind.

Jane Brennan promised to keep an eye on Mary and so Joseph took the trip to see his father buried. The July day was warm and bright and the railway station was hot. Joseph watched as he waved Mary goodbye from the window of the railway carriage. His daughter seemed much more content of late and he fervently hoped that she would cope whilst he was away. She had been offered the chance to go with him, but did not enjoy the smell and noise of the railways and had declined his offer. She was sad that her grandfather had passed away, but had not really known him. He seemed a distant figure, infrequently mentioned and seldom seen, and Mary did not relish the thought of meeting again with distant cousins. She knew that she would be fine staying with Jane, who now worked for her father as their own house servant. Mary enjoyed helping out with the chores and it was good to have someone to talk to during the day when her father was at work. There had been discussions about whether or not Mary should eventually get a position as a servant, but so far she had resisted the idea. Her father had also been more supportive towards her since the events of the previous Christmas and she was beginning to develop a closer bond with him. Mary had never understood why she had been sent to the workhouse and the fact that her father did not even go to see her as he had promised, had left a wound in her heart. He had made no mention of his reasons and she had never dared to broach the subject.

Mary's doll was left mostly in her bedroom where she sometimes went to talk to it when she felt sad about anything; but the doll rarely came into the parlour where visitors or other lodgers could see it. Joseph had tried to talk to her again about her own baby, but Mary did not want to discuss the subject. What had happened in the workhouse was her secret and would remain so. It would seem that they both had secrets which neither knew about, but which lay heavily on both their minds.

Mary enjoyed the time she spent with Jane, pretending to be the 'lady of the house' and the time went all too quickly. Joseph was back within a couple of days, bringing with him a surprise for them all. Jane had been employed all day in cleaning the house from top to bottom and she was rubbing the windows with an old piece of newspaper when she saw Joseph strolling down the street towards the house. By his side was a tall young man with a ruddy appearance and curly brown hair which refused to be tamed. They were smiling and joking with each other and it was obvious to Jane that the young man was well known to his companion. Jumping down from the step she was stood on, Jane shouted to Mary, to tell her that her father was returning. Mary was in the kitchen trying to make a large meat pie for the evening meal, and her hands and arms were covered with flour up to her elbows. Her apron was dusted with the white powder and her hair, although contained in a cap, was also touched with white at the front.

Joseph opened the door to his home and bade the young man to follow him. When Mary saw the visitor, she smiled shyly and went to her father's side.

"Mary, do you remember who this is?" asked Joseph.

Mary nodded, but remained silent. Jane bobbed a curtsey to the young man and introduced herself.

"Good afternoon sir, I am Jane, lodger and servant here." She waited for him to speak, but Joseph interrupted her.

"This is my nephew, Job. He has come to visit us for a while whilst he is looking for employment. Mary, come and say hello to your cousin!"

The introductions completed, Mary and Jane went back into the kitchen to continue the preparations for the evening meal. The lodgers who paid for their meals would soon be in from their places of employment and be ready for a good hearty meal.

"By, he's a good looking lad isn't he?" commented Jane. Mary said nothing. She was very shy and it had been a long time since she had seen her cousin and really did not know him well. The two men continued to talk together, leaving Jane to prepare Job a bed in the room shared by Joseph and several of the other male lodgers. Space was short now and they would not be able to take on any new lodgers until someone moved out and heaven only knew when that would be. Many of Joseph's lodgers were tinkers who stayed for a few months and then moved on. It was rare for anyone to stay for longer than a few months and when they did, Joseph welcomed the chance to keep hold of his paying guests. However, as a relative, it was more than likely that Job would not pay any rent.

The attraction between Job and Jane grew over the next few months and it was obvious that Job's attraction to Jane was essentially a physical one. Job had succeeded in finding himself employment as a house painter and for the first time in many a while had cash to spare. He took Jane to the theatre where they were entertained by bawdy music hall artists. Joseph was none too happy about the influence Job was having on his servant who had previously been of excellent character. Jane was becoming more interested in her own appearance than anything else and she seemed to abandon her friendship with Mary.

Things seemed to come to a head when Joseph caught the pair 'in flagrante' one Sunday afternoon. He had been on one of his rare visits to church with Mary and on entering the house could hear loud giggling from the upstairs rooms. Slowly, he crept up the stairs trying not to let the floorboards creak, and as he stood on the landing, the sounds that he heard disgusted him. Loud moans and the distinct thudding of the bed could be clearly heard from within one of the bedrooms. Joseph opened the door without any warning to the occupiers, interrupting the sexual exploits of the couple before him. They were both naked on the bed, the covers strewn all around the floor as were their clothes which had obviously been hastily abandoned.

"Cover yourselves!" Joseph demanded. "This is not a house of ill-repute and I will not have it treated so! Job, you have taken advantage of my hospitality and will leave my home immediately and take your slut with you!"

Jane began to sob, suddenly realising that she was now without both home and employment. Joseph turned and as he did, he saw the figure of Mary standing in the doorway, her face ashen.

"My James," she whispered, the memory of her own passionate liaison now being brought to the forefront of her mind. Joseph ushered her down the stairs and into the front parlour where he made her stay until both Job and Jane had left the house. The incident had been yet another reminder of Mary's secret and during the course of the next few weeks, she fell deeper into a melancholy she had not suffered for a long while. Her doll became the focus of her attention and her days were spent rocking her and talking to her as if she was a real baby. The threat of a mental breakdown was becoming apparent and Joseph knew that he must take action if she was to recover. A new housekeeper was quickly employed, but she was older than Jane had been and Mary could not form the same attachment with her.

Joseph had heard that the spring waters which were to be found in several places in the town could be beneficial to one's health, but partly because he was rather scathing of their so called healing properties and partly because he had never felt the need, he had not sampled them. Mary's need was great and he was willing to try anything to make her mood change. Joseph did not know whether or not the waters could soothe a person's mood, but it was worth a try. He too was beginning to feel the effects of Mary's melancholy and just lately he had been reminded of Hannah and their baby. Was the child thriving, he wondered? When he had discovered his nephew and his servant in bed together, not only had the act disgusted him, but it had somehow reminded him of his own sexual abstinence.

He had not lain with a woman in a long time and he missed the warmth of a naked body beside him and the release of tension that lovemaking could bring.

The spring of 1884 not only brought the awakening of plants and animals after a harsh winter, but the revival of hope that Mary would improve. Joseph had begun to walk with her each Sunday to the well close to the park where they would each take a drink of the waters. The water was icy cold which left a rush of exhilaration to the head and they drank freely of it, trusting in its healing properties.

Chapter 22

Buxton 1900

Mary opened the curtains onto a bright summer's day. She felt content and as she made breakfast for Mrs Flint, she reflected on the luck which had brought her to the home of this kindly old woman. Only five years previously, she had still been living with her father and his house full of lodgers and his housekeeper whom she disliked intensely. Joseph had employed Emily Duffy to be his housekeeper, the latest in a string of women to take up the role. Somehow, this woman was different. She had managed to curry favour with Joseph and within months had begun to warm his bed. It had been obvious from the start that she did not like Mary, ignoring her whenever Joseph was out at work and pointing the finger of blame at her whenever any mishap occurred. Emily had brought with her two small children and they too had managed to direct her father's affections away from her. She had felt lonely and misunderstood.

**

Taking the Buxton Spring waters had made little difference to Mary. She had no direction in life and often wished that she was back in the workhouse, for even though she had been a virtual prisoner, she had been kept active and always had Annie to turn to. Her father's attentions had now turned away from her and her life held little purpose. Her bed was the only place where she felt secure and gradually Mary began to spend longer there in the mornings, often not rising until almost noon. The friction that this caused between

Mrs Duffy and herself became unbearable and Mary decided to leave home for good.

Joseph was completely unaware of the plight his daughter felt herself tangled up in, and the news that Mary had left the house carrying a small valise, came as a complete surprise.

"Why did you not stop her?" he demanded of his housekeeper as the news began to sink in. "You know she is not herself!"

Emily Duffy did not see why she should have done anything to stop this woman who although was not as bright as many, had her own mind and was capable of making her own decisions.

"She cannot be made a prisoner Joseph. She is a grown woman," she simpered; her arm around his shoulders. Her own thoughts were far from the pretence she made to Joseph. Good riddance was what she really thought! Now at least, she would not have to compete for Joseph's affections. But Joseph could not leave his daughter to face the world alone and so much to Emily's displeasure; he set off to see if he could find her.

The railway station was a desolate place for Mary, in spite of the fact that she was surrounded by people. As panic began to rise in her throat, and she felt the sudden urge to visit the privy; Mary realised that she could not make this venture alone. The waiting room too was crowded and she had to wait her turn to relieve herself; by which time, it was almost too late. Feeling somewhat calmer afterwards, Mary returned to the platform where she sat and tried to think what she should do. The money she had would not take her far, she was sure; and when she arrived at her destination, would she have enough to find lodgings? Which platform would her train depart from? Where would she get the ticket? The questions kept on pounding through her head until she felt faint. Her pale face was clammy and a sudden tiredness made her find rest on one of the benches nearby.

Joseph's first thought had been to try the railway station. He realised that Mary would try to go back to Lancashire if she could, but also knew that she would find the journey very frightening on her own. Relief coursed through him as he saw her sat on a bench on the platform and as he approached her, he could also see that she was relieved to see him too. Mary stood as he approached and thinking her father would be angry with her, began to cry. Onlookers would have assumed that this was a husband and wife, albeit a wife younger than her husband; not a father and daughter. Joseph hugged his daughter; now an adult approaching her late forties, and sat her down on the bench to recover.

"Why do you need to go away Mary?" he asked her.

Mary looked at her father with tears still streaming down her face and simply said, "You don't want me, now you have Emily."

Sadness filled his heart and although he loved his daughter, he knew that there was some truth in what she had said and felt ashamed. Without speaking, he helped her from the bench, guiding her elbow towards the station entrance. Mary paused to take in the fresher air and the feelings of panic and dizziness retreated.

"Always remember that you are my daughter and I love you," whispered Joseph unconvincingly. He squeezed her arm and they set off back to Bennett Street.

On arriving back at their home, Joseph took Emily into the kitchen to speak to her, explaining what had happened. The blame for Mary's departure had been firmly placed on her shoulders and Emily felt annoyed. She must keep Joseph's attention on her and the one place she knew that she could make him forget his troubles was in their bed, so once they had retired for the night she undressed slowly and climbed into bed. Joseph was mesmerised by her body, still young looking and inviting. Emily explored every part of his body which by now was taut with desire and he made love to her with a passion that he had forgotten was possible.

After their lovemaking that night as they were relaxing in the after-glow of their delightful union, she planted the germ of an idea into Joseph's mind.

"Perhaps what Mary needs is more company. It might be suitable for all of us, if she were to find employment as a lady's companion where she would have light duties, but the company of another woman who needs her."

Although Emily's idea had been entirely selfish, she had actually found the very solution to Mary's problem, and within a matter of days, Joseph had used his own contacts within the building trade to see if he could find a suitable person. He had not held much hope initially of solving his problem so soon, for realistically, who in the building trade, unless they were a property owner, would have the means to employ a servant?

George Flint had lived with his mother for some time until the previous month when he had married. The money he earned as a house painter had just about allowed him to rent his own house where he now lived with his new wife, but in doing so, he had left his mother to take in lodgers to supplement her income. Jane Flint was getting on in years and her health was not good, but she was determined to continue to look after her two lodgers even after George had left. What her son had not realised; was that she too needed the company and so when he suggested that she should employ a servant who could also be a companion, she agreed.

As Mary put on her hat and coat, Emily fussed around her like a mother hen. Mary was nervous; that was obvious and what she needed was a calming influence, not the anxiety caused by Emily's false concerns. Joseph took her arm and as Mary looked back at the house she had called home for almost twenty years, Emily smiled at her and closed the door. Now she would have Joseph all to herself, and if she was clever, his money too!

Nervously, Mary put one foot in front of the other and walked by her father's side. They passed along Bennet Street, turning the corner onto Byron Street and then left onto London Road. The walk was only minutes, and as they approached the house she was to live and work in, Mary felt paralysed with fear. Joseph took hold of the door knocker and rapped loudly on the front door. Within a few seconds, the face of an old lady appeared and all of Mary's worries seemed to evaporate. No words were spoken initially, just the welcoming smile and kindly expression that said she would be fine. After arrangements had been made for the payment of Mary's wage, and with a promise of a day off each week to visit her father, Mary said her goodbyes and turned to face the woman she knew would take care of her, even though it was she who was employed to be the servant.

Sunday was to be Mary's day off, and so the first Sunday after the start of her employment, she waited patiently for her father to arrive. He would take her back home for the day and she hoped that he would have missed her, but no sooner had they arrived, than Emily had begun to find fault. Joseph had planned to take Mary to the park, but the weather was inclement and so this outing was postponed. In no time at all, it was time for her to go back to Mrs Flint's house and her day off with her father was over. What Mary had been expecting, she really did not know, maybe that the relationship with her father would improve and they would strengthen the tenuous bond they already had? The following weeks and months made little difference to their relationship and gradually, Mary decided to stay with Mrs Flint, with whom she had begun to develop a warm friendship.

Jane Flint thought the world of Mary. That she was slower than some of the servants she had employed in the past, was certain; but Mary had a warmth of character that made Jane feel a growing bond between them; and a vulnerability that needed the protection the older woman could give. They were a good match: the servant and the employer, and it often seemed to the onlooker that they were in fact mother and daughter. Mary respected Jane and always knew what the older woman needed. She loved looking after her and her life had improved ten-fold. In fact, Mary did not think about her role as that of servant, but as a friend and was happy to do as much of the housework as she was asked to do.

Mary turned to glance at the old lady lying in her bed and suddenly noticed her increased frailty. Her health was not as robust as once it had been, and Jane looked pale and small as she lay in her bed. Mary gently woke her and persuaded her to eat some breakfast and after helping her to dress, they set about the day's chores. Under Jane's guidance, Mary had blossomed and was now responsible for most of the heavy housework as well as making the meals. Today was Sunday however, and Jane declared that she needed some air.

In spite of her advancing years and poor health, Jane Flint still loved to walk in the park. Sunday was a day when many of the town's inhabitants took the air to walk off their lunch and perhaps contemplate upon the teachings they had heard that very morning in church. Although Jane did not always go to church these days, she still enjoyed the strolls she took in the park. This pastime was very popular and in her younger years, she had been known to meet a male acquaintance whilst meandering the pathways which led to the small lake or even the bandstand. Couples strolled arm in arm whispering their secrets and laughing together, often with the company of a brother or parent to act as chaperone, for it would not have been seemly for a young woman to meet secretly with a man unless their purpose was less than proper.

Mary took her arm as they walked slowly towards the bandstand. The bright, cheery sound that the band played, could be heard quite a distance from the bandstand, but was an indication that they were almost at their destination. The seats surrounding the platform, on which the band played, were almost full and Mary took Jane towards the back of the audience where they found two seats close together. Jane was exhausted, but happy.

"This always reminds me of happy times," she said to Mary. "I used to meet my husband, who was still my fiancé then, and we would sit and listen to the music and talk of our plans for the future we hoped to have."

Jane let her gaze fall on the audience, seeing the many young couples doing exactly that; and as Mary followed her gaze, she saw a couple of familiar faces, laughing and smiling at each other in the way that only lovers do. As if following a sixth sense, the man turned and looked behind him and the expression on his face changed to one of embarrassment as he recognised his daughter sat only a few rows behind him. Mary knew that her father also enjoyed a walk in the park, but somehow it was the realisation that he was still engaged in an intimate relationship with the housekeeper which had saddened her. She had not seen him now for many months as their Sunday visits had not been a success and Mary had put her father and his housekeeper from her mind.

Jane too had witnessed the exchange of glances, so the minute she had regained her composure and a little of her strength, she suggested to Mary that they continue their walk around the park in a different direction. By the time they had reached the lake, Jane was too tired to go any further and they sat for some time watching the ducks and their comical antics together.

The visit to the park was to be Jane's last. As autumn came and then passed into winter, she became unable to leave the house. Her limbs had stiffened and she now needed a stick to keep her mobile. The new-year brought with it a national tragedy. Towards the end of January in 1901, the old queen passed away whilst staying at her home in the Isle of Wight. At the ripe old age of eighty-one, Queen Victoria had been the longest serving monarch of Great Britain having reigned for a total of sixty-three years. Nationally there was an outpouring of mourning with the wearing of black clothes, and Jane and Mary were no exception. However, unlike the period of mourning for Prince Albert; the new King, Victoria's son Edward, had declared that mourning for his mother should be limited for a period of no more than three months. Black and purple banners were to be seen everywhere in shop windows declaring their respect and heartfelt loss at her passing.

The day of the Royal Funeral at the beginning of February was bitterly cold and in Buxton, the snow fell silently as if to mark the passing of such a well-loved monarch. It was a Saturday, but in spite of the loss to trade, there were many shopkeepers who closed for the day. The atmosphere of sadness was felt in many households and the home of Jane Flint was one of these. On the day of the funeral, the curtains were kept closed and they prayed for the soul of the departed Queen. By evening, Jane too was feeling unwell and she went to bed early complaining of pains in her chest.

The end of mourning for the old queen also brought with it a return to better weather and Jane's health began to improve. George Flint employed another servant to help Mary and when lodgers left, they were not replaced. Mary had never been happier and although she was employed as Jane's companion, she always felt like part of the family and began to look upon Jane as a daughter would her mother. When George came to visit, he often brought news of her father and did not understand why Mary could not bring herself to visit him. After all, he was past his sixtieth year and was no longer a young man. Mary would smile and accept his news with apparent ease. Only Jane understood her companion's feelings.

When winter once again brought its blanket of snow, Mary's refined world of embroidery, afternoon tea and sedate walks in the park came to an end. Jane suffered a repeat of the chest problems which had almost brought her to death the year before; but this time she did not recover. Mary nursed her aged friend through many days of fever and coughing, until the fever abated and although the false hope of a recovery was present, Jane died in her sleep. She was buried just over a year after the death of the old queen and Mary was forced once more to return to live with her father.

Stepping reluctantly over the threshold of the house in Bennett St, Mary was surprised to be greeted by her father. Where were Emily and her two children? Joseph held out his arms to receive his daughter and warmly embraced her. She could hear voices coming from the front parlour and assumed that the woman who warmed her father's bed was entertaining the lodgers in there. She hurriedly walked into the kitchen and the welcome warmth which it held. Joseph took her coat and valise and placed them at the bottom of the stairs; the coat itself having been hooked over the large knob of the bannister rail.

"Where is Emily?" enquired Mary quietly.

"Emily no longer lives here," replied her father. "I caught her trying to steal from me and dismissed her." Joseph did not tell his daughter the full truth; that since the day he had seen her in the park with Jane, he had seen through the façade which Emily had erected to gain access to his feelings and ultimately his money. When she had also noticed Mary sat behind them in the park that day, Emily had made scathing remarks about his 'backward' daughter. Whether it was the setting of the park or not, it reminded him of the occasions when he had protected Mary from the hurtful words she had endured whilst they had lived in Hyde; and he saw Emily's shallow pretence for what it really was. Within days both her and her children had left the house and never returned. Joseph had waited patiently now for many months; a proud man who could not bring himself to visit Mary and apologise; but here she was now and he fervently hoped that she would stay.

Chapter 23

Buxton, Summer 1903

Joseph welcomed the stranger with unusual familiarity. Mary could not understand why this man, whom he had only just met, was greeted so warmly.

"Mary, come and meet Mr Ashworth. He has come all the way from Rawtenstall and is on his way to visit his family in London….."

Mary did not hear the rest of the introduction, focussing only on the fact that he had come from Rawtenstall. Why did this name stir up bad feelings? She sat on the sofa beside him nodding politely at the unclear mutterings of conversation she could vaguely hear.

Rawtenstall… the workhouse! The realisation of where she had heard this familiar name brought Mary to her senses and she looked intently at the man before her. That there were several of the board of guardians named Ashworth, she was certain, but his face was not familiar. Perhaps her father had asked the man to come and take her away again?

Mary was brought from her reverie by the loud voice of her father urgently speaking her name.

"Mary! Mary! What is amiss? Are you sick?"

Mary glanced at her father and then back at Mr Ashworth, her fingers all the while plucking at her gown in an agitated fashion.

"The workhouse…" she whispered.

Joseph understood immediately her concerns and tried to calm her.

"No, Mr Ashworth has no links with the workhouse, but has lived for many years in Rawtenstall and knows it well. We have been discussing the state of the new shoe industry which has almost engulfed the cotton mills in the district and he has with him the local newspaper which he bought only this morning. He is to stay only for one night before he continues his travels on towards London."

In reality, Joseph was relieved that they had no acquaintances in common. Although he was curious about any local news Mr Ashworth might have, he did not want to rake up the past and was anxious to leave his previous life undisclosed. It was by chance that he had been questioned by Mr Ashworth at the station that very day; asking about lodgings in the town and been only too pleased to offer his own lodging house as a solution, but remained very vague when his guest enquired about his life in Rawtenstall. When Mr Ashworth finally said his goodbyes the next morning, he left behind his copy of The Bacup Times and it was with this, that Joseph entertained himself that morning over breakfast. The news was mainly about the closure of mills and the reopening of the same premises again as slipper factories. Little anecdotes of the drunken behaviour in the town's less respectable districts added a bit of spice to the mundane reading of the news it contained.

Joseph turned his attention to the section which contained notices of births, marriages and deaths. A mug of tea in one hand and the other firmly fixed on the large broadsheet before him, Joseph was drawn to one such notice and he had to quickly put the tea back onto the table in order not to spill any. As he read, he felt sick, but was unable to turn his eyes away from the death section of the notices in the newspaper.

On July 30th 1903
At her home in Woodlea Cottages Waterfoot
Hannah Freeman aged 63.

Interment at St Nicholas, Newchurch, on August 1ˢᵗ at 2pm.

Friends and family of the deceased will please accept this invitation.

Mary looked intently at her father as the newspaper began to shake and the tears fell slowly from his eyes.

"Whatever is wrong father?" she enquired, taking the newspaper from his hands and slowly placing it on the table. Joseph did not answer her; but recovering his composure quickly, he took the paper and disappeared up to his bedchamber. There were things he must do. One thing was certain, that he would never reveal his true plans to Mary.

Newchurch, Summer 1903

The end of July had been hot and sticky, with the threat of thunderstorms ever lingering in the air. As Joseph caught the earliest train he could manage, the storm clouds were also gathering in Newchurch. The station was crowded with passengers trying to get a seat on this early morning train to Manchester and by the time he climbed up into the carriage, there were no seats available. Standing cramped in a corner of the carriage near the doorway, he heard the whistle blow and the platform filled with steam, as he clung on to the hand-strap which hung from the ceiling. It would be a tedious journey and quite what he would do when he arrived in Newchurch; he was not sure. His only purpose at that moment was to say his goodbyes to the courageous woman who had once been his wife; and God help him, he would get there in time! The emotions which he felt almost swamped him and he felt physically sick. Regrets and 'if only's' bombarded him until he could not think straight; shame for the way in which he treated Hannah and had never ever thought it necessary to apologise; and the overwhelming need to see the child she had borne him at least once before he himself died.

At last he managed to get a seat in the connecting train from Manchester to Rawtenstall and he suddenly felt tired. He had brought nothing with him but a small amount of money, having given little thought to when he would return; and as the train finally chugged its way through a familiar landscape, he glanced at his pocket watch. Just gone noon! If he hurried, he should still be able to get to the churchyard in time.

Ernest's happiness in his recent marriage had been diminished by his mother's dreadful illness. She had been unwell for some time and kept the details of her complaint away from her sons; the problem being of an intimate feminine nature. However, by the early summer of 1903, it was obvious to her sons that she was very unwell and the doctor had diagnosed a cancer of the womb. There was nothing which could be done for her; and so in spite of the constant attentions of the two sons she had closest to her, she died thinking of the husband who had abandoned her. Arthur nursed her through the last few weeks of her life and sent for his brother John Richard who lived in Rishton, to come and say his own goodbyes. Ernest loved his mother immensely, but he had never known his father. His other elder brothers were in fact only half brothers, but had all been brought up together by the same spirited mother. Hannah had never told Ernest the complete truth about his father, and he began to realise that when she died, the secrets she had kept hidden for many years would die with her.

"Mother, do you want me to send for father?" he

asked her. "Surely now is the time to make your peace with him."

What he hoped more than anything was to find out the truth about the man who had fathered him, yet never been there to look up to as a father. He knew nothing about him except his name, that he had been a carpenter and that he had disappeared just before his son had been born.

Hannah opened her eyes to her youngest son, but was too weak to reply to his question. She did not know where Joseph was even if she had wanted to speak to him. Let the past stay in the past; Ernest would not gain anything from knowing his father now. As she once more closed her eyes, she dreamed about Joseph. He walked towards her, smiling and as he approached, Hannah could see that he was smiling at a young lady close by. None of this seemed to matter; the fact that she had seen him again was enough and she was content. Behind Joseph was another familiar face; that of William her first beloved husband. What happy times they had shared only to have him taken from her in his prime. Gradually, as the afternoon light faded, so too did Hannah's hold on life and she went to greet her cherished husband and the two children which had passed on before her. She was at peace now; leaving the only legacy she had for her sons: the memories of a wonderful mother, and a courageous, strong woman.

The beautiful weather which had not seen a drop of rain in July changed on the first of August. The rain poured down and threatened to dampen the spirits of the mourning party even more. There would be no fancy funeral, only a simple burial at the church where Hannah's husband William had been laid to rest. It had been her greatest regret that she would never be allowed to lie beside him in death, as she had in life. The Booth family had never accepted Joseph as her husband and had made it clear that although William was to be buried in the family plot, she would not be allowed to join him. The coffin was loaded onto the horse driven hearse, with a few flowers covering the top of the coffin. Arthur and Ernest sat just in front of it, with Ernest's pregnant wife right at the front next to the driver, her pregnancy allowing her the priority seat. The journey was short, and the other family mourners walked behind, their heads bowed in respect.

Hannah's eldest son John Richard had brought his family to say goodbye to their elderly grandmother and he walked with them just behind the coffin. His wife Edith had already borne him five children, four of whom still survived and they too walked in silent procession holding hands with each other and taking comfort from their mother who was close by. As John turned proudly to look at his growing family, he was filled with pride at this new generation of 'Booths' who would carry on the family name, and knew that his mother would have been equally proud.

The air was chilly inside the church in spite of the warmth of the previous weeks. The rain had not stopped and the funeral party were quite soaked through. The wind could be heard from inside the church, and Ernest for one, was not looking forward to going back outside to bury his mother. She would have no fancy memorial stone as there was no money put aside for this, and her grave would be marked by a simple cross for now. Perhaps there would be money for this at a later date?

When the party finally set foot outside again, there was no let-up in the weather and the family were in a hurry to return to the relative warmth of the church doorway. The burial place had been prepared and the coffin eventually lowered into its final resting place. Ernest and his brothers each added their own clod of earth as the rector spoke the final words of the interment and Hannah's body was finally laid to rest. The women and children left their men to say their final prayers for their mother and went to wait in the shelter of the church doorway. By this time, the wind had eased and although the rain continued to fall, it felt more like a soft, enveloping curtain of dampness than the gusty blasts which had pelted them earlier.

"How I wish my father was here now!" barked Ernest unexpectedly.

"Well Ernest," joined in John, "he isn't and I think you should have realised by now that he was a selfish bastard who gave no thought to anyone but himself. I never liked him even as a child."

Ernest turned to reply to his brother. "Why have you never spoken about him before John?"

The brothers slowly began to walk towards the church as they spoke. "There was always something about him I didn't like, but mother thought I was being awkward, so I did not feel it was my place to say anything to you. He was always nice when mother was about, but had no time for us when she was not there. He was lazy and I know he hit mother a few times when he was drunk, but she would not have a bad word spoken about him. When he left, he took all our money and mother struggled for a long time to pay the rent because of him!"

Ernest paused and looked back at the burial site. "Mother was better off without him, the sly bastard! I am glad he didn't come back. I hope he rots in hell!"

A rustle in the shrubs a short distance away made Ernest turn once more and a prickle of uneasiness made him shiver. John and Arthur had begun to walk towards the church, back to their women folk and Ernest stood alone. Was there someone hiding in the bushes? Or was it just his imagination? For one fleeting moment, he thought that perhaps his father had come back to say his final farewells to his wife, Ernest's mother; but Ernest dismissed the thought almost as soon as it had invaded his mind. No! He was just imagining things because he had been talking about him to his brothers. It was unlikely that he even knew of Hannah's death, let alone the date and time of her burial. Giving the misty graveyard one last glance and whispering a last goodbye to his mother, he too walked back to the church door and re-joined his family. He was unaware that his instincts had been correct and that Joseph had indeed been hiding behind a gravestone at the lower end of the graveyard and had heard every word that passed between him and his brothers.

When Joseph had alighted from the train, he hurriedly set off for the tram which would take him into Waterfoot. Half an hour later, he was walking from the centre of Waterfoot, head bowed against the rain which was pelting down and running in rivulets down his face and neck. He pulled the collar of his coat up, trying to protect himself from the elements as he quickened his pace along the road which led him to Newchurch. The church itself was on the top of a hill, and Joseph was no longer a young man, so by the time he reached the church gates, he was out of breath and ready for a rest. The churchyard was empty and as he sheltered in the doorway of the church, he could hear the service which was taking place inside. In spite of the dreadful weather, Joseph was not cold. The walk up the hill had made him hot and he took off his hat and undid the top buttons of his coat whilst he sheltered from the rain. Relief engulfed him as he knew that he had indeed managed to get to the churchyard in time to see Hannah laid to rest. His son would be inside the church at that very moment, solemnly paying his respects to his mother and Joseph had an overwhelming desire to comfort him. Questions would need to be answered and he did not know whether he could give the answers that would be required, so yet again, he lacked the courage to face the past.

A hymn was being sung and Joseph knew that the burial procession would soon be leaving the church. He looked around to see if he could find a freshly dug grave; one in which his wife might be laid to rest; and saw the two grave diggers leaving their work behind. Not wanting to invade the privacy of the grieving family he took his place behind a tall memorial stone not far away and waited for Hannah and her family to arrive at the grave. The rector led the party out of the church, and he could see that carrying her coffin were four men, one of whom was quite obviously one of the grave diggers. As they got closer, he realised that the other three were Hannah's sons. He could vaguely recognise the features of the eldest son John, even though it had been many years since he had seen him. The other two must be Arthur, who was still a baby when Joseph left, and of course his own son whose name he did not know.

Standing around the deep grave were also faces he did not recognise. A pregnant woman was holding onto the arm of the man he assumed was his son. She must be his wife! Sadness overcame him and Joseph knew that he would never know his future grandchild if he did not step out now and make himself known, but fear of rejection and the admissions of abandonment and selfishness that he must make, held him back. When the body had finally been placed in the ground and the final words spoken; the women took the children, who by this time were beginning to cry with the effects of the weather, back to the shelter of the church door. The pregnant woman turned towards her husband.

"Try not to be too long Ernest. The children are

soaked to the skin and we should be getting back to the house. Hannah would not want you to get a chill from standing at her graveside."

So, his son was called Ernest...

Ernest stood in silence for a few minutes beside the grave with his brothers looking on. Their conversation was brief, but Joseph knew that they were indeed discussing him. Ernest's words, 'I hope he rots in Hell!' were like an arrow in his heart and he knew that he would never be able to face the demons which had plagued him for so many years, and be a true father to his son. When Hannah's sons finally left the graveyard, Joseph knelt by her freshly dug grave looking down at the coffin and wished that he too was lying there beside her. He could never redress the wrongs he had perpetrated and knew that he must live with the fact that his son did not want to know him. The burden of his guilt would stay with him for ever and he could tell no one, for who would forgive him now?

Chapter 24

The darkness of the night wrapped itself around Joseph's shoulders like a shroud. He was exhausted and had found himself standing outside 'The Queen's Arms' in Rawtenstall, shivering. His clothes were soaked and he could not wait to rid himself of their chilly burden. Once inside the lobby, he booked a room for the night and wearily trudged up the stairs. Without a thought for anything but sleep, he undressed and hung his clothes near the warm fire to dry and climbed into bed. His mind racing with the events of the day, sleep did not come easily to Joseph; but when it did, he surrendered his body to the depths of the mattress and slept heavily.

The following day was mild and still; like the calm after a storm, and it was almost nine in the morning when Joseph finally rose from his bed. He felt hot and his body ached, but he knew that he must make his way home as Mary would be concerned about him.

The train arrived in Buxton in the late afternoon and a feverish Joseph made his way home. Every footstep was an effort and he took a cab from the station to Bennett St, something which he would not ordinarily have done as it cost precious funds, which he did not like to spend when he could walk. The August day had been bright and clear with a promise of a warm evening. Joseph shivered as he stepped out of the cab and opened the gate to his front garden path. Mary saw her father from inside the house and quickly opened the door to allow him to enter.

"Father, where have you been? I expected you home by last evening and I have been so worried about you." She noticed his fevered brow and that although he was wearing his coat and the afternoon was still warm, he was shivering. Mary took his coat from him, still damp from the torrential rain of the previous day, and ushered him into the parlour where he sat on the sofa staring into the fire grate. Once again, she spoke to him.

"Father, you are ill and have a fever. You must go up to bed at once and I will bring you a drink."

Joseph did not reply, but stood up and walked slowly upstairs to his room where he undressed slowly, put on his night shift and got into bed. Within minutes, the housekeeper had taken over from Mary and was fussing around his bedside trying to make him comfortable. The fever took its hold and by evening he was thrashing in his bed, deliriously talking about someone named Hannah. Mary stayed by his bedside for most of the night, half expecting the worst to happen and mopping his fevered brow. The fever raged all the next day and Mary allowed the housekeeper to take her turn at nursing him. When at last the fever broke and Joseph was calmer, Mary looked at her father wondering who this woman was, whose name he had so often mentioned in the rages of his fever. Joseph although quiet, was still a little agitated and his eyes which appeared sunken into their sockets, darted around the room as if looking for someone.

"What is it Father?" asked Mary quietly. "There is no one in the room but the two of us." His grey face seemed to relax and he sank back into a sleep which claimed him for several hours, during which time he continually called for Hannah. When he awoke, Mary sat by his bedside feeling a sense of disquiet which she had never felt before.

"Who is Hannah?" she asked him.

Joseph said nothing and turned his head away so that she would not see the distress written upon his face. He did not want to hear that name again, nor did he want to remember the events of the previous few days. The housekeeper interrupted the awkward silence and bustled into the room bearing a bowl of soup and began immediately to spoon feed her employer. She liked living in this house and did not want him to die. In her experience, when a fever took its hold, it often led to something worse and occasionally a dreadful illness such as pneumonia.

During the course of the next few days, Joseph gained in strength, partly due to the attentions of his housekeeper, and was soon well enough to leave his bed and rest on the sofa in the parlour. There were many questions which Mary needed to ask him about his absence, but which at the moment he was unwilling to answer. There seemed to be an atmosphere between father and daughter which made it difficult to talk and each time Mary began to quiz him about where he had been, Joseph refused to answer.

Although Joseph gained his strength, his disposition did not change. He became morose and disinclined to converse with anyone. The work he had enjoyed as a joiner became onerous to him and he began to work less and less, relying more on the paltry savings he had accumulated and the small income he had from his lodgers. Mary found that their roles had changed somewhat, she trying to encourage him to go out and get the air; and he being more inclined to stay indoors and become more depressed. Mary stopped asking him about his sudden absence; the subject tending to make him agitated and irritable.

The Christmas of 1903 was welcomed as usual with decorations and a goose, but not with the jollity which previous years had seen. Mary remembered the time when her father had bought her a doll, the Christmas following her return from the workhouse all those years ago and realised just how things had changed. She felt lonely. In spite of the fact that the house was full of paying guests who came and went like the seasons, she had never managed to make a firm friend of anyone except Mrs Flint, her dead employer. Her father rarely spoke to her now and she was always suspicious of any housekeeper after Emily Duffy, which meant that she had no one to talk to.

The doll had been put away in a cupboard in her bedroom, and on a cold snowy day early in 1904, Mary went to find her. Pulling her from the box where she had been stored, Mary smiled to herself as she stroked the doll's head and manipulated the arms and legs into a pose which would allow it to be cuddled. The clothes it wore were dusty and creased, so Mary took them down to the scullery where she filled a small bowl with water and carefully pared off a few shavings of soap from the block which was kept near the sink. Once she had managed to work the water into a foamy lather she immersed the clothes into the bowl and gently started to wash them. In no time at all, the dress and undergarments were washed, so she pulled down the drying rack from above the fire and placed them carefully on there to dry.

Mary had been unaware of the eyes which had watched her as she tenderly laundered the doll's clothes until she saw a movement out of the corner of her eye. When she turned to identify the watcher, she saw a flash of an apron and cap and knew that it had been the housekeeper. Mary did not want to explain about the doll and so went straight to her bedroom where she sat with the doll for several minutes. Her loneliness became almost too much for her and as she sat and cradled the toy which had been her substitute for a baby, the tears fell relentlessly onto its naked body. Mary curled up onto the bed and was soon sleeping; her arms still cradling the doll. When she finally awoke, Mary knew in her heart that she would never have the love of a real child, and instinctively felt that her father could not give her the parental affection she really needed. How she wished that Mrs Flint had not died. That old lady, who was no relation whatsoever, had shown her more affection than anyone else had in the last few years. It was then that she decided to look for employment as a general servant again, in the hopes that she might find an end to her loneliness. At the age of almost fifty, she knew that throughout her life many people had thought her an idiot, and she remembered the many instances when she had been bullied in her early adulthood. She knew that in her childhood she had been very slow to learn; and that she did not have the scholarly capacity which most women of her age had, but she did not think she was stupid. It was this description which her father had so cruelly given to her when she was first taken into the workhouse and she could never forgive him for that.

Hannah's face, distorted in agony appeared before him, and Joseph could not get away from it. He could not understand what she was trying to tell him and the distress he felt at witnessing her pain was unbearable. She seemed to be saying his name and he tried to answer, but the words would not come, and as her outstretched arm came towards him he too struggled to touch her hand one last time. As quickly as it had materialised, her tormented face disappeared and he was calm again. When at last he awoke, it was not Hannah's face which he saw before him, but the face of his daughter Mary and he was disappointed. Joseph closed his eyes again to get away from the words which she spoke.

"Who is Hannah?"

He could not speak to Mary about Hannah; not now, not ever. What he really wanted to do at this moment was die himself and he willed the darkness to take hold; but his time had not come and within a few hours, he was more lucid and ready to take the soup which his housekeeper had in her hands. His new housekeeper was not like Emily had been, and he was glad. The soup tasted good and when he had finished, he lay back on the pillow once more and allowed sleep to take hold. That he was not going to die now, he was certain; but the thought of facing the future was not something which he relished and did not want to think about.

In the days that followed, Joseph allowed himself to be led to the parlour where he was sat in the chair close to the window so that he could see the comings and goings outside. Mary continued her mission to question him about his visit to Waterfoot, but he could not talk to her. Every time she came to speak to him, he had to turn his face away from her as he could not bear the shame and guilt he felt about his dead wife and their son; nor could he bear to tell Mary about them. The rejection he had felt when his son had said those terrible words, 'I hope he rots in hell', would stay with him for the rest of his life. His reluctance to speak soon had the desired effect and before long, Mary stopped speaking to him, instead turning once more to the doll which had been bought for her as a Christmas gift all those years ago. He knew that she was lonely, but could not bring himself to do anything about it. After all, even though she was his daughter, she was an adult and it should not be his responsibility to take care of her. He was almost seventy and could not manage the emotional upheaval which it brought.

When Mary finally spoke to her father in the early summer of 1904, he was not surprised when she informed him that she was going to find herself a place as a domestic servant. Mary's reading skills were basic and so she had come to her father to ask his help in reading the newspaper advertisements which might help her secure employment. This he did, and for a few days, it seemed as if all was well with father and daughter. To the delight of the housekeeper, they could often be seen pouring over the newspaper looking for a suitable position and chatting as if nothing had been wrong. Finally a position as a general servant was found where Mary would once again be looking after an old spinster, and a letter was written giving Mrs Flint's son as a reference. The address given was another house on London Road and so Mary would not have far to walk if she decided to return home on her days off. Mary did not really expect this to happen and so when the day came for her to start her new employment, she set off alone carrying only her valise, determined to be independent from now on.

Mary's new employer was Miss Ada Briggs, who as her title would suggest had never been married, and Mary hoped that this would give them something in common. When she took hold of the door knocker and rapped hard on the door, Mary began to have her doubts. 'It is probably only nerves,' she thought to herself, trying to be sensible. Within seconds, the door was opened to reveal a tall, wiry looking woman dressed from head to toe in black. Mary assumed that someone in this lady's family must have died and the clothes were mourning dress. The house was dark. Brown painted woodwork seemed to cover the house and where the walls were visible, they were covered with thick, dark green wallpaper which must have been beautiful when new, but which was now discoloured in places by the smoke from the oil lamps which still lit the house. This was not a modern house by any means and before Mary had the opportunity to see any more of the downstairs, Miss Briggs had indicated by a flick of her hand, that Mary was to pick up her valise and follow her up the stairs. Not a word was spoken between them until they reached the landing.

Miss Briggs pointed to the small room at the end of the small landing and said shortly, "This is your room. Put your valise inside and come down to the kitchen. There is work to do!"

Mary did as she had been asked; only glancing round her bedroom, which was only just big enough to hold a bed, and a small chest in which to put her belongings. Again, the room was dim, shaded even further by the dark velvet curtains which draped across the window. Quickly pulling them back to reveal the daylight, Mary then descended the stairs and went straight to the kitchen.

"Do you know how to make a stew, girl?" asked Miss Briggs sternly.

Mary, somewhat taken aback by the old woman's curt manner nodded her head in reply.

"Speak, girl! Don't nod at me as I am sure you have a voice!"

"Yes Miss," replied Mary, a lump already forming in her throat and feeling ready to cry. Mrs Flint had never spoken to Mary like this and she knew she must be brave. Miss Briggs left the room and Mary began to prepare the meal. Little did she know that by the time she left this woman's employ, she would be an expert at making stews as this was to be her staple diet whilst being employed at her dark, dingy, home. After they had eaten their meal, Mary was asked to clear away and wash the dishes, tidy the kitchen and parlour before she was allowed to sit down.

The evening dragged, as Mary; although allowed to sit in the back parlour, was not engaged in conversation. She longed for the womanly conversations she had shared with Mrs Flint, but her new employer was not to be drawn into any sociable banter.

Mary excused herself and decided to go to bed.

Perhaps things would be better in the morning. She could not go back to her father now and so she knew that she must put up with her lot and hope that her circumstances would improve. On reaching the relative privacy of her bedroom, Mary found that the room had only a single candle to lighten the darkness and so she undressed and got into bed. The cold sheets and thin blankets hardly kept her warm and she spent a restless night, tossing and turning, eventually putting on her stockings and underskirt over her nightdress to keep her warm. The room held the chill of winter in spite of the relative warmth of early summer and when morning came, Mary could not wait to get to the kitchen and begin the task of making a hot drink and some breakfast.

Mary sat at the kitchen table with a mug of tea in her hands and thought about her predicament. She could leave this very day and return to the loneliness of her father's house; or she could stay and hope that at least she would eventually make a friend of the bitter old maid who now employed her. Deciding to do the latter, she went into the front parlour and opened the curtains to let in the light. When she turned to face the rest of the room, she was amazed by what she saw. The room was filled with ornaments and grand clocks of all sizes. Hardly a surface could be seen as each was topped with one or more of these delights. Mary went over to a small table and gently picked up a porcelain dog. It was the most delicate thing she had ever handled and as she turned it over and over in her hands, taking in every detail, a loud voice brought her out of her daydreams.

"Put that down, girl!"

Mary, almost dropping the dog in fright, immediately put the dog back on the table and took a step back.

"Why have you opened the curtains so far back? They let in too much light and people might see my precious things!"

Miss Briggs went over to the curtains and began to adjust them so that only a small chink of daylight was allowed into the room. It was many weeks before Mary understood the many obsessions which Miss Briggs had and this was only one of them. Each ornament was to be dusted daily with great care and the clocks, of which there were many, were to be wound regularly; some once a day, and some weekly. Every penny was accounted for and Miss Briggs sat each Friday with her household accounts making sure that money had not been wasted. She did the shopping herself; never allowing Mary access to any cash except what was her due. This was paid to Mary each Friday evening and she dutifully put it away until the day when she might need it.

Mary was kept busy from morning to night, and she was glad by the time they had eaten supper, for some time of her own. Although Miss Briggs remained a stickler for routine, this in fact helped Mary to settle eventually into her new way of life. She remained quite lonely in spite of the company she had in her employer, as her friendship was not required, only her duties as a servant, but Mary had become a stronger woman both physically and mentally since the day she went to work for Ada Briggs.

Chapter 25

Buxton May 1908

The newspaper lay before Joseph unopened on the table. Beside it was a letter which had been delivered that very morning and he glanced from one to the other, trying to decide which to open first. The newspaper contained details of the recently held Olympic Games which had taken place at the White City Stadium and were opened by the King himself. Information about the final medal count which put Great Britain in the lead was of no real interest to Joseph and so he decided to open his letter. He did not get many personal letters these days as most of his own family were no longer alive and so he was fully expecting to receive bad news.

The writing on the envelope was not familiar to him, being rather untidy and only just legible, but he took his letter opener and sliced the envelope open. The address at the top of the page was vaguely familiar, being one in Halifax, and he glanced down to the bottom of the page to see first who the sender was. It was from his sister Emma whom he had not set eyes on for many years; the last time being at their father's funeral; and so he was anxious to find out why she was writing to him after such a long time. His intuition had been correct. Emma had written to tell him that his son Fred was critically ill.

'………..*he has pneumonia and is gravely ill, being unlikely to survive more than a couple of days. It is probable that by the time you receive this letter, he will have passed away. Fred has been asking for you and I know that if you could come up and see him before he*

*dies, it would make a dying man happy. Bring Mary
Ellen with you- it is a long time since we last met and I
am sure that she would like the opportunity to say
goodbye to her brother.*

Your loving sister,

Emma'

Joseph read the letter several times and then placed
it back in the envelope on the table. He had not seen his
son for many years and had only communicated by
letter once or twice since then. Theirs had never been a
close relationship. It had been even longer since Mary
Ellen saw her brother and he did not really know
whether or not she would want to go and see him, but
he knew that he must give her the chance. The old
feelings of failure were resurrected at that moment, and
he could only think that he had been a bad father to all
of his children. Not one of them had really loved him
and he knew that instead of being surrounded by a
loving family in his old age, he would remain a lonely
old man.

Joseph was not certain of the address which had
been Mary's home for some time now as he had not
seen her since the day she left. He had assumed that she
was well and that her employment had been a
satisfactory one as she had not returned home, but he
knew that the house was on London Road and not far
from the house where he had found Mary employment
with Mrs Flint almost ten years ago. He wandered
slowly along the busy road, for this residential street
was also now a busy thoroughfare into the town of
Buxton, and looked for the house where Mrs Flint had
lived. Once he had located that house, he knew that the
house where Mary should be living would not be many

doors away. Taking his chance, he knocked at a door hoping to ask the resident about the possible whereabouts of a lady who might have a servant named Mary; and was surprised when Mary actually opened the door.

"Good morning Mary," he said. "Can I come in and speak to your mistress please?"

Mary, unable to speak with the shock of seeing her father again after so long, opened the door further to allow him to enter.

"Who is it girl?" shouted a voice from inside the house.

Mary showed her father into the front parlour and before Miss Briggs had time to speak, she introduced him.

"This is my father, Miss Briggs. He would like to speak to you."

Ada Briggs looked at the old man in front of her. "Well, what do you want? I thought that Mary's father was dead. She never speaks of you and so what is your business?"

Joseph was exhausted by this time, both from the strain of the emotion he felt that day, and also the walk which had brought him to this house. He was not a fit man any longer and his bones ached. Seeing his discomfort, Ada told him to be seated and sat in the chair opposite.

"I am afraid that I have come with some bad news for Mary. My son, her brother Fred, is very ill and asking to see us. My sister has written a letter which I have received this very day, to ask us to go and visit him before it is too late. He may have passed away by the time we get there and so time is of the greatest importance."

Ada looked at Joseph intently. "I take it that you require Mary to leave with you today?"

"We will need to catch the train today and so with your permission, and if Mary is willing to accompany me, then yes, she will need to leave immediately." He looked back at Mary to see if there was any sign of distress on her face which might acknowledge her feelings for her brother. Mary however seemed more in a state of shock upon seeing her father than distressed at the news that her brother was seriously ill. She had never had much of a relationship with Fred, having met only a few times since they were young adults.

Ada Briggs interrupted his thoughts. "Well girl! What do you want to do? Are you to leave with your father and visit this brother or not?"

"I will go with him," she replied simply.

Ada got up from her seat and walked over to Mary, putting her arm on her shoulder and for the first time showing Mary that she was capable of warm feelings, said quietly, "I think you have made the right decision Mary. Better to go and see him now whilst there is a possibility of saying goodbye, than regretting it later."

It was an uneasy silence which accompanied Joseph and his daughter to the station. Few words were spoken, but Mary carried herself with dignity and looked upon her father now as an elderly man needing her company. Neither one felt the need, nor the inclination, to question each other about the past; and by the time they reached Halifax, they had begun to relax in the unspoken bond they had created.

Taking his sister's address from his pocket, Joseph hailed one of the horse drawn cabs which were lined up outside the station. Within minutes, they were on their way and their destination was in sight. Emma had been unsure of their intentions, but was happy to see her brother and his daughter when they appeared at her door.

When she opened the door to them, they instantly

knew that they had arrived too late. Emma was wearing the traditional black attire of a woman in mourning and although she greeted them with a smile, it hid the sadness she felt at her nephew's passing. Fred was buried along with the rest of his family; his only mourners being his father, sister and aunt. Mary and her father remained with Emma for a couple of days after the funeral, but Mary was in a hurry to return to her employer in case she was dismissed for taking too much time off.

Not for the first time, and certainly not for the last time, Joseph was made to think of his role as a father. His only surviving offspring was now Mary. He had outlived all the others except Hannah's son, and he was as good as dead to him. His own life held little meaning for him now and he suddenly felt very old and lonely. Joseph had no inclination to work any longer, and no need for the money it brought. He had just enough to live on from the income generated by taking in lodgers and his housekeeper saw to their needs. With a mundane routine set every day, Joseph became more depressed and almost a recluse.

As Mary helped her father into the cab which took them from the station to Bennett Street, she began to despise the old man who had been her father. He was no longer capable of looking after anyone and she knew that she had done the right thing in finding employment with Miss Briggs, even though the work was hard and she was still sometimes lonely. Once she had seen Joseph into the house, she hurriedly walked off towards London Road and the home she now shared with Ada Briggs. At least she felt needed there.

Ada greeted her with a warm smile and Mary knew that even though she hadn't spoken the words, she had been missed. Her life with Miss Briggs would never be as companionable as the one she had experienced with

Jane Flint, but in spite of her gruff exterior, Mary knew that Miss Briggs would always be a friend.

Chapter 26

Chapel-en-le-Frith, Derbyshire. 1912

The lump that Mary could feel in her throat had grown. She knew that for certain because each time she looked at her reflection in the mirror, her neck looked more grotesque than the last time. She lay on the narrow bed in the long ward she shared with so many other patients in the Infirmary. When she had brought herself to this place; a place which she had vowed would never feature in her life again; it had been as a last resort....

Ada Briggs had died some months previously, and Mary had no other choice but to go back to her father or a room in the workhouse would beckon once more. Neither was what she wanted, but her father was old and becoming more frail. As she lay in bed, her thoughts returned to the day when she had returned to Bennett Street for the last time. Not knowing whether to knock at the door; for she had felt like a stranger, or to go straight in; was a decision that was taken from her, when an unfamiliar person came out of the front door almost falling over Mary in his efforts to leave.

"In a hurry, sorry!" he muttered under his breath, leaving the front door wide open for Mary to enter. Through the passageway which led through the ground floor of the house, Mary could see her father hunched over his walking stick, hobbling from the kitchen to the parlour. His eyes were fixed on the floor and he did not notice her until she had entered the house and was standing almost next to him.

"Hello father," she said quietly. "How are you?"

Joseph strained his head to look up at her; the expression on his face showing no emotion. He grunted some sort of a reply which Mary could not hear and continued on his way to the parlour where he slumped down in an armchair.

"What do you want?" he muttered, this time more clearly.

It was obvious to Mary that he neither expected her to visit, nor needed her company. "Miss Briggs passed away last week and I have no employment now, so I thought that I might come home again for a while." She stood motionless for several minutes, waiting for some reply or reaction to the fact that she had come home, but none came. The housekeeper entered the room and offered her some tea and enquired whether or not she would be staying. Mary did not know what she should do and did not have anywhere else to go, so she took her bags up to the room she had shared so long ago with other female lodgers and sat on the bed and cried. How could she stay here? It was obvious that if she did, her life would yet again become meaningless. Sitting on the edge of the bed with her head propped in her hands, she tried to think clearly. Hers would be a life without the affection of her father and no meaningful role to play in his household. Unable to return to the parlour to speak to her father, she undressed and climbed between the clean sheets which felt cool against her warm body. Sleeping was difficult; her pounding head spinning with the combination of the difficult decisions she needed to make and the uncomfortable heat which continued to plague the whole of her body.

Mary woke up the following morning with a sore throat, the dry scratchy feeling making her reach immediately for a glass of water. Although she had no fever, she did not feel herself and decided to stay in bed for the day. Although it had been difficult for her to sleep during the night, try as she might, sleep just would not come to her during the day. By the late afternoon, Mary decided that she must get up and try to shake herself out of the morose feeling she had. She was not hungry and could not eat, as the soreness in her throat made it difficult to swallow, so a cordial of lemon and sugar was prescribed for her by the kindly housekeeper. Hoping to feel improved by the morning, Mary returned to her bed later in the evening armed with more cordial and a menthol rub to ease her breathing. For almost a week Mary suffered with the soreness in her throat and a tickly cough which would not allow her to rest.

"I almost feel as if I have something stuck in my throat," she croaked to the housekeeper as more of the cordial was poured. "Perhaps I have swallowed a piece of food which has not gone down."

The housekeeper looked in her mouth and could see nothing, but Mary kept on rubbing at her neck almost as if it might help the uncomfortable feeling to go. She felt sick and had been unable to eat anything. The very thought of food passing between her lips made her want to gag. The doctor was brought but could see nothing wrong with her throat apart from the usual redness which comes with infected tonsils. The only thing he prescribed was a lozenge which might ease the soreness in the throat.

By the time Mary was beginning to feel better, she realised that her father had not spoken a word to her in the whole time she had been ill, nor had he, to her knowledge, enquired after her health. He had grumbled when the doctor's bill had arrived, but seemed not to notice Mary's presence in the house. Mary possessed very little money of her own and could not have paid the doctor's bill herself, and felt frustrated that she was dependent on her father. There seemed only one way out; to get another post as a domestic servant as soon as possible.

Mary's own health eventually determined her future. The bouts of throat infections became more frequent, she lost weight and it was soon obvious that she would not be able to take up any form of employment. In desperation, she decided that she must find a room somewhere in a lodging house, but soon realised that she could not afford even that. When the doctor was at last sent for again, Joseph became agitated once more at the thought of having to pay more money for what seemed like a trivial ailment. Examining Mary's throat, the doctor seemed concerned. He prodded gently around her neck, feeling either side of her windpipe and up into the jaw line. Mary winced as he pressed the right side of her neck and it was obvious that it was a tender spot. There was little sign of real inflammation in her throat, but her condition puzzled him. Her weight loss had become quite dramatic, the result of a severe loss of appetite and the inexplicable inability to swallow properly. She was able to eat small amounts of softened food, but the desire to eat had been lost in the fear of choking upon any lump of food. Besides that, Mary's voice was quite husky and it had become an effort for her to talk normally.

The doctor spoke gently to Mary, trying not to panic her. "Mary, I am not really sure what the problem is, but I would like you to come into hospital where we can treat you better and I can ask other doctors to examine your neck."

Mary knew that the hospital he spoke of was actually the Infirmary in the workhouse at Chapel-en-le-Frith. The very thought of being confined within the walls of a workhouse again made her shiver, but what choice did she have? She had no money to pay for private treatment and so a bed in the workhouse hospital seemed the only answer. If she stayed with her father, it was likely that her illness would recur; this much had been pointed out to her by the doctor. Surely it was better to seek treatment and then hopefully she would be able to return at a later date. The doctor had offered to arrange for the ambulance which served the surrounding district to collect her, but Mary did not feel that her condition was serious enough to warrant such treatment. However, she was grateful that her father's housekeeper had offered to accompany her on the train as she was beginning to feel rather unwell at the thought of once more being in the workhouse, even if it was as a patient.

Again she found herself packing up her belongings into the now battered valise which had been well used these past years, and saying goodbye to her father. Joseph was sat in his favourite chair next to the window in the parlour. The room was strangely silent except for the ticking of the clock on the mantle; most of the lodgers being out at work for the day. He turned to look at Mary as she entered the room; her face and neck wrapped up warmly with a muffler and her warm coat fastened tightly to the neck. His expression only gave a hint of what lay behind his eyes; the sadness and frustration he still felt, but a stubborn pride which had stopped him from admitting to his daughter, that he still loved her, deep in his heart.

"Goodbye father. The doctor has insisted that I be treated at the workhouse infirmary. I don't know when I will see you again; perhaps when I am recovered from this ailment which has shadowed me these last months, then I will return."

She walked over to put her arms around his shoulders in an embrace, for she had a strange feeling that she may not return and would probably never see her father again; but Joseph was unable to stand and she gently planted a kiss on the top of his head in the place where his hair was almost gone. The words he had spoken to her many years past echoed in her mind; '...You will never need to return to the workhouse as long as we are living here...' Turning to the door, she took a final glance back at the old man in the chair and saw him slowly put his hand upon his head in the very spot where she had kissed him.

Mary had never enjoyed train journeys, but this one was always going to be difficult. It wasn't far from Buxton to Chapel, the train only stopping at one other station, that of Doveholes where extensive lime works were carried out. Her thoughts being only of her forthcoming stay in the workhouse; Mary was unable to enjoy the beautiful view from the carriage window and before long they alighted from the train and were heading by horse drawn omnibus for the Infirmary. The doctor had given her a letter which would explain her treatment so far and she held it firmly in her hand. With trepidation, they made their way towards the forbidding looking building; all the time looking for the Infirmary entrance. The doctor had told her that she was to go to the North side of the workhouse itself where the Infirmary buildings were located and so they wandered around the outside of the grey stone walls which held the poorest of society. Eventually they arrived at a set of doors which Mary assumed would lead her into the Infirmary and made her way inside.

By this time, the stress of the journey and anticipation of what was to come had made Mary feel sick. Her face was clammy and pale and her neck ached. She had not eaten all day and it was well after tea time. As she entered the hospital, her head began to spin and the unfamiliar surroundings began to blur. Her companion immediately held on to her arm and she suddenly found herself sat on the floor as she had been unable to support Mary's dead weight.

"Somebody help me please," shouted the

housekeeper, panicking at the sight of the pallid face in front of her.

Nurses immediately appeared and Mary was taken away to the ward where she would spend a considerable amount of time. When she finally came round from her faint, Mary was being helped into bed; her clothes taken from her and a large calico shift thrust over her head. As she lay under the cocoon of a warm blanket, fatigue finally overcame her and she drifted off into a deep sleep; her last thoughts being of her father.

Joseph's housekeeper, Mrs White, was a kindly woman in her late forties who managed his household with ease. She often had five or more boarders to feed and kept the house in good order. She had become acutely aware of the strained relationship between Joseph and his daughter whilst trying to engage him in conversation about his family; and had liked Mary the instant she had met her. Leaving her at the Infirmary was a difficult thing for her as she too had a daughter and could not bear the thought of her being all alone without any family to give her some support; but she knew that she must. On returning home, Mrs White tried to engage Joseph once more in conversation about his daughter, but without success. He rarely spoke to anyone now, except for giving orders as to what meal he would like or issue orders about other housekeeping problems.

When Joseph heard his front door open very late on the evening Mrs White returned from the workhouse, he seemed to have no thought other than the fact that he had not eaten all day. His stomach growled with hunger and even though he could easily have made himself a basic meal of bread and cheese, he had waited until his housekeeper returned. Ignoring his rude manner, Mrs White made Joseph his meal and left him to his temper alone in the dining room. She was both physically and emotionally drained from the arduous journey and the scenes she had witnessed in the Infirmary, and longed for the comfort of her bed. Any dirty dishes would have to wait until the next day and so would Joseph. He had not even asked her how his daughter had been, and she could not understand his callousness. The smell in the ward had made her feel sick to the stomach and she could still hear the sounds of patients groaning and begging for help even now; but she was thankful that Mary had been asleep when she had left and could only pray that she would be well looked after.

Chapter 27

Joseph stumbled around the parlour looking for something. He was unsure exactly what he was looking for, but knew that he would recognise it when he saw it. Life had become very confusing and although every so often he had snatches of a memory, he found that he forgot everyday things. Only a day or so ago, he thought that Mary had visited him, but he did not know where she had gone. Sitting in his chair, his head gradually fell sideways onto the winged arm of the chair and he fell asleep. His dreams were always the same; of a beautiful woman and the baby she carried in her arms. She had no name, but he always knew that they had been lovers and the warmth that he felt after waking was almost always dispelled by the realisation that she was not with him.

On the day that his daughter had said goodbye to him and left to go into the Infirmary, he had felt unusually confused. He knew her face and that she was his daughter, but he could not remember her name. Sitting in his chair by the window, he racked his brains to bring her name to the forefront of his mind, but could not. When his housekeeper returned from her outing, he could not remember why she had needed to go out and felt extremely cross with her for leaving him alone without any food for the whole day.

"Where have you been woman?" he demanded. "I am hungry!" He often addressed her as 'woman' to hide the fact that he could rarely remember her name either, a fact that distressed him. The frustration he felt with his dulling memory made him feel bad tempered and he could not help himself when his bad manners took over. When at last he was fed, he waited to see if his housekeeper would return for the dirty plates; and when she did not continue to wait on him, he took hold of his stick and banged on the floor as loudly as he could. His anger took hold and he threw the plate which had held his meal, onto the floor, smashing it into several pieces. The housekeeper still did not appear and Joseph was compelled to leave the mess and climb the stairs to bed.

Mrs White was up early the next morning, and had cleared the mess which Joseph had left before any of the lodgers had risen. There was no visible evidence of his temper and unless they had heard his tantrums, they would never have known that he had been so distressed. When Joseph finally came downstairs for his breakfast long after the rest of the household was up and out to work, he had completely forgotten about the previous day and appeared calm and quite lucid. However, in the days and weeks which followed, Mrs White became increasingly concerned about his erratic behaviour and fluctuating memory. The only thing that he wanted to do was sit and gaze out of the window and watch the people walk by.

When the weather improved and the sun began to shine, he seemed to be calmer and Mrs White encouraged him to sit on a small wooden chair in the tiny garden that fronted the house. At least he would be able to get some fresh air and the opportunity to chat with passers-by. He often fell asleep and was sometimes the object of fun for children as they threw small stones at him to try and wake him up. Most of the time he was unaware of these childish pranks and the children never used the stones to hit him, merely to land close by and give him a fright.

Spring turned to summer and Joseph's face became a nut brown colour from spending so much time outdoors. He looked healthier, but his outward appearance did not accurately portray his wellbeing; only Mrs White knew that by now he had to have the majority of his needs cared for by her. She was not his wife and should not be expected to dress and feed him, but this is what she had to do in order to maintain his outward appearance of dignity. However, by the time the winter months arrived and the new year of 1913 entered, Joseph could no longer sit and enjoy the mild weather, so she knew that she must get help. When the doctor arrived to examine Joseph, his comments on Joseph's senility came as no surprise. He could see a big change in Joseph's emotional and behavioural patterns since he had made his last visit several months previously, when he had been to see Mary, and he was shocked.

"Mrs White, you have done an excellent job in caring for Mr Freeman, but he is, I am afraid, becoming senile; and his condition will only get more severe. It is possible that he will become aggressive and you should no longer be looking after him."

When the housekeeper heard this news, she began to cry. Although Joseph was a burden to her and she had found it very difficult during these last few months, she had developed an affectionate bond with the old man and felt sad that he would be reduced to ending his days as his daughter was, in the Infirmary. The doctor made all the necessary arrangements for his transportation to Chapel-en-le-Frith and Mrs White once more made the journey with him, albeit this time in an ambulance, not the train, for Joseph could not be trusted to behave in a suitable manner with other passengers.

The Infirmary greeted Joseph with kindness and he was allocated a bed in a ward where other elderly men were being treated. Some sat on their beds, while others lay asleep on chairs and Joseph seemed confused about his reason for being with all these strange people. His agitation was evident and he was finally given some sedation to help him sleep and to remain calm. Mrs

White said her goodbyes and decided that whilst she was at the Infirmary, she would ask if she could visit Mary.

The women's ward that had become Mary's home, was full of very sick people and Mary herself was not really fit to see any visitors, so the housekeeper was politely refused entry and asked to enquire another day. Mrs White set off home again wondering how she was going to run the house without the money which Joseph gave to her each week for shopping.

During the spring and summer of 1912, Mary's health had fluctuated with bouts of severe discomfort and pain, mingled with short periods of reasonable good health. When she felt well enough, Mary would return to the workhouse dormitories where the old familiar routines fell into place. She did not feel quite as anxious as she once had and knew that although the medical care was basic, at least she had some relief from the discomfort and pain she sometimes felt.

The new year of 1913 brought her news that her condition was terminal, the doctors having given her the diagnosis which scared everyone: that of cancer. Her tumour was in her throat and she knew that it was growing fast. Swallowing had become quite difficult and although she tried to eat, she had continued to lose weight. Mary was unaware of her father's plight and had no knowledge of the fact that he too was now a resident of the Infirmary, until he arrived at her bedside.

In one of his more lucid moments, Joseph became conscious of the fact that he was in the same hospital that his daughter had gone to all those months before. He could not remember why she was there, but thought that if he could see her, his mind might be put at ease. Arriving at her bedside, he could see that the person who lay in the bed was very sick. A raucous, gasping noise came from her mouth and although she was partially propped up on a pillow, he could see that she was struggling to take a breath. This was not the young woman he remembered and for several minutes he refused to believe that this prone figure was actually his daughter.

"Miss Freeman has cancer of the throat," whispered the nurse. "She is very ill."

Sudden memories came flooding back of times in the park, laughter at Christmas and most distressingly, of a violent incident with another man. He could not bear to see his daughter so ill and in such obvious pain, so he immediately rose from the seat beside her bed and, clutching his chest, staggered off down the ward and out of sight. Mary opened her eyes just in time to glimpse the sight of a frail old man standing momentarily beside the bed and thought for just a second that she had seen her father.

Stabbing pains seared through Joseph's chest making him clutch violently at his night shirt. Visions of Mary's sickly pallor and the awful noise made by her laboured breathing made him feel terrible. She was dreadfully ill and he had not known about it! Why had no one ever informed him that she was so ill? Falling onto his bed, he sobbed out loud. The pain in his chest was unbearable and he gasped with its intensity.

As the heart attack struck its fatal blow; Joseph's heart finally gave out and he breathed his last breath; his last thoughts being of the woman lying in a bed only yards away and of the fact that he would also end his life in a place which he had condemned his daughter to live in, so many years ago. He was surprisingly lucid; his memories strangely vivid; almost as if he was finally being punished for the selfish actions which had caused so many people such heartache. Joseph's death on the 21st of January 1913 in the Infirmary at the workhouse in Chapel-en-le-Frith, brought to an end a life which had caused pain and suffering, but one which had never intended to do harm. Joseph had been weak and he had died a man without great means and tortured by his own wrong doings.

Mary outlived her father by a matter of days. On January 30th, her life came to an end. She was exhausted by the efforts made to simply breathe. Her tumour had become too large to allow her windpipe to function correctly and she had been unable to swallow properly for some time. The sight of a familiar old man standing at her bedside gave her one last glimmer of hope that perhaps her father did actually love her and after he left her, she gradually fell into a state of unconsciousness which flickered between life and death for several days. Neither Joseph nor Mary had much money and they were buried, days apart in an unmarked grave with no ceremony. Theirs was a funeral which no one attended, as no one knew of their passing; but at least they would be together in death.

Epilogue

When Joseph Clarke Freeman died in January 1913, he did not leave a will, and Mary who died only nine days later, did not have the opportunity to make any claim on his estate such as it was. The letters of administration which later dealt with a claim on his estate said, that he was 'a widower not possessed of real estate leaving Mary Ellen Freeman spinster his lawful daughter *and only next of kin and the only person entitled in distribution to his personal estate* who has since died without taking upon herself letters of administration of his estate.'

The secret that he had kept from his own Freeman family, of his marriage to Hannah Booth and the birth of their son Ernest truly went with him to his grave and it is obvious from this document that he had not divulged their existence to anyone else within his family. Seventeen years after his death, his nephew Harry Freeman Whitehead made a claim on Mary Ellen's estate, becoming her administrator and thus gained access to what little money Joseph had left which amounted to £262.4s.11d. – not a fortune.

Ernest Freeman of course was alive and well in 1913, living in Rossendale with his wife and daughter. According to the 1911 census, he was a heel fitter in a slipper factory. My father can also remember his great uncle Ernest sitting at his workbench mending shoes! Ernest had known who his father was, having wrangled with his mother over the use of the Freeman versus Booth surname. In the 1881 census she was still calling herself by the surname Freeman but stated that she was a widow. In the 1891 census both Hannah and Ernest were using the surname Booth, Hannah still classing herself as a widow. However, by the 1901 census she and Ernest were both using the surname Freeman and

Hannah once again said she was married. Perhaps between the 1891 and 1901 census' she found out that Joseph was indeed alive and came clean to Ernest about his father, or maybe Ernest just insisted on using his real father's name; the name on his birth certificate, and so Hannah did the same. What seems possible is that she thought Joseph had died sometime after he had left; but just as likely is the idea that she classed herself as a widow to 'save face.' When Ernest was old enough to make decisions for himself, he must have had some influence on Hannah's decision to change her name back again to Freeman. We will never know what went through her mind during those years, but the evidence from census returns, her marriage certificate to Joseph and Ernest's birth certificate naming Joseph as his father are undisputed sources of evidence which proves the relationship between them.

This story is my version of the events which formed Joseph Clark Freeman's life, using actual records where possible and piecing the rest together like a jigsaw puzzle with a bit of imagination!

www.ingramcontent.com/pod-product-compliance
Lightning Source LLC
Chambersburg PA
CBHW021005260626
47169CB00006B/1955